POLLYANNA GROWS UP

ELEANOR HODGMAN PORTER (1868–1920) was born Eleanor Hodgman in New Hampshire, USA, into an old New England family; she married John Porter in 1892. She was blessed with a fine singing voice, and studied for several years at the prestigious New England Conservatory of Music.

She began publishing books in 1907, and even wrote a series of three novels about a young girl called 'Miss Billy'. But at the same time a different girl was forming in her mind, and in 1913 *Pollyanna* was published and Pollyanna Whittier was introduced to the reading public. The book was an overnight success: over a million copies were sold in a short space of time and the book has continued to delight young readers ever since.

The demand for a sequel was immense, and two years later the equally successful *Pollyanna Grows Up* was published. These two books became popularly known as the 'Glad Books', because this is Pollyanna's favourite word. She faces the good times, as well as the bad times (such as those following her road accident), with optimism, and even succeeds in infecting grumpy adults like her maiden aunt Polly with cheerfulness. Her outlook is that of Eleanor Porter herself, who said: 'I have never believed that we ought to deny discomfort and pain and evil; I have merely thought that it is far better to greet the unknown with a cheer.'

The two Pollyanna books were so famous, and so much loved, that after Eleanor Porter's death other writers were commissioned to continue the tale. In all, ten further books were written by four other writers. However, any success these books enjoyed was due only to their reflection of the two classic originals, *Pollyanna* and *Pollyanna Grows Up*.

Some other Puffin Classics to enjoy

POLLYANNA
Eleanor H. Porter

HEIDI
Johanna Spyri

REBECCA OF SUNNYBROOK FARM
Kate Douglas Wiggen

EIGHT COUSINS
GOOD WIVES
JACK AND JILL
JO'S BOYS
LITTLE MEN
LITTLE WOMEN
Louisa May Alcott

ELEANOR H. PORTER

Pollyanna Grows Up

PUFFIN BOOKS

To
My Cousin Walter

PUFFIN BOOKS

Published by the Penguin Group
Penguin Books Ltd, 27 Wrights Lane, London W8 5TZ, England
Penguin Books USA Inc., 375 Hudson Street, New York, New York 10014, USA
Penguin Books Australia Ltd, Ringwood, Victoria, Australia
Penguin Books Canada Ltd, 10 Alcorn Avenue, Toronto, Ontario, Canada M4V 3B2
Penguin Books (NZ) Ltd, 182–190 Wairau Road, Auckland 10, New Zealand

Penguin Books Ltd, Registered Offices: Harmondsworth, Middlesex, England

First published in Great Britain by George G. Harrap & Co. Ltd 1927
Published in Puffin Books 1984
Reissued in this edition 1996
6

Filmset by Datix International Limited, Bungay, Suffolk
Printed in England by Clays Ltd, St Ives plc
Set in 11/14 pt Monophoto Plantin

Contents

1

DELLA SPEAKS HER MIND

Della Wetherby tripped up the somewhat imposing steps of her sister's Commonwealth Avenue home and pressed an energetic finger against the electric-bell button. From the tip of her wing-trimmed hat to the toe of her low-heeled shoe she radiated health, capability, and alert decision. Even her voice, as she greeted the maid that opened the door, vibrated with the joy of living.

'Good morning, Mary. Is my sister in?'

'Y-yes, ma'am, Mrs Carew is in,' hesitated the girl; 'but – she gave orders she'd see no one.'

'Did she? Well, I'm no one,' smiled Miss Wetherby, 'so she'll see me. Don't worry – I'll take the blame,' she nodded, in answer to the frightened remonstrance in the girl's eyes. 'Where is she – in her sitting-room?'

'Y-yes, ma'am; but – that is, she said –' Miss Wetherby, however, was already half-way up the broad stairway; and, with a despairing backward glance, the maid turned away.

In the hall above Della Wetherby unhesitatingly walked towards a half-open door, and knocked.

'Well, Mary,' answered a 'dear-me-what-now' voice. 'Haven't I – Oh, Della!' The voice grew suddenly warm with love and surprise. 'You dear girl, where did you come from?'

'Yes, it's Della,' smiled that young woman blithely, already half-way across the room. 'I've come from an over-Sunday at the beach with two of the other nurses, and I'm on my way back to the Sanatorium now. That is, I'm here now, but I shan't be long. I stepped in for – this,' she finished, giving the owner of the 'dear-me-what-now' voice a hearty kiss.

Mrs Carew frowned and drew back a little coldly. The slight touch of joy and animation that had come into her face fled, leaving only a dispirited fretfulness that was plainly very much at home there.

'Oh, of course! I might have known,' she said. 'You never stay – here.'

'Here!' Della Wetherby laughed merrily, and threw up her hands; then, abruptly, her voice and manner changed. She regarded her sister with grave, tender eyes. 'Ruth, dear, I couldn't – I just couldn't live in this house. You know I couldn't,' she finished gently.

Mrs Carew stirred irritably.

'I'm sure I don't see why not,' she fenced.

Della Wetherby shook her head.

'Yes, you do, dear. You know I'm entirely out of sympathy with it all: the gloom, the lack of aim, the insistence on misery and bitterness.'

'But I *am* miserable and bitter.'

'You ought not to be.'

'Why not? What have I to make me otherwise?'

Della Wetherby gave an impatient gesture.

'Ruth, look here,' she challenged. 'You're thirty-three years old. You have good health – or would have, if you treated yourself properly – and you certainly have an abundance of time and a superabundance of money. Surely anybody would say you ought to find *something* to do this glorious morning besides sitting moped up in this tomb-like house with instructions to the maid that you'll see no one.'

'But I don't *want* to see anybody.'

'Then I'd *make* myself want to.'

Mrs Carew sighed wearily and turned away her head.

'Oh, Della, why won't you ever understand? I'm not like you. I can't – forget.'

A swift pain crossed the other woman's face.

'You mean – Jamie, I suppose. I don't forget – that, dear. I couldn't, of course. But moping won't help us – find him.'

'As if I hadn't *tried* to find him, for eight long years – and by something besides moping,' flashed Mrs Carew indignantly, with a sob in her voice.

'Of course you have, dear,' soothed the other quickly; 'and we shall keep on hunting, both of us, till we do find him – or die. But *this* sort of thing doesn't help.'

'But I don't want to do – anything else,' murmured Ruth Carew drearily.

For a moment there was silence. The younger woman sat regarding her sister with troubled, disapproving eyes.

'Ruth,' she said at last, with a touch of exasperation, 'forgive me, but – are you always going to be like this? You're widowed, I'll admit; but your married life lasted only a year, and your husband was much older than yourself. You were little more than a child at the time, and that one short year can't seem much more than a dream now. Surely that ought not to embitter your whole life!'

4 POLLYANNA GROWS UP

'No, oh, no,' murmured Mrs Carew still drearily.

'Then *are* you going to be always like this?'

'Well, of course, if I could find Jamie –'

'Yes, yes, I know; but, Ruth dear, isn't there any-thing in the world but Jamie – to make you *any* happy?'

'There doesn't seem to be, that I can think of,' sighed Mrs Carew indifferently.

'Ruth!' ejaculated her sister, stung into something very like anger. Then suddenly she laughed. 'Oh, Ruth, Ruth, I'd like to give you a dose of Pollyanna. I don't know anyone who needs it more!'

Mrs Carew stiffened a little.

'Well, what pollyanna may be I don't know, but whatever it is, I don't want it,' she retorted sharply, nettled in her turn. 'This isn't your beloved Sanato-rium, and I'm not your patient to be dosed and bossed, please remember.'

Della Wetherby's eyes danced, but her lips remained unsmiling.

'Pollyanna isn't a medicine, my dear,' she said de-murely, '– though I've heard some people call her a tonic. Pollyanna is a little girl.'

'A child? Well, how should I know?' retorted the other, still aggrievedly. 'You have your "belladonna", so I'm sure I don't see why not "pollyanna". Besides, you're always recommending something for me to take, and you distinctly said "dose" – and dose usually means medicine of a sort.'

'Well, Pollyanna *is* a medicine – of a sort,' smiled Della. 'Anyway, the Sanatorium doctors all declare that she's better than any medicine they can give. She's a little girl, Ruth, twelve or thirteen years old, who was at the Sanatorium all last summer and most of the winter. I didn't see her but a month or two, for she left soon after I arrived. But that was long enough for me to come fully under her spell. Besides, the whole Sanatorium is still talking Pollyanna, and playing her game.'

'*Game!*'

'Yes,' nodded Della, with a curious smile. 'Her "Glad Game". I'll never forget my first introduction to it. One feature of her treatment was particularly disagreeable and even painful. It came every Tuesday morning, and very soon after my arrival it fell to my lot to give it to her. I was dreading it, for I knew from past experience with other children what to expect: fretfulness and tears, if nothing worse. To my unbounded amazement she greeted me with a smile and said she was glad to see me: and, if you'll believe it, there was never so much as a whimper from her lips through the whole ordeal, though I knew I was hurting her cruelly.

'I fancy I must have said something that showed my surprise, for she explained earnestly: "Oh, yes, I used to feel that way too, and I did dread it so, till I happened to think 'twas just like Nancy's wash-days, and I could be gladdest of all on *Tuesdays*, 'cause there wouldn't be another one for a whole week."'

'Why, how extraordinary!' frowned Mrs Carew, not quite comprehending. 'But I'm sure I don't see any *game* to that.'

'No, I didn't, till later. Then she told me. It seems she was the motherless daughter of a poor minister in the West, and was brought up by the Ladies' Aid Society and missionary barrels. When she was a tiny girl she wanted a doll, and confidently expected it in the next barrel; but there turned out to be nothing but a pair of little crutches.

'The child cried, of course, and it was then that her father taught her the game of hunting for something to be glad about in everything that happened; and he said she could begin right then by being glad she didn't *need* the crutches. That was the beginning. Pollyanna said it was a lovely game, and she'd been playing it ever since; and that the harder it was to find the glad part, the more fun it was, only when it was too *awful* hard, like she had found it sometimes.'

'Why, how extraordinary!' murmured Mrs Carew, still not entirely comprehending.

'You'd think so – if you could see the results of that game in the Sanatorium,' nodded Della; 'and Dr Ames says he hears she's revolutionized the whole town where she came from, just the same way. He knows Dr Chilton very well – the man that married Pollyanna's aunt. And, by the way, I believe that marriage was one of her ministrations. She patched up an old lovers' quarrel between them.

'You see, two years ago or more, Pollyanna's father died, and the little girl was sent east to this aunt. In October she was hurt by an automobile, and was told she could never walk again. In April Dr Chilton sent her to the Sanatorium, and she was there till last March – almost a year. She went home practically cured. You should have seen the child! There was just one cloud to mar her happiness; that she couldn't *walk* all the way there. As near as I can gather, the whole town turned out to meet her with brass bands and banners.

'But you can't *tell* about Pollyanna. One has to *see* her. And that's why I say I wish you could have a dose of Pollyanna. It would do you a world of good.'

Mrs Carew lifted her chin a little.

'Really, indeed, I must say I beg to differ with you,' she returned coldly. 'I don't care to be "revolution-ized", and I have no lovers' quarrel to be patched up; and if there is *anything* that would be insufferable to me, it would be a little Miss Prim with a long face preaching to me how much I had to be thankful for. I never could bear –' But a ringing laugh interrupted her.

'Oh, Ruth, Ruth,' choked her sister gleefully. 'Miss Prim, indeed – *Pollyanna!* Oh, oh, if only you could see that child now! But there, I might have known. I *said* one couldn't *tell* about Pollyanna. And of course you won't be apt to see her. But – Miss Prim, indeed!' And off she went into another gale of laughter. Almost at once, however, she sobered and gazed at her sister with the old troubled look in her eyes.

'Seriously, dear, can't anything be done?' she pleaded. 'You ought not to waste your life like this. Won't you try to get out a little more, and – meet people?'

'Why should I, when I don't want to? I'm tired of – people. You know society always bored me.'

'Then why not try some sort of work – charity?'

Mrs Carew gave an impatient gesture.

'Della, dear, we've been all over this before. I do give money – lots of it, and that's enough. In fact, I'm not sure but it's too much. I don't believe in pauperiz-ing people.'

'But if you'd give a little of yourself, dear,' ventured

Della gently. 'If you could only get interested in something outside of your own life it would help so much; and –'

'Now, Della, dear,' interrupted the elder sister restively, 'I love you, and I love to have you come here; but I simply cannot endure being preached to. It's all very well for you to turn yourself into an angel of mercy and give cups of cold water, and bandage up broken heads, and all that. Perhaps *you* can forget Jamie that way; but I couldn't. It would only make me think of him all the more, wondering if he had anyone to give him water and bandage up his head. Besides, the whole thing would be very distasteful to me – mixing with all sorts and kinds of people like that.'

'Did you ever try it?'

'Why, no, of course not!' Mrs Carew's voice was scornfully indignant.

'Then how can you know – till you do try?' asked the young nurse, rising to her feet a little wearily. 'But I must go, dear. I'm to meet the girls at the South Station. Our train goes at twelve-thirty. I'm sorry if I've made you cross with me,' she finished, as she kissed her sister good-bye.

'I'm not cross with you, Della,' sighed Mrs Carew; 'but if you only would understand!'

One minute later Della Wetherby made her way through the silent, gloomy halls, and out to the street. Face, step, and manner were very different from what they had been when she tripped up the steps less than half an hour before. All the alertness, the springiness, the joy of living, were gone. For half a block she listlessly dragged one foot after the other. Then, suddenly, she threw back her head and drew a long breath.

'One week in that house would kill me,' she shuddered. 'I don't believe even Pollyanna herself could so much as make a dent in the gloom! And the only thing she could be glad for there would be that she didn't have to stay.'

That this avowed disbelief in Pollyanna's ability to bring about a change for the better in Mrs Carew's home was not Della Wetherby's real opinion, however, was quickly proved; for no sooner had the nurse reached the Sanatorium than she learned something that sent her flying back over the fifty-mile journey to Boston the very next day.

So exactly as before did she find circumstances at her sister's home that it seemed almost as if Mrs Carew had not moved since she left her.

'Ruth,' she burst out eagerly, after answering her sister's surprised greeting, 'I just *had* to come, and you must, this once, yield to me and let me have my way. Listen! You can have that little Pollyanna here, I think, if you will.'

'But I won't,' returned Mrs Carew, with chilly promptness.

Della Wetherby did not seem to have heard. She plunged on excitedly.

'When I got back yesterday I found that Dr Ames had had a letter from Dr Chilton, the one who married Pollyanna's aunt, you know. Well, it seems in it he said he was going to Germany for the winter for a special course, and was going to take his wife with him, if he could persuade her that Pollyanna would be all right in some boarding-school here meantime. But

Mrs Chilton didn't want to leave Pollyanna in just a school, and so he was afraid she wouldn't go. And now, Ruth, there's our chance. I want *you* to take Pollyanna this winter, and let her go to some school around here.'

'What an absurd idea, Della! As if I wanted a child here to bother with!'

'She won't bother a bit. She must be nearly or quite thirteen by this time, and she's the most capable little thing you ever saw.'

'I don't like "capable" children,' retorted Mrs Carew perversely – but she laughed; and because she did laugh her sister took sudden courage and redoubled her efforts.

Perhaps it was the suddenness of the appeal, of the novelty of it. Perhaps it was because the story of Pollyanna had somehow touched Ruth Carew's heart. Perhaps it was only her unwillingness to refuse her sister's impassioned plea. Whatever it was that finally turned the scale, when Della Wetherby took her hurried leave half an hour later she carried with her Ruth Carew's promise to receive Pollyanna into her home.

'But just remember,' Mrs Carew warned her at parting, 'just remember that the minute that child begins to preach to me and to tell me to count my mercies, back she goes to you, and you may do what you please with her. *I* shan't keep her!'

'I'll remember – but I'm not worrying any,' nodded the younger woman, in farewell. To herself she whispered, as she hurried away from the house: 'Half my job is done. Now for the other half – to get Pollyanna to come. But she's just got to come. I'll write that letter so they can't help letting her come!'

2

Some Old Friends

In Beldingsville that August day Mrs Chilton waited until Pollyanna had gone to bed before she spoke to her husband about the letter that had come in the morning mail. For that matter, she would have had to wait, anyway, for crowded office hours and the doctor's two long drives over the hills had left no time for domestic conferences.

It was about half-past nine, indeed, when the doctor entered his wife's sitting-room. His tired face lighted at sight of her, but at once a perplexed questioning came to his eyes.

'Why, Polly dear, what is it?' he asked concernedly.

His wife gave a rueful laugh.

'Well, it's a letter – though I didn't mean you should find out by just looking at me.'

'Then you mustn't look so I can,' he smiled. 'But what is it?'

Mrs Chilton hesitated, pursed her lips, then picked up a letter near her.

'I'll read it to you,' she said. 'It's from a Miss Della Wetherby at Dr Ames' Sanatorium.'

'All right. Fire away,' directed the man, throwing himself at full length on to the couch near his wife's chair.

But his wife did not at once 'fire away'. She got up first and covered her husband's recumbent figure with a grey worsted afghan. Mrs Chilton's wedding-day was but a year behind her. She was forty-two now. It seemed sometimes as if into that one short year of wifehood she had tried to crowd all the loving service and 'babying' that had been accumulating through twenty years of lovelessness and loneliness. Nor did the doctor – who had been forty-five on his wedding-day, and who could remember nothing but loneliness and lovelessness – on his part object in the least to this concentrated 'tending'. He acted, indeed, as if he quite enjoyed it – though he was careful not to show it too ardently; he had discovered that Mrs Polly had for so long been Miss Polly that she was inclined to retreat in a panic and dub her ministrations 'silly' if they were received with too much notice and eagerness. So he contented himself now with a mere pat of her hand as she gave the afghan a final smooth, and settled herself to read the letter aloud.

My dear Mrs Chilton [Della Wetherby had written],

Just six times I have commenced a letter to you, and torn it up; so now I have decided not to 'commence' at all, but just to tell you what I want at once. I want Pollyanna. May I have her?

I met you and your husband last March when you came on to take Pollyanna home, but I presume you don't remember me. I am asking Dr Ames (who does know me very well) to write your husband, so that you may (I hope) not fear to trust your dear little niece to us.

I understand that you would go to Germany with your husband but for leaving Pollyanna; and so I am making so bold as to ask you to let us take her. Indeed, I am begging you to let us have her, dear Mrs Chilton. And now let me tell you why.

My sister, Mrs Carew, is a lonely, broken-hearted, discontented, unhappy woman. She lives in a world of gloom, into which no sunshine penetrates. Now I believe that if anything on earth can bring the sunshine into her life, it is your niece, Pollyanna. Won't you let her try? I wish I could tell you what she has done for the Sanatorium here, but nobody could *tell*. You would have to see it. I long ago discovered that you can't *tell* about Pollyanna. The minute you try to, she sounds priggish and preachy, and – impossible. Yet you and I know she is anything but that. You just have to bring Pollyanna on to the scene and let her speak for herself. And so I want to take her to my sister – and let her speak for herself. She would attend school, of course, but meanwhile I truly believe she would be healing the wound in my sister's heart.

I don't know how to end this letter. I believe it's harder than it was to begin it. I'm afraid I don't want to end it at all. I just want to keep talking and talking, for fear, if I stop, it'll give you a chance to say no. And so, if you *are* tempted to say that dreadful word, won't you please consider that – that I'm still talking, and telling you how much we want and need Pollyanna.

Hopefully yours,
Della Wetherby

'There!' ejaculated Mrs Chilton, as she laid the letter down. 'Did you ever read such a remarkable letter, or hear of a more preposterous, absurd request?'

'Well, I'm not so sure,' smiled the doctor. 'I don't think it's absurd to want Pollyanna.'

'But – but the way she puts it – healing the wound

in her sister's heart and all that. One would think the child was some sort of – medicine!'

The doctor laughed outright, and raised his eyebrows.

'Well, I'm not so sure but she is, Polly. I *always* said I wished I could prescribe her and buy her as I would a box of pills; and Charlie Ames says they always made it a point at the Sanatorium to give their patients a dose of Pollyanna as soon as possible after their arrival, during the whole year she was there.'

'"Dose", indeed!' scorned Mrs Chilton.

'Then – you don't think you'll let her go?'

'Go? Why, of course not! Do you think I'd let that child go to perfect strangers like that? – and such strangers! Why, Thomas, I should expect that that nurse would have her all bottled and labelled with full directions on the outside how to take her, by the time I'd got back from Germany.'

Again the doctor threw back his head and laughed heartily, but only for a moment. His face changed perceptibly as he reached into his pocket for a letter.

'I heard from Dr Ames myself, this morning,' he said, with an odd something in his voice that brought a puzzled frown to his wife's brow. 'Suppose I read you my letter now.'

Dear Tom [he began],

Miss Della Wetherby has asked me to give her and her sister a 'character', which I am very glad to do. I have known the Wetherby girls from babyhood. They come from a fine old family, and are thoroughbred gentlewomen. You need not fear on that score.

There were three sisters, Doris, Ruth, and Della. Doris

married a man named John Kent, much against the family's wishes. Kent came from good stock, but was not much himself, I guess, and was certainly a very eccentric, disagreeable man to deal with. He was bitterly angry at the Wetherbys' attitude towards him, and there was little communication between the families until the baby came. The Wetherbys worshipped the little boy, James – 'Jamie', as they called him. Doris, the mother, died when the boy was four years old, and the Wetherbys were making every effort to get the father to give the child entirely up to them, when suddenly Kent disappeared, taking the boy with him. He has never been heard from since, though a world-wide search has been made.

The loss practically killed old Mr and Mrs Wetherby. They both died soon after. Ruth was already married and widowed. Her husband was a man named Carew, very wealthy, and much older than herself. He lived but a year or so after marriage, and left her with a young son who also died within a year.

From the time little Jamie disappeared, Ruth and Della seemed to have but one object in life, and that was to find him. They have spent money like water, and have all but moved heaven and earth; but without avail. In time Della took up nursing. She is doing splendid work, and has become the cheerful, efficient, sane woman that she was meant to be – though still never forgetting her lost nephew, and never leaving unfollowed any possible clue that might lead to his discovery.

But with Mrs Carew it is quite different. After losing her own boy, she seemed to concentrate all her thwarted mother-love on her sister's son. As you can imagine, she was frantic when he disappeared. That was eight years ago – for her, eight long years of misery, gloom, and bitterness. Everything that money can buy, of course, is at her command; but nothing pleases her, nothing interests her. Della feels that the time has come when she must be gotten out of herself, at all hazards; and Della believes that your wife's sunny little niece, Pollyanna, possesses the magic key that will unlock the door to a new existence for her. Such being the case, I hope you will see your way clear to granting her request. And may I add that I too, personally, would appreciate the favour; for Ruth Carew and her sister are very old, dear friends of my wife and myself; and what touches them touches us.

As ever yours,

Charlie

The letter finished, there was a long silence, so long a silence that the doctor uttered a quiet, 'Well, Polly?'

Still there was silence. The doctor, watching his wife's face closely, saw that the usually firm lips and chin were trembling. He waited then quietly until his wife spoke.

'How soon – do you think – they'll expect her?' she asked at last.

In spite of himself Dr Chilton gave a slight start.

'You mean – that you *will* let her go?' he cried.

His wife turned indignantly.

'Why, Thomas Chilton, what a question! Do you suppose, after a letter like that, I could do anything *but* let her go? Besides, didn't Dr Ames himself ask us to? Do you think, after what that man has done for Pollyanna, that I'd refuse him *anything* – no matter what it was?'

'Dear, dear! I hope now that the doctor won't take it into his head to ask for – for *you*, my love,' murmured the husband of a year, with a whimsical smile. But his wife only gave him a deservedly scornful glance, and said:

'You may write Dr Ames that we'll send Pollyanna; and ask him to tell Miss Wetherby to give us full instructions. It must be some time before the tenth of next month, of course, for you sail then; and I want to see the child properly established myself before I leave, naturally.'

'When will you tell Pollyanna?'

'Tomorrow, probably.'

'What will you tell her?'

'I don't know – exactly; but not any more than I can't help, certainly. Whatever happens, Thomas, we don't want to spoil Pollyanna; and no child could help being spoiled if she once got it into her head that she was a sort of – of –'

'Of medicine-bottle with a label of full instructions for taking?' interpolated the doctor, with a smile.

'Yes,' sighed Mrs Chilton. 'It's her unconsciousness that saves the whole thing. *You* know that, dear.'

'Yes, I know,' nodded the man.

'She knows, of course, that you and I and half the town are playing the game with her, and that we – we are wonderfully happier because we *are* playing it.' Mrs Chilton's voice shook a little, then went on more steadily. 'But if, consciously, she should begin to be anything but her own natural, sunny, happy little self, playing the game that her father taught her, she would be – just what that nurse said she sounded like – "impossible". So, whatever I tell her, I shan't tell her that she's going down to Mrs Carew's to cheer her up,' concluded Mrs Chilton, rising to her feet with decision, and putting away her work.

'Which is where I think you're wise,' approved the doctor.

Pollyanna was told the next day; and this was the manner of it.

'My dear,' began her aunt, when the two were alone together that morning, 'how would you like to spend next winter in Boston?'

'With you?'

'No; I have decided to go with your uncle to Germany. But Mrs Carew, a dear friend of Dr Ames, has asked you to come and stay with her for the winter, and I think I shall let you go.'

Pollyanna's face fell.

'But in Boston I won't have Jimmy, or Mr Pendleton, or Mrs Snow, or anybody that I know, Aunt Polly.'

'No, dear; but you didn't have them when you came here – till you found them.'

Pollyanna gave a sudden smile.

'Why, Aunt Polly, so I didn't! And that means that down to Boston there are some Jimmys and Mr Pendletons and Mrs Snows waiting for me that I don't know, doesn't it?'

'Yes, dear.'

'Then I can be glad of that. I believe now, Aunt Polly, you know how to play the game better than I do. I never thought of the folks down there waiting for me to know them. And there's such a lot of 'em, too! I saw some of them when I was there two years ago with Mrs Gray. We were there two whole hours, you know, on my way here from out West.

'There was a man in the station – a perfectly lovely man who told me where to get a drink of water. Do you suppose he's there now? I'd like to know him. And there was a nice lady with a little girl. They live in Boston. They said they did. The little girl's name was Susie Smith. Perhaps I could get to know them. Do you suppose I could? And there was a boy, and another lady with a baby – only they lived in Honolulu, so probably I couldn't find them there now. But there'd be Mrs Carew, anyway. Who is Mrs Carew, Aunt Polly? Is she a relation?'

'Dear me, Pollyanna!' exclaimed Mrs Chilton, half laughingly, half despairingly. 'How do you expect anybody to keep up with your tongue, much less your thoughts, when they skip to Honolulu and back again in two seconds! No, Mrs Carew isn't any relation to us. She's Miss Della Wetherby's sister. Do you remember Miss Wetherby at the Sanatorium?'

Pollyanna clapped her hands.

'*Her* sister? Miss Wetherby's sister? Oh, then she'll be lovely, I know. Miss Wetherby was. I loved Miss Wetherby. She had little smile-wrinkles all around her eyes and mouth, and she knew the *nicest* stories. I only had her two months, though, because she only got there a little while before I came away. At first I was sorry that I hadn't had her all the time, but afterwards I was glad; for you see if I *had* had her all the time, it would have been harder to say good-bye than 'twas when I'd only had her a little while. And now it'll seem as if I had her again, 'cause I'm going to have her sister.'

Mrs Chilton drew in her breath and bit her lip.

'But, Pollyanna dear, you must not expect that they'll be quite alike,' she ventured.

'Why, they're *sisters*, Aunt Polly,' argued the little

girl, her eyes widening; 'and I thought sisters were always alike. We had two sets of 'em in the Ladies' Aiders. One set was twins, and *they* were so alike you couldn't tell which was Mrs Peck and which was Mrs Jones, until a wart grew on Mrs Jones's nose, then of course we could, because we looked for the wart the first thing. And that's what I told her one day when she was complaining that people called her Mrs Peck, and I said if they'd only look for the wart as I did, they'd know right off. But she acted real cross – I mean displeased, and I'm afraid she didn't like it – though I don't see why; for I should have thought she'd been glad there was something they could be told apart by, 'specially as she was the president, and didn't like it when folks didn't *act* as if she was the president – best seats and introductions and special attentions at church suppers, you know. But she didn't, and afterwards I heard Mrs White tell Mrs Rawson that Mrs Jones had done everything she could think of to get rid of that wart, even to trying to put salt on a bird's tail. But I don't see how *that* could do any good. Aunt Polly, *does* putting salt on a bird's tail help the warts on people's noses?'

'Of course not, child! How you do run on, Pollyanna, especially if you get started on those Ladies' Aiders!'

'Do I, Aunt Polly?' asked the little girl ruefully. 'And does it plague you? I don't mean to plague you, honestly, Aunt Polly. And, anyway, if I do plague you about those Ladies' Aiders, you can be kind o' glad, for if I'm thinking of the Aiders, I'm sure to be thinking how glad I am that I don't belong to them any longer, but have got an aunt all my own. You can be glad of that, can't you, Aunt Polly?'

'Yes, yes, dear, of course I can, of course I can,' laughed Mrs Chilton, rising to leave the room, and feeling suddenly very guilty that she was conscious sometimes of a little of her old irritation against Pollyanna's perpetual gladness.

During the next few days, while letters concerning Pollyanna's winter stay in Boston were flying back and forth, Pollyanna herself was preparing for that stay by a series of farewell visits to her Beldingsville friends.

Everybody in the little Vermont village knew Pollyanna now, and almost everybody was playing the game with her. The few who were not were not refraining because of ignorance of what the Glad Game was. So to one house after another Pollyanna carried the news now that she was going down to Boston to spend the winter; and loudly rose the clamour of regret and remonstrance, all the way from Nancy in Aunt Polly's own kitchen to the great house on the hill where lived John Pendleton.

Nancy did not hesitate to say – to every one except her mistress – that *she* considered this Boston trip all foolishness, and that for her part she would have been glad to take Miss Pollyanna home with her to 'The Corners', she would, she would; and then Mrs Polly could have gone to Germany all she wanted to.

On the hill John Pendleton said practically the same thing, only he did not hesitate to say it to Mrs Chilton herself. As for Jimmy, the twelve-year-old boy whom John Pendleton had taken into his home because Pollyanna wanted him to, and whom he had now adopted – because he wanted to himself – as for Jimmy, Jimmy was indignant, and he was not slow to show it.

'But you've just come,' he reproached Pollyanna, in a tone of voice a small boy is apt to use when he wants to hide the fact that he has a heart.

'Why, I've been here ever since the last of March. Besides, it isn't as if I was going to stay. It's only for this winter.'

'I don't care. You've just been away for a whole year, 'most, and if I'd s'posed you was going away again right off, the first thing, I wouldn't have helped one mite to meet you with flags and bands and things, that day you come from the Sanatorium.'

'Why, Jimmy Bean!' ejaculated Pollyanna, in amazed disapproval. Then, with a touch of superiority born of hurt pride, she observed, 'I'm sure I didn't *ask* you to meet me with bands and things – and you made two mistakes in that sentence. You shouldn't say "you was"; and I think "you come" is wrong. It doesn't sound right, anyway.'

'Well, who cares if I did?'

Pollyanna's eyes grew still more disapproving.

'You *said* you did – when you asked me this summer to tell you when you said things wrong, because Mr Pendleton was trying to make you talk right.'

'Well, if you'd been brought up in an 'sylum without any folks that cared, instead of by a whole lot of old women who didn't have anything to do but tell you how to talk right, maybe you'd say "you was", and a whole lot more worse things, Pollyanna Whittier!'

'Why, Jimmy Bean!' flared Pollyanna. 'My Ladies' Aiders weren't old women – that is, not many of them, so very old,' she corrected hastily, her usual proclivity for truth and literalness superseding her anger; 'and –'

'Well, I'm not Jimmy Bean, either,' interrupted the boy, uptilting his chin.

'You're – not – Why, Jimmy Be– What do you mean?' demanded the little girl.

'I've been adopted, *legally*. He's been intending to do it all along, he says, only he didn't get to it. Now he's done it. I'm to be called Jimmy Pendleton, and I'm to call him Uncle John, only I ain't – are not – I mean, I *am* not used to it yet, so I hain't – haven't begun to call him that, much.'

The boy still spoke crossly, aggrievedly, but every trace of displeasure had fled from the little girl's face at his words. She clapped her hands joyfully.

'Oh, how splendid! Now you've really got *folks* – folks that care, you know. And you won't ever have to explain that he wasn't *born* your folks, 'cause your name's the same now. I'm so glad, *glad*, GLAD!'

The boy got up suddenly from the stone wall where they had been sitting, and walked off. His cheeks felt hot, and his eyes smarted with tears. It was to Pollyanna that he owed it all – this great good that had come to him; and he knew it. And it was to Pollyanna that he had just now been saying . . .

He kicked a small stone fiercely, then another, and another. He thought those hot tears in his eyes were going to spill over and roll down his cheeks in spite of himself. He kicked another stone, then another; then he picked up a third stone and threw it with all his might. A minute later he strolled back to Pollyanna still sitting on the stone wall.

'I bet you I can hit that pine-tree down there before you can,' he challenged airily.

'Bet you can't,' cried Pollyanna, scrambling down from her perch.

The race was not run after all, for Pollyanna remembered just in time that running fast was yet one of the forbidden luxuries for her. But so far as Jimmy was concerned, it did not matter. His cheeks were no longer hot, his eyes were not threatening to overflow with tears. Jimmy was himself again.

3

A DOSE OF POLLYANNA

As the 8th of September approached – the day Pollyanna was to arrive – Mrs Ruth Carew became more
and more nervously exasperated with herself. She declared that she had regretted just *once* her promise to
take the child – and that was ever since she had given
it. Before twenty-four hours had passed she had,
indeed, written to her sister demanding that she be
released from the agreement; but Della had answered
that it was quite too late, as already both she and Dr
Ames had written the Chiltons.

Soon after that had come Della's letter saying that
Mrs Chilton had given her consent, and would in a
few days come to Boston to make arrangements as to
school, and the like. So there was nothing to be done,
naturally, but to let matters take their course. Mrs
Carew realized that, and submitted to the inevitable,
but with poor grace. True, she tried to be decently
civil when Della and Mrs Chilton made their expected
appearance; but she was very glad that limited time
made Mrs Chilton's stay of very short duration, and
full to the brim of business.

It was well, indeed, perhaps, that Pollyanna's arrival
was to be at a date no later than the 8th; for time,
instead of reconciling Mrs Carew to the prospective

new member of her household, was filling her with angry impatience at what she was pleased to call her 'absurd yielding to Della's crazy scheme'.

Nor was Della herself in the least unaware of her sister's state of mind. If outwardly she maintained a bold front, inwardly she was very fearful as to results; but on Pollyanna she was pinning her faith, and because she did pin her faith on Pollyanna, she determined on the bold stroke of leaving the little girl to begin her fight entirely unaided and alone. She contrived, therefore, that Mrs Carew should meet them at the station upon their arrival; then, as soon as greetings and introductions were over, she hurriedly pleaded a previous engagement and took herself off. Mrs Carew, therefore, had scarcely time to look at her new charge before she found herself alone with the child.

'Oh, but, Della, Della, you mustn't – I can't,' she called agitatedly after the retreating figure of the nurse.

But Della, if she heard, did not heed; and, plainly annoyed and vexed, Mrs Carew turned back to the child at her side.

'What a shame! She didn't hear, did she?' Pollyanna was saying, her eyes, also, wistfully following the nurse. 'And I didn't *want* her to go now a bit. But then, I've got you, haven't I? I can be glad for that.'

'Oh, yes, you've got me – and I've got you,' returned the lady, not very graciously. 'Come, we go this way,' she directed, with a motion towards the right.

Obediently Pollyanna turned and trotted at Mrs Carew's side, through the huge station; but she looked up once or twice rather anxiously into the lady's unsmiling face. At last she spoke hesitatingly.

'I expect maybe you thought – I'd be pretty,' she hazarded, in a troubled voice.

'P-pretty?' repeated Mrs Carew.

'Yes – with curls, you know, and all that. And of course you did wonder how I *did* look, just as I did you. Only I *knew* you'd be pretty and nice, on account of your sister. I had her to go by, and you didn't have anybody. And of course I'm not pretty on account of the freckles, and it *isn't* nice when you've been expecting a *pretty* little girl, to have one come like me; and –'

'Nonsense, child!' interrupted Mrs Carew, a trifle sharply. 'Come, we'll see to your trunk now, then we'll go home. I had hoped that my sister would come with us; but it seems she didn't see fit – even for this one night.'

Pollyanna smiled and nodded.

'I know; but she couldn't, probably. Somebody wanted her, I expect. Somebody was always wanting her at the Sanatorium. It's a bother, of course, when folks do want you all the time, isn't it? – 'cause you can't have yourself when you want yourself, lots of times. Still, you can be kind of glad for that, for it *is* nice to be wanted, isn't it?'

There was no reply – perhaps because for the first time in her life Mrs Carew was wondering if anywhere in the world there was anyone who really wanted her – not that she *wished* to be wanted, of course, she told herself angrily, pulling herself up with a jerk, and frowning down at the child by her side.

Pollyanna did not see the frown. Pollyanna's eyes were on the hurrying throngs about them

'My! what a lot of people,' she was saying happily. 'There's even more of them than there was the other time I was here; but I haven't seen anybody, yet, that I saw then, though I've looked for them everywhere. Of course the lady and the little baby lived in Honolulu, so probably they *wouldn't* be here; but there was a little girl, Susie Smith – she lived right here in Boston. Maybe you know her though. Do you know Susie Smith?'

'No, I don't know Susie Smith,' replied Mrs Carew drily.

'Don't you? She's awfully nice, and *she's* pretty – black curls, you know; the kind I'm going to have when I go to heaven. But never mind; maybe I can find her for you so you *will* know her. Oh, my! what a perfectly lovely automobile! And are we going to ride in it?' broke off Pollyanna, as they came to a pause before a handsome limousine, the door of which a liveried chauffeur was holding open.

The chauffeur tried to hide a smile – and failed. Mrs Carew, however, answered with the weariness of one to whom 'rides' are never anything but a means of locomotion from one tiresome place to another probably quite as tiresome.

'Yes, we're going to ride in it.' Then 'Home, Perkins,' she added to the deferential chauffeur.

'Oh, my, is it yours?' asked Pollyanna, detecting the unmistakable air of ownership in her hostess's manner. 'How perfectly lovely! Then you must be rich – awfully – I mean *exceedingly* rich, more than the kind that just has carpets in every room and ice-cream Sundays, like the Whites – one of my Ladies' Aiders, you know. (That is, *she* was a Ladies' Aider.) I used to think *they* were rich, but I know now that being really rich means you've got diamond rings and hired girls and sealskin coats, and dresses made of silk and velvet for every day, and an automobile. Have you got all those?'

'Why, y-yes, I suppose I have,' admitted Mrs Carew, with a faint smile.

'Then you are rich, of course,' nodded Pollyanna wisely. 'My Aunt Polly has them too, only her automobile is a horse. My! but don't I just love to ride in these things!' exulted Pollyanna, with a happy little bounce. 'You see, I never did before, except the one that ran over me. They put me *in* that one after they'd got me out from under it; but of course I didn't know about it, so I couldn't enjoy it. Since then I haven't been in one at all. Aunt Polly doesn't like them. Uncle Tom does, though, and he wants one. He says he's got to have one, in his, business. He's a doctor, you know, and all the other doctors in town have got them now. I don't know how it will come out. Aunt Polly is all stirred up over it. You see, she wants Uncle Tom to have what he wants, only she wants him to want what she wants him to want. See?'

Mrs Carew laughed suddenly.

'Yes, my dear, I think I see,' she answered demurely, though her eyes still carried – for them – a most unusual twinkle.

'All right,' sighed Pollyanna contentedly. 'I thought you would; still, it did sound sort of mixed when I said it. Oh, Aunt Polly says she wouldn't mind having an automobile, so much, if she could have the only one there was in the world, so there wouldn't be anyone else to run into her; but – My! what a lot of houses!' broke off Pollyanna, looking about her with round eyes of wonder. 'Don't they ever stop? Still, there'd have to be a lot of them for all those folks to live in, of course, that I saw at the station, besides all these here on the streets. And of course where there *are* more folks, there are more to know. I love folks. Don't you?'

'*Love folks!*'

'Yes, just folks, I mean. Anybody – everybody.'

'Well, no, Pollyanna, I can't say that I do,' replied Mrs Carew coldly, her brows contracted.

Mrs Carew's eyes had lost their twinkle. They were turned rather mistrustfully, indeed, on Pollyanna. To herself Mrs Carew was saying, 'Now for preachment number one, I suppose, on my duty to mix with my fellow-men, *à la* Sister Della!'

'Don't you? Oh, I do,' sighed Pollyanna. 'They're all so nice and so different, you know. And down here there must be such a lot of them to be nice and different. Oh, you don't know how glad I am so soon that I came! I knew I would be, anyway, just as soon as I found out you were *you* – that is, Miss Wetherby's sister, I mean. I love Miss Wetherby so I knew I should you too; for of course you'd be alike – sisters, so – even if you weren't twins like Mrs Jones and Mrs Peck – and they weren't quite alike, anyway, on account of the wart. But I reckon you don't know what I mean, so I'll tell you.'

And thus it happened that Mrs Carew, who had been steeling herself for a preachment on social ethics, found herself, much to her surprise and a little to her discomfiture, listening to the story of a wart on the nose of one Mrs Peck, Ladies' Aider.

By the time the story was finished the limousine had turned into Commonwealth Avenue, and Pollyanna immediately began to exclaim at the beauty of a street which had such a 'lovely big long yard all the way up and down through the middle of it', and which was all the nicer, she said, 'after all those little narrow streets'.

'Only I should think every one would want to live on it,' she commented enthusiastically.

'Very likely; but that would hardly be possible,' retorted Mrs Carew, with uplifted eyebrows.

Pollyanna, mistaking the expression on her face for one of dissatisfaction that her own home was not on the beautiful Avenue, hastened to make amends.

'Why, no, of course not,' she agreed. 'And I didn't mean that the narrower streets weren't just as nice,' she hurried on; 'and even better, maybe, because you could be glad you didn't have to go so far when you wanted to run across the way to borrow eggs or soda, and – Oh, but *do* you live here?' she interrupted herself, as the car came to a stop before the imposing Carew doorway. 'Do you live here, Mrs Carew?'

'Why, yes, of course I live here,' returned the lady, with just a touch of irritation.

'Oh, how glad, *glad* you must be to live in such a perfectly lovely place!' exulted the little girl, springing to the sidewalk and looking eagerly about her. 'Aren't you glad?'

Mrs Carew did not reply. With unsmiling lips and frowning brow she was stepping from the limousine.

For the second time in five minutes Pollyanna hastened to make amends.

'Of course I don't mean the kind of glad that's sinfully proud,' she explained, searching Mrs Carew's face with anxious eyes. 'Maybe you thought I did, same as Aunt Polly used to sometimes. I don't mean the kind that's glad because you've got something somebody else can't have; but the kind that just – just makes you want to shout and yell and bang doors, you know, even if it isn't proper,' she finished, dancing up and down on her toes.

The chauffeur turned his back precipitately, and busied himself with the car. Mrs Carew, still with unsmiling lips and frowning brow, led the way up the broad stone steps.

'Come, Pollyanna,' was all she said crisply.

It was five days later that Della Wetherby received the letter from her sister, and very eagerly she tore it open. It was the first that had come since Pollyanna's arrival in Boston.

My dear Sister [Mrs Carew had written],

For pity's sake, Della, why didn't you give me some sort of an idea what to expect from this child you have insisted upon my taking? I'm nearly wild – and I simply can't send her away. I've tried to three times, but every time, before I get the words out of my mouth, she stops them by telling me what a perfectly lovely time she is having, and how glad she is to be here, and how good I am to let her live with me while her Aunt Polly has gone to Germany. Now how, pray, in the face of that, can I turn around and say 'Well, won't you please go home; I don't want you'? And the absurd part of it is, I don't believe it has ever entered her head that I don't *want* her here; and I can't seem to make it enter her head, either.

Of course if she begins to preach, and to tell me to count my blessings, I *shall* send her away. You know I told you, to begin with, that I wouldn't permit that. And I won't. Two or three times I have thought she was going to (preach, I mean), but so far she has always ended up with some ridiculous story about those Ladies' Aiders of hers; so the sermon gets sidetracked – luckily for her, if she wants to stay.

But, really, Della, she is impossible. Listen. In the first place she is wild with delight over the house. The very first day she got here she begged me to open every room; and she was not satisfied until every shade in the house was up, so that she might 'see all the perfectly lovely things', which, she declared, were even nicer than Mr John Pendleton's – whoever he may be, somebody in Beldingsville, I believe. Anyhow he isn't a Ladies' Aider. I've found out that much.

Then, as if it wasn't enough to keep me running from room to room (as if I were the guide on a 'personally conducted'), what did she do but discover a white satin evening gown that I hadn't worn for years, and beseech me to put it on. And I did put it on – why, I can't imagine, only that I found myself utterly helpless in her hands.

But that was only the beginning. She begged then to see everything that I had, and she was so perfectly funny in her stories of the missionary barrels, which she used to 'dress out of', that I had to laugh – though I almost cried, too, to think of the wretched things that poor child had to wear. Of course gowns led to jewels, and she made such a fuss over my two or three rings that I foolishly opened the safe, just to see her eyes pop out. And, Della, I thought that child would go crazy. She put on to me every ring, brooch, bracelet, and necklace that I owned, and insisted on fastening both diamond tiaras in my hair (when she found out what they were), until there I sat, hung with pearls and diamonds and emeralds, and feeling like a heathen goddess in a Hindu temple, especially when that preposterous child began to dance round and round me, clapping her hands and chanting, 'Oh, how perfectly lovely, how perfectly lovely! How I would love to hang you on a string in the window – you'd make such a beautiful prism!'

I was just going to ask her what on earth she meant by

that when down she dropped in the middle of the floor and began to cry. And what do you suppose she was crying for? Because she was so glad she'd got eyes that could see! Now what do you think of that?

Of course this isn't all. It's only the beginning. Pollyanna has been here four days, and she's filled every one of them full. She already numbers among her friends the ash-man, the policeman on the beat, and the paper-boy, to say nothing of every servant in my employ. They seem actually bewitched with her, every one of them. But please do not think *I* am, for I'm not. I would send the child back to you at once if I didn't feel obliged to fulfil my promise to keep her this winter. As for her making me forget Jamie and my great sorrow – that is impossible. She only makes me feel my loss all the more keenly – because I have her instead of him. But, as I said, I shall keep her – until she begins to preach. Then back she goes to you. But she hasn't preached yet.

Lovingly but distractedly yours,
Ruth

'"Hasn't preached yet", indeed!' chuckled Della Wetherby to herself, folding up the closely written sheets of her sister's letter. 'Oh, Ruth, Ruth! and yet you admit that you've opened every room, raised every shade, decked yourself in satin and jewels – and Pollyanna hasn't been there a week yet. But she hasn't preached – oh, no, she hasn't preached!'

4

The Game and Mrs Carew

Boston, to Pollyanna, was a new experience, and certainly Pollyanna, to Boston – such part of it as was privileged to know her – was very much of a new experience.

Pollyanna said she liked Boston, but that she did wish it was not quite so big.

'You see,' she explained earnestly to Mrs Carew, the day following her arrival, 'I want to see and know it *all*, and I can't. It's just like Aunt Polly's company dinners; there's so much to eat – I mean, to see – that you don't eat – I mean, see – anything, because you're always trying to decide what to eat – I mean, to see.

'Of course you can be glad there *is* such a lot,' resumed Pollyanna, after taking breath, ' 'cause a whole lot of anything is nice – that is, *good* things; not such things as medicine and funerals, of course! – but at the same time I couldn't used to help wishing Aunt Polly's company dinners could be spread out a little over the days when there wasn't any cake and pie; and I feel the same way about Boston. I wish I could take part of it home with me up to Beldingsville so I'd have *something* new next summer. But of course I can't. Cities aren't like frosted cake – and, anyhow, even the cake didn't keep very well. I tried it, and it dried up, 'specially the frosting. I reckon the time to take frosting and good times is while they are going; so I want to see all I can now while I'm here.'

Pollyanna, unlike the people who think that to see the world one must begin at the most distant point, began her 'seeing Boston' by a thorough exploration of her immediate surroundings – the beautiful Commonwealth Avenue residence which was now her home. This, with her school-work, fully occupied her time and attention for some days.

There was so much to see, and so much to learn; and everything was so marvellous and so beautiful, from the tiny buttons in the wall that flooded the rooms with light, to the great silent ballroom hung with mirrors and pictures. There were so many delightful people to know, too, for besides Mrs Carew herself there were Mary, who dusted the drawing-rooms, answered the bell, and accompanied Pollyanna to and from school each day; Bridget, who lived in the kitchen and cooked; Jennie, who waited at table, and Perkins, who drove the automobile. And they were all so delightful – yet so different!

Pollyanna had arrived on a Monday, so it was almost a week before the first Sunday. She came downstairs that morning with a beaming countenance.

'I love Sundays,' she sighed happily.

'Do you?' Mrs Carew's voice had the weariness of one who loves no day.

'Yes, on account of church, you know, and Sunday school. Which do you like best, church or Sunday school?'

'Well, really, I –' began Mrs Carew, who seldom went to church and never went to Sunday school.

''Tis hard to tell, isn't it?' interposed Pollyanna, with luminous but serious eyes. 'But you see *I* like church best, on account of Father. You know he was a minister, and of course he's really up in heaven with Mother and the rest of us, but I try to imagine him down here, lots of times; and it's easiest in church, when the minister is talking. I shut my eyes and imagine it's Father up there; and it helps lots. I'm so glad we can imagine things, aren't you?'

'I'm not so sure of that, Pollyanna.'

'Oh, but just think how much nicer our *imagined* things are than our really truly ones – that is, of course, yours aren't, because your *real* ones are so nice.' Mrs Carew angrily started to speak, but Pollyanna was hurrying on. 'And of course *my* real ones are ever so much nicer than they used to be. But all that time I was hurt, when my legs didn't go, I just had to keep imagining all the time, just as hard as I could. And of course now there are lots of times when I do it – like about Father, and all that. And so today I'm just going to imagine it's Father up there in the pulpit. What time do we go?'

'*Go?*'

'To church, I mean.'

'But, Pollyanna, I don't – that is, I'd rather not –' Mrs Carew cleared her throat and tried again to say that she was not going to church at all; that she almost never went. But with Pollyanna's confident little face and happy eyes before her, she could not do it.

'Why, I suppose – about quarter-past ten – if we walk,' she said then, almost crossly. 'It's only a little way.'

Thus it happened that Mrs Carew on that bright

September morning occupied for the first time in months the Carew pew in the very fashionable and elegant church to which she had gone as a girl, and which she still supported liberally – so far as money went.

To Pollyanna that Sunday morning service was a great wonder and joy. The marvellous music of the vested choir, the opalescent rays from the jewelled windows, the impassioned voice of the preacher, and the reverent hush of the worshipping throng filled her with an ecstasy that left her for a time almost speechless. Not until they were nearly home did she fervently breathe:

'Oh, Mrs Carew, I've just been thinking how glad I am we don't have to live but just one day at a time!'

Mrs Carew frowned and looked down sharply. Mrs Carew was in no mood for preaching. She had just been obliged to endure it from the pulpit, she told herself angrily, and she would *not* listen to it from this chit of a child. Moreover, this 'living one day at a time' theory was a particularly pet doctrine of Della's. Was not Della always saying: 'But you only have to live one minute at a time, Ruth, and anyone can endure anything for one minute at a time!'

'Well?' said Mrs Carew now tersely.

'Yes. Only think what I'd do if I had to live yesterday and today and tomorrow all at once,' sighed Pollyanna. 'Such a lot of perfectly lovely things, you know. But I've had yesterday, and now I'm living today, and I've got tomorrow still coming, and next Sunday, too. Honestly, Mrs Carew, if it wasn't Sunday now, and on this nice quiet street, I should just dance and shout and yell. I couldn't help it. But it's being Sunday, so I shall have to wait till I get home and then take a hymn – the most rejoicingest hymn I can think of. What is the most rejoicingest hymn? Do you know, Mrs Carew?'

'No, I can't say that I do,' answered Mrs Carew faintly, looking very much as if she were searching for something she had lost. For a woman who expects, because things are so bad, to be told that she need stand only one day at a time, it is disarming, to say the least, to be told that, because things are so good, it is lucky she does not *have* to stand but one day at a time!

On Monday, the next morning, Pollyanna went to school for the first time alone. She knew the way perfectly now, and it was only a short walk. Pollyanna enjoyed her school very much. It was a small private school for girls, and was quite a new experience in its way; but Pollyanna liked new experiences.

Mrs Carew, however, did not like new experiences, and she was having a good many of them these days. For one who is tired of everything to be in so intimate a companionship with one to whom everything is a fresh and fascinating joy must needs result in annoyance, to say the least. And Mrs Carew was more than annoyed. She was exasperated. Yet to herself she was forced to admit that if anyone asked her why she was exasperated, the only reason she could give would be 'Because Pollyanna is so glad' – and even Mrs Carew would hardly like to give an answer like that.

To Della, however, Mrs Carew did write that the word 'glad' had got on her nerves, and that sometimes she wished she might never hear it again. She still admitted that Pollyanna had not preached – that she had not even once tried to make her play the game.

What the child did do, however, was invariably to take Mrs Carew's 'gladness' as a matter of course, which, to one who *had* no gladness, was most provoking.

It was during the second week of Pollyanna's stay that Mrs Carew's annoyance overflowed into irritable remonstrance. The immediate cause thereof was Pollyanna's glowing conclusion to a story about one of her Ladies' Aiders.

'She was playing the game, Mrs Carew. But maybe you don't know what the game is. I'll tell you. It's a lovely game.'

But Mrs Carew held up her hand.

'Never mind, Pollyanna,' she demurred. 'I know all about the game. My sister told me, and – and I must say that I – I should not care for it.'

'Why, of course not, Mrs Carew!' exclaimed Pollyanna in quick apology. 'I didn't mean the game for you. You couldn't play it, of course.'

'I *couldn't* play it!' ejaculated Mrs Carew, who, though she *would* not play this silly game, was in no mood to be told that she *could* not.

'Why, no, don't you see?' laughed Pollyanna gleefully. 'The game is to find something in everything to be glad about; and you couldn't even begin to hunt, for there isn't anything about you but what you *could* be glad about. There wouldn't *be* any game to it for you! Don't you see?'

Mrs Carew flushed angrily. In her annoyance she said more than perhaps she meant to say.

'Well, no, Pollyanna, I can't say that I do,' she differed coldly. 'As it happens, you see, I can find nothing whatever to be – glad for.'

For a moment Pollyanna stared blankly. Then she fell back in amazement.

'Why, *Mrs Carew!*' she breathed.

'Well, what is there – for me?' challenged the woman, forgetting all about, for the moment, that she was never going to allow Pollyanna to 'preach'.

'Why, there's – there's everything,' murmured Pollyanna, still with that dazed unbelief. 'There – there's this beautiful house.'

'It's just a place to eat and sleep – and I don't want to eat and sleep.'

'But there are all these perfectly lovely things,' faltered Pollyanna.

'I'm tired of them.'

'And your automobile that will take you anywhere.'

'I don't want to go anywhere.'

Pollyanna quite gasped aloud.

'But think of the people and things you could see, Mrs Carew.'

'They would not interest me, Pollyanna.'

Once again Pollyanna stared in amazement. The troubled frown on her face deepened.

'But, Mrs Carew, I don't see,' she urged. 'Always, before, there have been *bad* things for folks to play the game on, and the badder they are the more fun 'tis to get them out – find the things to be glad for, I mean. But where there *aren't* any bad things, I shouldn't know how to play the game myself.'

There was no answer for a time. Mrs Carew sat with her eyes out the window. Gradually the angry rebellion on her face changed to a look of hopeless sadness. Very slowly then she turned and said:

'Pollyanna, I had thought I wouldn't tell you this;

but I've decided that I will. I'm going to tell you why nothing that I have can make me – glad.' And she began the story of Jamie, the little four-year-old boy who, eight long years before, had stepped as into another world, leaving the door fast shut between.

'And you've never seen him since – anywhere?' faltered Pollyanna, with tear-wet eyes, when the story was done.

'Never.'

'But we'll find him, Mrs Carew – I'm sure we'll find him.'

Mrs Carew shook her head sadly.

'But I can't. I have looked everywhere, even in foreign lands.'

'But he must be somewhere.'

'He may be – dead, Pollyanna.'

Pollyanna gave a quick cry.

'Oh, no, Mrs Carew. Please don't say that! Let's imagine he's alive. We *can* do that, and that'll help; and when we get him *imagined* alive we can just as well imagine we're going to find him. And that'll help a whole lot more.'

'But I'm afraid he's – dead, Pollyanna,' choked Mrs Carew.

'You don't know it for sure, do you?' besought the little girl anxiously.

'N-no.'

'Well, then, you're just imagining it,' maintained Pollyanna, in triumph. 'And if you can imagine him dead, you can just as well imagine him alive, and it'll be a whole lot nicer while you're doing it. Don't you see? And some day, I'm just sure you'll find him. Why, Mrs Carew, you *can* play the game now! You can play it on Jamie. You can be glad every day, for every day brings you just one day nearer to the time when you're going to find him. See?'

But Mrs Carew did not 'see'. She rose drearily to her feet and said:

'No, no, child! You don't understand – you don't understand. Now run away, please, and read, or do anything you like. My head aches. I'm going to lie down.'

And Pollyanna, with a troubled, sober face, slowly left the room.

5

POLLYANNA TAKES A WALK

It was on the second Saturday afternoon that Pollyanna took her memorable walk. Heretofore Pollyanna had not walked out alone, except to go to and from school. That she would ever attempt to explore Boston streets by herself, never occurred to Mrs Carew, hence she naturally had never forbidden it. In Beldingsville, however, Pollyanna had found – especially at the first – her chief diversion in strolling about the rambling old village streets in search of new friends and new adventures.

On this particular Saturday afternoon Mrs Carew had said, as she often did say: 'There, there, child, run away; please do. Go where you like and do what you like, only don't, please, ask me any more questions today!'

Until now, left to herself, Pollyanna had always found plenty to interest her within the four walls of the house; for, if inanimate things failed, there were yet Mary, Jennie, Bridget, and Perkins. Today, however, Mary had a headache, Jennie was trimming a new hat, Bridget was making apple pies, and Perkins was nowhere to be found. Moreover it was a particularly beautiful September day, and nothing within the house was so alluring as the bright sunlight and balmy air outside. So outside Pollyanna went and dropped herself down on the steps.

For some time she watched in silence the well-dressed men, women, and children, who walked briskly by the house, or else sauntered more leisurely through the parkway that extended up and down the middle of the Avenue. Then she got to her feet, skipped down the steps, and stood looking, first to the right, then to the left.

Pollyanna had decided that she too would take a walk. It was a beautiful day for a walk, and not once, yet, had she taken one at all – not a *real* walk. Just going to and from school did not count. So she would take one today. Mrs Carew would not mind. Had she not told her to do just what she pleased so long as she asked no more questions? And there was the whole long afternoon before her. Only think what a lot one might see in a whole long afternoon! And it really was such a beautiful day. She would go – this way! And with a little whirl and skip of pure joy, Pollyanna turned and walked blithely down the Avenue.

Into the eyes of those she met Pollyanna smiled joyously. She was disappointed – but not surprised – that she received no answering smile in return. She was used to that now – in Boston. She still smiled, however, hopefully: there might be some one, some-time, who would smile back.

Mrs Carew's home was very near the beginning of Commonwealth Avenue, so it was not long before Pollyanna found herself at the edge of a street crossing her way at right angles. Across the street, in all its autumn glory, lay what to Pollyanna was the most beautiful 'yard' she had ever seen – the Boston Public Garden.

For a moment Pollyanna hesitated, her eyes longingly fixed on the wealth of beauty before her. That it was the private grounds of some rich man or woman, she did not for a moment doubt. Once, with Dr Ames at the Sanatorium, she had been taken to call on a lady who lived in a beautiful house surrounded by just such walks and trees and flower-beds as these.

Pollyanna wanted now very much to cross the street and walk in those grounds, but she doubted if she had the right. To be sure, others were there, moving about, she could see; but they might be invited guests, of course. After she had seen two women, one man, and a little girl unhesitatingly enter the gate and walk briskly down the path, however, Pollyanna concluded that she too might go. Watching her chance, she skipped nimbly across the street and entered the Garden.

It was even more beautiful close at hand than it had been at a distance. Birds twittered over her head, and a squirrel leaped across the path ahead of her. On benches here and there sat men, women, and children. Through the trees flashed the sparkle of the sun on water; and from somewhere came the shouts of children and the sound of music.

Once again Pollyanna hesitated; then, a little timidly, she accosted a handsomely dressed young woman coming towards her.

'Please, is this – a party?' she asked.

The young woman stared.

'A party!' she repeated dazedly.

'Yes'm. I mean, is it all right for me – to be here?'

'For you to be here? Why, of course. It's for – for everybody!' exclaimed the young woman.

'Oh, that's all right, then. I'm glad I came,' beamed Pollyanna.

The young woman said nothing; but she turned back and looked at Pollyanna still dazedly as she hurried away.

Pollyanna, not at all surprised that the owner of this beautiful place should be so generous as to give a party to everybody, continued on her way. At the turn of the path she came upon a small girl and a doll-carriage. She stopped with a glad little cry, but she had not said a dozen words before from somewhere came a young woman with hurrying steps and a disapproving voice; a young woman who held out her hand to the small girl, and said sharply:

'Here, Gladys, Gladys, come away with me. Hasn't Mama told you not to talk to strange children?'

'But I'm not strange children,' explained Pollyanna in eager defence. 'I live right here in Boston now, and –' But the young woman and the little girl dragging the doll-carriage were already far down the path; and with a half-stifled sigh Pollyanna fell back. For a moment she stood silent, plainly disappointed; then resolutely she lifted her chin and went forward.

'Well, anyhow, I can be glad for that,' she nodded to herself, 'for now maybe I'll find somebody even nicer – Susie Smith, perhaps, or even Mrs Carew's Jamie. Anyhow, I can *imagine* I'm going to find them; and if I don't find *them*, I can find *somebody*!' she finished, her wistful eyes on the self-absorbed people all about her.

Undeniably Pollyanna was lonesome. Brought up by

her father and the Ladies' Aid Society in a small Western town, she had counted every house in the village her home, and every man, woman, and child her friend. Coming to her aunt in Vermont at eleven years of age, she had promptly assumed that conditions would differ only in that the homes and the friends would be new, and therefore even more delightful, possibly, for they would be 'different' – and Pollyanna did so love 'different' things and people! Her first and always her supreme delight in Beldingsville, therefore, had been her long rambles about the town and the charming visits with the new friends she had made. Quite naturally, in consequence, Boston, as she first saw it, seemed to Pollyanna even more delightfully promising in its possibilities.

Thus far, however, Pollyanna had to admit that in one respect, at least, it had been disappointing: she had been here nearly two weeks and she did not yet know the people who lived across the street, or even next door. More inexplicable still, Mrs Carew herself did not know many of them, and not any of them well. She seemed, indeed, utterly indifferent to her neighbours, which was most amazing from Pollyanna's point of view; but nothing she could say appeared to change Mrs Carew's attitude in the matter at all.

'They do not interest me, Pollyanna,' was all she would say; and with this, Pollyanna – whom they did interest very much – was forced to be content.

Today, on her walk, however, Pollyanna had started out with high hopes, yet thus far she seemed to be destined to be disappointed. Here all about her were people who were doubtless most delightful – if she only knew them. But she did not know them. Worse yet, there seemed to be no prospect that she would know them, for they did not apparently wish to know her; Pollyanna was still smarting under the nurse's sharp warning concerning 'strange children'.

'Well, I reckon I'll just have to show 'em that I'm not strange children,' she said at last to herself, moving confidently forward again.

Pursuant of this idea Pollyanna smiled sweetly into the eyes of the next person she met, and said blithely:

'It's a nice day, isn't it?'

'Er – what? Oh, y-yes, it is,' murmured the lady addressed, as she hastened on a little faster.

Twice again Pollyanna tried the same experiment, but with like disappointing results. Soon she came upon the little pond that she had seen sparkling in the sunlight through the trees. It was a beautiful pond, and on it were several pretty little boats full of laughing children. As she watched them, Pollyanna felt more and more dissatisfied to remain by herself. It was then that, spying a man sitting alone not far away, she advanced slowly towards him and sat down on the other end of the bench. Once Pollyanna would have danced unhesitatingly to the man's side and suggested acquaintanceship with a cheery confidence that had no doubt of a welcome; but recent rebuffs had filled her with unaccustomed diffidence. Covertly she looked at the man now.

He was not very good to look at. His garments, though new, were dusty, and plainly showed lack of care. They were of the cut and style (though Pollyanna of course did not know this) that the State gives its prisoners as a freedom suit. His face was a pasty white, and was adorned with a week's beard. His hat was pulled far down over his eyes. With his hands in his pockets he sat idly staring at the ground.

For a long minute Pollyanna said nothing; then hopefully she began:

'It *is* a nice day, isn't it?'

The man turned his head with a start.

'Eh? Oh – er – what did you say?' he questioned, with a curiously frightened look around to make sure the remark was addressed to him.

'I said 'twas a nice day,' explained Pollyanna in hurried earnestness; 'but I don't care about that especially. That is, of course I'm glad it's a nice day, but I said it just as a beginning to things, and I'd just as soon talk about something else – anything else. It's only that I wanted you to talk – about something, you see.'

The man gave a low laugh. Even to Pollyanna the laugh sounded a little queer, though she did not know (as did the man) that a laugh to his lips had been a stranger for many months.

'So you want me to talk, do you?' he said a little sadly. 'Well, I don't see but what I shall have to do it, then. Still, I should think a nice little lady like you might find lots nicer people to talk to than an old duffer like me.'

'Oh, but I like old duffers,' exclaimed Pollyanna quickly; 'that is, I like the *old* part, and I don't know what a duffer is, so I can't dislike that. Besides, if you are a duffer, I reckon I like duffers. Anyhow, I like you,' she finished, with a contented little settling of herself in her seat that carried conviction.

'Humph! Well, I'm sure I'm flattered,' smiled the man ironically. Though his face and words expressed polite doubt, it might have been noticed that he sat a little straighter on the bench. 'And, pray, what shall we talk about?'

'It's – it's infinitesimal to me. That means I don't care, doesn't it?' asked Pollyanna, with a beaming smile. 'Aunt Polly says that, whatever I talk about, anyhow, I always bring up at the Ladies' Aiders. But I reckon that's because they brought me up first, don't you? We might talk about the party. I think it's a perfectly beautiful party – now that I know some one.'

'P-party?'

'Yes – this, you know – all these people here today. It *is* a party, isn't it? The lady said it was for everybody, so I stayed – though I haven't got to where the house is, yet, that's giving the party.'

The man's lips twitched.

'Well, little lady, perhaps it is a party, in a way,' he smiled; 'but the "house" that's giving it is the city of Boston. This is the Public Garden – a public park, you understand, for everybody.'

'Is it? Always? And I may come here any time I want to? Oh, how perfectly lovely! That's even nicer than I thought it could be. I'd worried for fear I couldn't ever come again, after today, you see. I'm glad now, though, that I didn't know it just at the first, for it's all the nicer now. Nice things are nicer when you've been worrying for fear they won't be nice, aren't they?'

'Perhaps they are – if they ever turn out to be nice at all,' conceded the man, a little gloomily.

'Yes, I think so,' nodded Pollyanna, not noticing the gloom. 'But isn't it beautiful – here?' she gloried. 'I wonder if Mrs Carew knows about it – that it's for anybody, so. Why, I should think everybody would want to come here all the time, and just stay and look around.'

The man's face hardened.

'Well, there are a few people in the world who have got a job – who've got something to do besides just to come here and stay and look around; but I don't happen to be one of them.'

'Don't you? Then you can be glad for that, can't you?' sighed Pollyanna, her eyes delightedly following a passing boat.

The man's lips parted indignantly, but no words came. Pollyanna was still talking.

'I wish *I* didn't have anything to do but that. I have to go to school. Oh, I like school; but there's such a whole lot of things I like better. Still, I'm glad I *can* go to school. I'm 'specially glad when I remember how last winter I didn't think I could ever go again. You see, I lost my legs for a while – I mean, they didn't go; and you know you never know how much you use things, till you don't have 'em. And eyes, too. Did you ever think what a lot you do with eyes? I didn't till I went to the Sanatorium. There was a lady there who had just got blind the year before. I tried to get her to play the game – finding something to be glad about, you know – but she said she couldn't; and if I wanted to know why I might tie up my eyes with my handkerchief for just one hour. And I did. It was awful. Did you ever try it?'

'Why, n-no, I didn't.' A half-vexed, half-baffled expression was coming to the man's face.

'Well, don't. It's awful. You can't do anything – not anything that you want to do. But I kept it on the whole hour. Since then I've been so glad, sometimes – when I see something perfectly lovely like this, you know – I've been so glad, I wanted to cry – 'cause I *could* see it, you know. She's playing the game now, though – that blind lady is. Miss Wetherby told me.'

'The – *game*?'

'Yes; the Glad Game. Didn't I tell you? Finding something in everything to be glad about. Well, she's found it now – about her eyes, you know. Her husband is the kind of a man that goes to help make the laws, and she had him ask for one that would help blind people, 'specially little babies. And she went herself and talked and told those men how it felt to be blind. And they made it – that law. And they said that she did more than anybody else, even her husband, to help make it, and that they didn't believe there would have been any law at all if it hadn't been for her. So now she says she's glad she lost her eyes, 'cause she's kept so many little babies from growing up to be blind like her. So you see she's playing it – the game. But I reckon you don't know about the game yet, after all; so I'll tell you. It started this way.' And Pollyanna, with her eyes on the shimmering beauty all about her, told of the little pair of crutches of long ago, which should have been a doll.

When the story was finished there was a long silence; then, a little abruptly, the man got to his feet.

'Oh, are you going away *now*?' she asked in open disappointment.

'Yes, I'm going now.' He smiled down at her a little queerly.

'But you're coming back some time?'

He shook his head – but again he smiled.

'I hope not – and I believe not, little girl. You see, I've made a great discovery today. I thought I was down and out. I thought there was no place for me anywhere – now. But I've just discovered that I've got two eyes, two arms, and two legs. Now I'm going to use them – and I'm going to *make* somebody understand that I know how to use them!'

The next moment he was gone.

'Why, what a funny man!' mused Pollyanna. 'Still, he was nice – and he was different, too,' she finished, rising to her feet and resuming her walk.

Pollyanna was now once more her usual cheerful self, and she stepped with the confident assurance of one who has no doubt. Had not the man said that this was a public park, and that she had as good a right as anybody to be there? She walked nearer to the pond and crossed the bridge to the starting-place of the little boats. For some time she watched the children happily, keeping a particularly sharp look-out for the possible black curls of Susie Smith. She would have liked to take a ride in the pretty boats herself, but the sign said 'Five cents' a trip, and she did not have any money with her. She smiled hopefully into the faces of several women, and twice she spoke tentatively. But no one spoke first to her, and those whom she addressed eyed her coldly, and made scant response.

After a time she turned her steps into still another path. Here she found a white-faced boy in a wheel-chair. She would have spoken to him, but he was so absorbed in his book that she turned away after a moment's wistful gazing. Soon then she came upon a pretty but sad-looking young girl sitting alone, staring at nothing, very much as the man had sat. With a contented little cry Pollyanna hurried forward.

'Oh, how do you do?' she beamed. 'I'm so glad I found you! I've been hunting ever so long for you,' she asserted, dropping herself down on the unoccupied end of the bench.

The pretty girl turned with a start, an eager look of expectancy in her eyes.

'Oh!' she exclaimed, falling back in plain disappointment. 'I thought – Why, what do you mean?' she demanded aggrievedly. 'I never set eyes on you before in my life.'

'No, I didn't you, either,' smiled Pollyanna; 'but I've been hunting for you, just the same. That is, of course, I didn't know you were going to be *you*, exactly. It's just that I wanted to find some one that looked lonesome, and that didn't have anybody. Like me, you know. So many here today have got folks. See?'

'Yes, I see,' nodded the girl, falling back into her old listlessness. 'But, poor little kid, it's too bad *you* should find it out – so soon.'

'Find what out?'

'That the lonesomest place in all the world is in a crowd in a big city.'

Pollyanna frowned and pondered.

'Is it? I don't see how it can be. I don't see how you can be lonesome when you've got folks all around you. Still –' she hesitated, and the frown deepened – 'I *was* lonesome this afternoon, and there *were* folks all around me; only they didn't seem to – to think – or notice.'

The pretty girl smiled bitterly.

'That's just it. They don't ever think – or notice, crowds don't.'

'But some folks do. We can be glad some do,' urged Pollyanna. 'Now when I –'

'Oh, yes, some do,' interrupted the other. As she spoke she shivered and looked fearfully down the path beyond Pollyanna. 'Some notice – too much.'

Pollyanna shrank back in dismay. Repeated rebuffs that afternoon had given her a new sensitiveness.

'Do you mean – me?' she stammered. 'That you wished I hadn't – noticed – you?'

'No, no, kiddie! I meant – some one quite different from you. Some one that hadn't ought to notice. I was glad to have you speak, only – I thought at first it was some one from home.'

'Oh, then you don't live here, either, any more than I do – I mean, for keeps.'

'Oh, yes, I live here now,' sighed the girl; 'that is, if you can call it living – what I do.'

'What do you do?' asked Pollyanna interestedly.

'Do? I'll tell you what I do,' cried the other, with sudden bitterness. 'From morning till night I sell fluffy laces and perky bows to girls that laugh and talk and *know* each other. Then I go home to a little back room up three flights just big enough to hold a lumpy cot-bed, a washstand with a nicked pitcher, one rickety chair, and me. It's like a furnace in the summer and an ice-box in the winter; but it's all the place I've got, and I'm supposed to stay in it – when I ain't workin'. But I've come out today. I ain't goin' to stay in that room, and I ain't goin' to go to any old library to read, neither. It's our last half-holiday this year – and an extra one, at that; and I'm going to have a good time –

for once. I'm just as young, and I like to laugh and
joke just as well as them girls I sell bows to all day.
Well, today I'm going to laugh and joke.'

Pollyanna smiled and nodded her approval.

'I'm glad you feel that way. I do, too. It's a lot more
fun – to be happy, isn't it? Besides, the Bible tells us to
– rejoice and be glad, I mean. It tells us to eight
hundred times. Probably you know about 'em, though
– the rejoicing texts.'

The pretty girl shook her head. A queer look came
to her face.

'Well, no,' she said drily. 'I can't say I *was* thinkin'
– of the Bible.'

'Weren't you? Well, maybe not; but, you see, *my*
father was a minister, and he –'

'A *minister*?'

'Yes. Why, was yours, too?' cried Pollyanna, answering something she saw in the other's face.

'Y-yes.' A faint colour crept up to the girl's
forehead.

'Oh, and has he gone like mine to be with God and
the angels?'

The girl turned away her head.

'No. He's still living – back home,' she answered,
half under her breath.

'Oh, how glad you must be,' sighed Pollyanna, enviously. 'Sometimes I get to thinking, if only I could
just *see* Father once – but you do see your father, don't
you?'

'Not often. You see, I'm down – here.'

'But you *can* see him – and I can't, mine. He's gone
to be with Mother and the rest of us up in heaven, and
– Have you got a mother, too – an earth mother?'

'Y-yes.' The girl stirred restlessly, and half moved as if to go.

'Oh, then you can see both of them,' breathed Pollyanna, unutterable longing on her face. 'Oh, how glad you must be! For there just isn't anybody, is there, that really *cares* and notices quite so much as fathers and mothers? You see I know, for I had a father until I was eleven years old; but for a mother I had the Ladies' Aiders for ever so long, till Aunt Polly took me. Ladies' Aiders are lovely, but of course they aren't like mothers, or even Aunt Pollys; and –'

On and on Pollyanna talked. Pollyanna was in her element now. Pollyanna loved to talk. That there was anything strange or unwise or even unconventional in this intimate telling of her thoughts and her history to a total stranger on a Boston park-bench did not once occur to Pollyanna. To Pollyanna all men, women, and children were friends, either known or unknown; and thus far she had found the unknown quite as delightful as the known, for with them there was always the excitement of mystery and adventure – while they were changing from the unknown to the known.

To this young girl at her side, therefore, Pollyanna talked unreservedly of her father, her Aunt Polly, her Western home, and her journey east to Vermont. She told of new friends and old friends, and of course she told of the game. Pollyanna almost always told everybody of the game, either sooner or later. It was, indeed, so much a part of her very self that she could hardly have helped telling of it.

As for the girl – she said little. She was not now sitting in her old listless attitude, however, and to her whole self had come a marked change. The flushed cheeks, frowning brow, troubled eyes, and nervously working fingers were plainly the signs of some inward struggle. From time to time she glanced apprehensively down the path beyond Pollyanna, and it was after such a glance that she clutched the little girl's arm.

'See here, kiddie, for just a minute don't you leave me. Do you hear? Stay right where you are! There's a man I know comin'; but no matter what he says, don't you pay no attention, and *don't you go*. I'm goin' to stay with *you*. See?'

Before Pollyanna could more than gasp her wonderment and surprise, she found herself looking up into the face of a very handsome young gentleman, who had stopped before them.

'Oh, here you are,' he smiled pleasantly, lifting his hat to Pollyanna's companion. 'I'm afraid I'll have to begin with an apology – I'm a little late.'

'It don't matter, sir,' said the young girl, speaking hurriedly. 'I – I've decided not to go.'

The young man gave a light laugh.

'Oh, come, my dear, don't be hard on a chap because he's a little late!'

'It isn't that, really,' defended the girl, a swift red flaming into her cheeks. 'I mean – I'm not going.'

'Nonsense!' The man stopped smiling. He spoke sharply. 'You said yesterday you'd go.'

'I know; but I've changed my mind. I told my little friend here – I'd stay with her.'

'Oh, but if you'd rather go with this nice young gentleman,' began Pollyanna anxiously; but she fell back silenced at the look the girl gave her.

'I tell you I had *not* rather go. I'm not going.'

'And, pray, why this sudden right-about face?'

demanded the young man, with an expression that made him suddenly look, to Pollyanna, not quite so handsome. 'Yesterday you said –'

'I know I did,' interrupted the girl feverishly. 'But I knew then that I hadn't ought to. Let's call it – that I know it even better now. That's all.' And she turned away resolutely.

It was not all. The man spoke again, twice. He coaxed, then he sneered with a hateful look in his eyes. At last he said something very low and angry, which Pollyanna did not understand. The next moment he wheeled about and strode away.

The girl watched him tensely till he passed quite out of sight, then, relaxing, she laid a shaking hand on Pollyanna's arm.

'Thanks, kiddie. I reckon I owe you – more than you know. Good-bye.'

'But you aren't going away *now*!' bemoaned Pollyanna.

The girl sighed wearily.

'I got to. He might come back, and the next time I might not be able to.' She clipped the words short and rose to her feet. For a moment she hesitated, then she choked bitterly: 'You see, he's the kind that – notices too much, and that hadn't ought to notice – *me* – at all!' With that she was gone.

'Why, what a funny lady,' murmured Pollyanna, looking wistfully after the vanishing figure. 'She was nice, but she was sort of different, too,' she commented, rising to her feet and moving idly down the path.

6

JERRY TO THE RESCUE

It was not long before Pollyanna reached the edge of
the Garden at a corner where two streets crossed. It
was a wonderfully interesting corner, with its hurrying
cars, automobiles, carriages, and pedestrians. A huge
red bottle in a drug-store window caught her eye, and
from down the street came the sound of a hurdy-gurdy.
Hesitating only a moment, Pollyanna darted across the
corner and skipped lightly down the street towards the
entrancing music.

Pollyanna found much to interest her now. In the
store windows were marvellous objects, and around
the hurdy-gurdy, when she had reached it, she found a
dozen dancing children, most fascinating to watch. So
altogether delightful, indeed, did this pastime prove to
be that Pollyanna followed the hurdy-gurdy for some
distance, just to see those children dance. Presently
she found herself at a corner so busy that a very big
man in a belted blue coat helped the people across the
street. For an absorbed minute she watched him in
silence; then a little timidly, she herself started to
cross.

It was a wonderful experience. The big, blue-coated
man saw her at once and promptly beckoned to her.
He even walked to meet her. Then, through a wide

lane with puffing motors and impatient horses on either hand, she walked unscathed to the farther kerb. It gave her a delightful sensation, so delightful that, after a minute, she walked back. Twice again, after short intervals, she trod the fascinating way so magically opened at the lifting of the big man's hand. But the last time her conductor left her at the kerb, he gave a puzzled frown.

'See here, little girl, ain't you the same one what crossed a minute ago?' he demanded. 'And again before that?'

'Yes, sir,' beamed Pollyanna. 'I've been across four times!'

'Well!' the officer began to bluster; but Pollyanna was still talking.

'And it's been nicer every time!'

'Oh-h, it has – has it?' mumbled the big man lamely. Then, with a little more spirit he sputtered: 'What do you think I'm here for – just to tote you back and forth?'

'Oh, no, sir,' dimpled Pollyanna. 'Of course you aren't just for me! There are all these others. I know what you are. You're a policeman. We've got one of you out where I live at Mrs Carew's, only he's the kind that just walks on the sidewalk, you know. I used to think you were soldiers, on account of your gold buttons and blue hats; but I know better now. Only I think you *are* a kind of a soldier, 'cause you're so brave – standing here like this, right in the middle of all these teams and automobiles, helping folks across.'

'Ho – ho! Brrrr!' spluttered the big man, colouring like a schoolboy and throwing back his head with a hearty laugh. 'Ho – ho! Just as if –' He broke off with a quick lifting of his hand. The next moment he was escorting a plainly very much frightened little old lady from kerb to kerb. If his step was a bit more pompous, and his chest a bit more full, it must have been only an unconscious tribute to the watching eyes of the little girl back at the starting-point. A moment later, with a haughtily permissive wave of his hand towards the chafing drivers and chauffeurs, he strolled back to Pollyanna.

'Oh, that was splendid!' she greeted him, with shining eyes. 'I love to see you do it – and it's just like the Children of Israel crossing the Red Sea, isn't it? – with you holding back the waves for the people to cross. And how glad you must be all the time, that you can do it! I used to think being a doctor was the very gladdest business there was, but I reckon, after all, being a policeman is gladder yet – to help frightened people like this, you know. And –' But with another 'Brrrr!' and an embarrassed laugh the big blue-coated man was back in the middle of the street, and Pollyanna was all alone on the kerbstone.

For only a minute longer did Pollyanna watch her fascinating 'Red Sea', then, with a regretful backward glance, she turned away.

'I reckon maybe I'd better be going home now,' she meditated. 'It must be 'most dinner-time.' And briskly she started to walk back by the way she had come.

Not until she had hesitated at several corners, and unwittingly made two false turns, did Pollyanna grasp the fact that 'going back home' was not to be so easy as she had thought it to be. And not until she came to a building, which she knew she had never seen before, did she fully realize that she had lost her way.

She was on a narrow street, dirty and ill-paved. Dingy tenement blocks and a few unattractive stores were on either side. All about were jabbering men and chattering women – though not one word of what they said could Pollyanna understand. Moreover, she could not help seeing that the people looked at her very curiously, as if they knew she did not belong there.

Several times, already, she had asked her way, but in vain. No one seemed to know where Mrs Carew lived; and the last two times, those addressed had answered with a gesture and a jumble of words which Pollyanna, after some thought, decided must be Dutch, the kind the Haggermans – the only foreign family in Beldingsville – used.

On and on, down one street and up another, Pollyanna trudged. She was thoroughly frightened now. She was hungry, too, and very tired. Her feet ached, and her eyes smarted with the tears she was trying so hard to hold back. Worse yet, it was unmistakably beginning to grow dark.

'Well, anyhow,' she choked to herself, 'I'm going to be glad I'm lost, 'cause it'll be so nice when I get found. I *can* be glad for that!'

It was at a noisy corner where two broader streets crossed that Pollyanna finally came to a dismayed stop. This time the tears quite overflowed, so that, lacking a handkerchief, she had to use the backs of both hands to wipe them away.

'Hullo, kid, why the weeps?' queried a cheery voice. 'What's up?'

With a relieved little cry Pollyanna turned to confront a small boy carrying a bundle of newspapers under his arm.

'Oh, I'm so glad to see you!' she exclaimed. 'I've so wanted to see some one who didn't talk Dutch!'

The small boy grinned.

'Dutch nothin'!' he scoffed. 'You mean Dago, I bet ye.'

Pollyanna gave a slight frown.

'Well, anyway, it – it wasn't English,' she said doubtfully; 'and they couldn't answer my questions. But maybe you can. Do you know where Mrs Carew lives?'

'Nix! You can search me.'

'Wha-at?' queried Pollyanna, still more doubtfully.

The boy grinned again.

'I say not in mine. I guess I ain't acquainted with the lady.'

'But isn't there anybody anywhere that is?' implored Pollyanna. 'You see, I just went out for a walk and I got lost. I've been ever and ever so far, but I can't find the house at all: and it's supper – I mean dinner-time and getting dark. I want to get back. I *must* get back.'

'Gee! Well, I should worry!' sympathized the boy.

'Yes, and I'm afraid Mrs Carew'll worry, too,' sighed Pollyanna.

'Gorry! if you ain't the limit,' chuckled the youth, unexpectedly. 'But, say, listen! Don't ye know the name of the street ye want?'

'No – only that it's some kind of an avenue,' desponded Pollyanna.

'A ave*noo*, is it? Sure, now, some class to that! We're doin' fine. What's the number of the house? Can ye tell me that? Just scratch your head!'

'Scratch – my – head?' Pollyanna frowned questioningly, and raised a tentative hand to her hair.

The boy eyed her with disdain.

'Aw, come off yer perch! Ye ain't so dippy as all that. I say, don't ye know the number of the house ye want?'

'N-no, except there's a seven in it,' returned Pollyanna, with a faintly hopeful air.

'Won't ye listen ter that?' gibed the scornful youth. 'There's a seven in it – an' she expects me ter know it when I see it!'

'Oh, I should know the house, if I could only see it,' declared Pollyanna eagerly; 'and I think I'd know the street, too, on account of the lovely long yard running right up and down through the middle of it.'

This time it was the boy who gave a puzzled frown.

'*Yard?*' he queried, 'in the middle of a street?'

'Yes – trees and grass, you know, with a walk in the middle of it, and seats, and –' But the boy interrupted her with a whoop of delight.

'Gee whiz! Commonwealth Avenue, sure as yer livin'! Wouldn't that get yer goat, now?'

'Oh, do you know – do you really?' besought Pollyanna. 'That sounded like it – only I don't know what you meant about the goat part. There aren't any goats there. I don't think they'd allow –'

'Goats nothin'!' scoffed the boy. 'You bet yer sweet life I know where 'tis! Don't I tote Sir James up there to the Garden 'most ev'ry day? An' I'll take *you*, too. Jest ye hang out here till I get on ter my job again, an' sell out my stock. Then we'll make tracks for that 'ere Avenue 'fore ye can say Jack Robinson.'

'You mean you'll take me – home?' appealed Pollyanna, still plainly not quite understanding.

'Sure! It's a cinch – if you know the house.'

'Oh yes, I know the house,' replied the literal Pollyanna, anxiously, 'but I don't know whether it's a – a
cinch, or not. If it isn't, can't you –'

But the boy only threw her another disdainful glance
and darted off into the thick of the crowd. A moment
later Pollyanna heard his strident call of 'Paper! paper!
Herald, Globe – paper, sir?'

With a sigh of relief Pollyanna stepped back into a
doorway and waited. She was tired, but she was happy.
In spite of sundry puzzling aspects of the case, she yet
trusted the boy, and she had perfect confidence that he
could take her home.

'He's nice, and I like him,' she said to herself,
following with her eyes the boy's alert, darting figure.
'But he does talk funny. His words *sound* English, but
some of them don't seem to make any sense with the
rest of what he says. But then, I'm glad he found me,
anyway,' she finished, with a contented little sigh.

It was not long before the boy returned, his hands
empty.

'Come on, kid. All aboard,' he called cheerily. 'Now
we'll hit the trail for the Avenue. If I was the real
thing, now, I'd tote ye home in style in a buzz-wagon;
but seein' as how I hain't got the dough, we'll have ter
hoof it.'

It was, for the most part, a silent walk. Pollyanna,
for once in her life, was too tired to talk, even of the
Ladies' Aiders; and the boy was intent on picking out
the shortest way to his goal. When the Public Garden
was reached, Pollyanna did exclaim joyfully:

'Oh, now I'm 'most there! I remember this place. I
had a perfectly lovely time here this afternoon. It's
only a little bit of a ways home now.'

'That's the stuff! Now we're gettin' there,' crowed the boy. 'What'd I tell ye? We'll just cut through here to the Avenue, an' then it'll be up ter you ter find the house.'

'Oh, I can find the house,' exulted Pollyanna, with all the confidence of one who has reached familiar ground.

It was quite dark when Pollyanna led the way up the broad Carew steps. The boy's ring at the bell was very quickly answered, and Pollyanna found herself confronted by not only Mary, but by Mrs Carew, Bridget and Jennie as well. All four of the women were white-faced and anxious-eyed.

'Child, child, where *have* you been?' demanded Mrs Carew, hurrying forward.

'Why, I – I just went to walk,' began Pollyanna, 'and I got lost, and this boy –'

'Where did you find her?' cut in Mrs Carew, turning imperiously to Pollyanna's escort, who was, at the moment, gazing in frank admiration at the wonders about him in the brilliantly lighted hall. 'Where did you find her, boy?' she repeated sharply.

For a brief moment the boy met her gaze unflinchingly; then something very like a twinkle came into his eyes, though his voice, when he spoke, was gravity itself.

'Well, I found her round Bowdoin Square, but I reckon she'd been doin' the North End, only she couldn't catch on ter the lingo of the Dagos, so I don't think she give 'em the glad hand, ma'am.'

'The North End – that child – alone! Pollyanna!' shuddered Mrs Carew.

'Oh, I wasn't alone, Mrs Carew,' fended Pollyanna.

'There was ever and ever so many people there, weren't there, boy?'

But the boy, with an impish grin, was disappearing through the door.

Pollyanna learned many things during the next half-hour. She learned that nice little girls do not take long walks alone in unfamiliar cities, nor sit on park-benches and talk to strangers. She learned, also, that it was only by a 'perfectly marvellous miracle' that she had reached home at all that night, and that she had escaped many, many very disagreeable consequences of her foolishness. She learned that Boston was not Beldingsville, and that she must not think it was.

'But, Mrs Carew,' she finally argued despairingly, 'I *am* here, and I didn't get lost for keeps. Seems as if I ought to be glad for that instead of thinking all the time of the sorry things that might have happened.'

'Yes, yes, child, I suppose so, I suppose so,' sighed Mrs Carew; 'but you have given me such a fright, and I want you to be sure, *sure*, SURE never to do it again. Now come, dear, you must be hungry.'

It was just as she was dropping off to sleep that night that Pollyanna murmured drowsily to herself:

'The thing I'm the very sorriest for of anything is that I didn't ask that boy his name nor where he lived. Now I can't ever say thank you to him!'

7

A NEW ACQUAINTANCE

Pollyanna's movements were most carefully watched over after her adventurous walk; and, except to go to school, she was not allowed out of the house unless Mary or Mrs Carew herself accompanied her. This, to Pollyanna, however, was no cross, for she loved both Mrs Carew and Mary, and delighted to be with them. They were, too, for a while, very generous with their time. Even Mrs Carew, in her terror of what might have happened, and her relief that it had not happened, exerted herself to entertain the child.

Thus it came about that, with Mrs Carew, Pollyanna attended concerts and matinées, and visited the Public Library and the Art Museum; and with Mary she took the wonderful 'Seeing Boston' trips, and visited the State House and the Old South Church.

Greatly as Pollyanna enjoyed the automobile, she enjoyed the trolley-cars more, as Mrs Carew, much to her surprise, found out one day.

'Do we go in the trolley-car?' Pollyanna asked eagerly.

'No. Perkins will take us,' answered Mrs Carew. Then, at the unmistakable disappointment in Pollyanna's face, she added in surprise: 'Why, I thought you liked the auto, child!'

'Oh, I do,' acceded Pollyanna hurriedly; 'and I wouldn't say anything, anyway, because of course I know it's cheaper than the trolley-car and –'

'"Cheaper than the trolley-car"!' exclaimed Mrs Carew, amazed into an interruption.

'Why, yes,' explained Pollyanna, with widening eyes; 'the trolley-car costs five cents a person, you know, and the auto doesn't cost anything, 'cause it's yours. And of course I *love* the auto, anyway,' she hurried on, before Mrs Carew could speak. 'It's only that there are so many more people in the trolley-car, and it's such fun to watch them! Don't you think so?'

'Well, no, Pollyanna, I can't say that I do,' responded Mrs Carew drily, as she turned away.

As it chanced, not two days later, Mrs Carew heard something more of Pollyanna and trolley-cars – this time from Mary.

'I mean, it's queer, ma'am,' explained Mary earnestly, in answer to a question her mistress had asked, 'it's queer how Miss Pollyanna just gets round *everybody* – and without half trying. It isn't that she *does* anything. She doesn't. She just – just looks glad, I guess, that's all. But I've seen her get into a trolley-car that was full of cross-looking men and women, and whimpering children, and in five minutes you wouldn't know the place. The men and women have stopped scowling and the children have forgot what they're cryin' for.

'Sometimes it's just somethin' that Miss Pollyanna has said to me, and they've heard it. Sometimes it's just the "Thank you", she gives when somebody insists on givin' us their seat – and they're always doin' that – givin' us seats, I mean. And sometimes it's the way she

smiles at a baby or a dog. All dogs everywhere wag
their tails at her, anyway, and all babies, big and little,
smile and reach out to her. If we get held up it's a
joke, and if we take the wrong car, it's the funniest
thing that ever happened. And that's the way 'tis
about everythin'. One just can't stay grumpy, with
Miss Pollyanna, even if you're only one of a trolley-car
full of folks that don't know her.'

'Hm-m; very likely,' murmured Mrs Carew, turning
away.

October proved to be, that year, a particularly warm,
delightful month, and as the golden days came and
went, it was soon very evident that to keep up with
Pollyanna's eager little feet was a task which would
consume altogether too much of somebody's time and
patience; and, while Mrs Carew had the one, she had
not the other, neither had she the willingness to allow
Mary to spend quite so much of *her* time (whatever
her patience might be) in dancing attendance to Pollyanna's whims and fancies.

To keep the child indoors all through those glorious
October afternoons was, of course, out of the question.
Thus it came about that, before long, Pollyanna found
herself once more in the 'lovely big yard' – the Boston
Public Garden – and alone. Apparently she was as free
as before, but in reality she was surrounded by a high
stone wall of regulations.

She must not talk to strange men or women; she
must not play with strange children; and under no
circumstances must she step foot outside the Garden
except to come home. Furthermore, Mary, who had
taken her to the Garden and left her, made very sure

that she knew the way home – that she knew just where Commonwealth Avenue came down to Arlington Street across from the Garden. And always she must go home when the clock in the church tower said it was half-past four.

Pollyanna went often to the Garden after this. Occasionally she went with some of the girls from school. More often she went alone. In spite of the somewhat irksome restrictions she enjoyed herself very much. She could *watch* the people even if she could not talk to them; and she could talk to the squirrels and pigeons and sparrows that so eagerly came for the nuts and grain which she soon learned to carry to them every time she went.

Pollyanna often looked for her old friends of that first day – the man who was so glad he had his eyes and legs and arms, and the pretty young lady who would not go with the handsome man; but she never saw them. She did frequently see the boy in the wheelchair, and she wished she could talk to him. The boy fed the birds and squirrels, too, and they were so tame that the doves would perch on his head and shoulders, and the squirrels would burrow in his pockets for nuts. But Pollyanna, watching from a distance, always noticed one strange circumstance: in spite of the boy's very evident delight in serving his banquet, his supply of food always ran short almost at once; and though he invariably looked fully as disappointed as did the squirrel after a nutless burrowing, yet he never remedied the matter by bringing more food the next day – which seemed most shortsighted to Pollyanna.

When the boy was not playing with the birds and squirrels he was reading – always reading. In his chair

were usually two or three worn books, and sometimes
a magazine or two. He was nearly always to be found
in one especial place, and Pollyanna used to wonder
how he got there. Then, one unforgettable day, she
found out. It was a school holiday, and she had come
to the Garden in the forenoon; and it was soon after
she reached the place that she saw him being wheeled
along one of the paths, by a snub-nosed, sandy-haired
boy. She gave a keen glance into the sandy-haired
boy's face, then ran towards him with a glad little cry.

'Oh, you – you! I know you – even if I don't know
your name. You found me! Don't you remember? Oh,
I'm so glad to see you! I've so wanted to say thank
you!'

'Gee, if it ain't the swell little lost kid of the Ave*noo*!'
grinned the boy. 'Well, what do you know about that!
Lost again?'

'Oh, no!' exclaimed Pollyanna, dancing up and down
on her toes in irrepressible joy. 'I can't get lost any
more – I have to stay right here. And I mustn't talk,
you know. But I can to you, for I *know* you; and I can
to him – after you introduce me,' she finished, with a
beaming glance at the lame boy, and a hopeful pause.

The sandy-haired youth chuckled softly, and tapped
the shoulder of the boy in the chair.

'Listen ter that, will ye? Ain't that the real thing,
now? Just you wait while I intro*dooce* ye!' And he
struck a pompous attitude. 'Madam, this is me friend,
Sir James, Lord of Murphy's Alley, and –' But the
boy in the chair interrupted him.

'Jerry, quit your nonsense!' he cried vexedly. Then
to Pollyanna he turned a glowing face. 'I've seen you
here lots of times before. I've watched you feed the

birds and squirrels – you always have such a lot for them! And I think *you* like Sir Lancelot the best, too. Of course, there's the Lady Rowena – but wasn't she rude to Guinevere yesterday – snatching her dinner right away from her like that?'

Pollyanna blinked and frowned, looking from one to the other of the boys in plain doubt. Jerry chuckled again. Then, with a final push he wheeled the chair into its usual position, and turned to go. Over his shoulder he called to Pollyanna:

'Say, kid, jest let me put ye wise ter somethin'. This chap ain't drunk nor crazy. See? Them's just names he's give his young friends here' – with a flourish of his arms towards the furred and feathered creatures that were gathering from all directions. 'An' they ain't even names of *folks*. They're just guys out of books. Are ye on? Yet he'd ruther feed them than feed hisself. Ain't he the limit? Ta-ta, Sir James,' he added, with a grimace, to the boy in the chair. 'Buck up, now – nix on the no-grub racket for you! See you later.' And he was gone.

Pollyanna was still blinking and frowning when the lame boy turned with a smile.

'You mustn't mind Jerry. That's just his way. He'd cut off his right hand for me – Jerry would; but he loves to tease. Where'd you see him? Does he know you? He didn't tell me your name?'

'I'm Pollyanna Whittier. I was lost and he found me and took me home,' answered Pollyanna, still a little dazedly.

'I see. Just like him,' nodded the boy. 'Don't he tote me up here every day?'

A quick sympathy came to Pollyanna's eyes.

'Can't you walk – at all – Sir J-James?'

The boy laughed gleefully.

'Sir James, indeed! That's only more of Jerry's non-sense. I ain't a "Sir".'

Pollyanna looked clearly disappointed.

'You aren't? Nor a – a lord, like he said?'

'I sure ain't.'

'Oh, I hoped you were – like Little Lord Fauntleroy, you know,' rejoined Pollyanna. 'And –'

But the boy interrupted her with an eager:

'Do *you* know Little Lord Fauntleroy? And do you know about Sir Launcelot, and the Holy Grail, and King Arthur and his Round Table, and the Lady Rowena, and Ivanhoe and all those? *Do* you?'

Pollyanna gave her head a dubious shake.

'Well, I'm afraid maybe I don't know *all* of 'em,' she admitted. 'Are they all – in books?'

The boy nodded.

'I've got 'em here – some of 'em,' he said. 'I like to read 'em over and over. There's always *something* new in 'em. Besides, I hain't got no others, anyway. These were Father's. Here, you little rascal – quit that!' He broke off in laughing reproof as a bushy-tailed squirrel leaped to his lap and began to nose in his pockets. 'Gorry, guess we'd better give them their dinner or they'll be tryin' to eat us,' chuckled the boy. 'That's Sir Lancelot. He's always first, you know.'

From somewhere the boy produced a small paste-board box which he opened guardedly, mindful of the numberless bright little eyes that were watching every move. All about him now sounded the whirr and flutter of wings, the cooing of doves, the saucy twitter of the sparrows. Sir Lancelot, alert and eager, occupied one arm of the wheelchair. Another bushy-tailed little fellow, less venturesome, sat back on his haunches five feet away. A third squirrel chattered noisily on a neighbouring tree-branch.

From the box the boy took a few nuts, a small roll, and a doughnut. At the latter he looked longingly, hesitatingly.

'Did you – bring anything?' he asked then.

'Lots – in here,' nodded Pollyanna, tapping the paper-bag she carried.

'Oh, then perhaps I *will* eat it today,' sighed the boy, dropping the doughnut back into the box with an air of relief.

Pollyanna, on whom the significance of this action was quite lost, thrust her fingers into her own bag, and the banquet was on.

It was a wonderful hour. To Pollyanna it was, in a way, the most wonderful hour she had ever spent, for she had found some one who could talk faster and longer than she could. This strange youth seemed to have an inexhaustible fund of marvellous stories of brave knights and fair ladies, of tournaments and battles. Moreover, so vividly did he draw his pictures that Pollyanna saw with her own eyes the deeds of valour, the knights in armour, and the fair ladies with their jewelled gowns and tresses, even though she was really looking at a flock of fluttering doves and sparrows and a group of frisking squirrels on a wide sweep of sunlit grass.

The Ladies' Aiders were forgotten. Even the Glad Game was not thought of. Pollyanna, with flushed cheeks and sparkling eyes, was trailing down the golden ages led by a romance-fed boy who – though she did not know it – was trying to crowd into this one short hour of congenial companionship countless dreary days of loneliness and longing.

Not until the noon bells sent Pollyanna hurrying homeward did she remember that she did not even yet know the boy's name.

'I only know it isn't Sir James,' she sighed to herself, frowning with vexation. 'But never mind. I can ask him tomorrow.'

8

Jamie

Pollyanna did not see the boy 'tomorrow'. It rained, and she could not go to the Garden at all. It rained the next day, too. Even on the third day she did not see him, for, though the sun came out bright and warm, and though she went very early in the afternoon to the Garden and waited long, he did not come at all. But on the fourth day he was there in his old place, and Pollyanna hastened forward with a joyous greeting.

'Oh, I'm so glad, *glad* to see you! But where've you been? You weren't here yesterday at all.'

'I couldn't. The pain wouldn't let me come yesterday,' explained the lad, who was looking very white.

'The *pain*! Oh, does it – ache?' stammered Pollyanna, all sympathy at once.

'Oh, yes, always,' nodded the boy, with a cheerfully matter-of-fact air. 'Most generally I can stand it and come here just the same, except when it gets *too* bad, same as 'twas yesterday. Then I can't.'

'But how can you stand it – to have it ache – always?' gasped Pollyanna.

'Why, I have to,' answered the boy, opening his eyes a little wider. 'Things that are so are *so*, and they can't be any other way. So what's the use thinking how they might be? Besides, the harder it aches one day, the nicer 'tis to have it let up the next.'

'I know. That's like the ga–' began Pollyanna; but the boy interrupted her.

'Did you bring a lot this time?' he asked anxiously. 'Oh, I hope you did! You see I couldn't bring them any today. Jerry couldn't spare even a penny for peanuts this morning and there wasn't really enough stuff in the box for me this noon.'

Pollyanna looked shocked.

'You mean – that you didn't have enough to eat – yourself? – for *your* luncheon?'

'Sure!' smiled the boy. 'But don't worry. 'Tisn't the first time – and 'twon't be the last. I'm used to it. Hi, there! Here comes Sir Lancelot.'

Pollyanna, however, was not thinking of squirrels.

'And wasn't there any more at home?'

'Oh, no, there's *never* any left at home,' laughed the boy. 'You see, Mumsey works out – stairs and washings – so she gets some of her feed in them places, and Jerry picks his up where he can, except nights and mornings; he gets it with us then – if we've got any.'

Pollyanna looked still more shocked.

'But what do you do when you don't have anything to eat?'

'Go hungry, of course.'

'But I never *heard* of anybody who didn't have *anything* to eat,' gasped Pollyanna. 'Of course Father and I were poor, and we had to eat beans and fishballs when we wanted turkey. But we had *something*. Why don't you tell folks – all these folks everywhere, that live in these houses?'

'What's the use?'

'Why, they'd give you something, of course!'

The boy laughed once more, this time a little queerly.

'Guess again, kid. You've got another one coming. Nobody I know is dishin' out roast beef and frosted cakes for the askin'. Besides, if you didn't go hungry once in a while, you wouldn't know how good 'taters and milk can taste; and you wouldn't have so much to put in your Jolly Book.'

'Your *what*?'

The boy gave an embarrassed laugh and grew suddenly red.

'Forget it! I didn't think, for a minute, but you was Mumsey or Jerry.'

'But what *is* your Jolly Book?' pleaded Pollyanna. 'Please tell me. Are there knights and lords and ladies in that?'

The boy shook his head. His eyes lost their laughter and grew dark and fathomless.

'No; I wish't there was,' he sighed wistfully. 'But when you – you can't even *walk*, you can't fight battles and win trophies, and have fair ladies hand you your sword, and bestow upon you the golden guerdon.' A sudden fire came into the boy's eyes. His chin lifted itself as if in response to a bugle-call. Then, as suddenly, the fire died, and the boy fell back into his old listlessness.

'You just can't do nothin',' he resumed wearily, after a moment's silence. 'You just have to sit and think; and times like that your *think* gets to be something awful. Mine did, anyhow. I wanted to go to school and learn things – more things than just Mumsey can teach me; and I thought of that. I wanted to run and play ball with the other boys; and I thought of that. I wanted to go out and sell papers with Jerry; and I thought of that. I didn't want to be taken care of all my life; and I thought of that.'

'I know, oh, I know,' breathed Pollyanna, with shining eyes. 'Didn't I lose *my* legs for a while?'

'Did you? Then you do know, some. But you've got yours again. I hain't, you know,' sighed the boy, the shadow in his eyes deepening.

'But you haven't told me yet about – the Jolly Book,' prompted Pollyanna, after a minute.

The boy stirred and laughed shamefacedly.

'Well, you see, it ain't much, after all, except to me. *You* wouldn't see much in it. I started it a year ago. I was feelin' 'specially bad that day. Nothin' was right. For a while I grumped it out, just thinkin'; and then I picked up one of Father's books and tried to read. And the first thing I see was this; I learned it afterwards, so I can say it now:

'Pleasures lie thickest where no pleasures seem;
    There's not a leaf that falls upon the ground
    But holds some joy, of silence or of sound.[1]

'Well, I was mad. I wished I could put the guy that wrote that in my place, and see what kind of joy he'd find in my "leaves". I was so mad I made up my mind I'd prove he didn't know what he was talkin' about, so I begun to hunt for them – the joys in my "leaves", you know. I took a little old empty notebook that Jerry had given me, and I said to myself that I'd write 'em

[1] Blanchard, 'Hidden Joys', in *Lyric Offerings*.

down. Everythin' that had anythin' about it that I
liked I'd put down in the book. Then I'd just show
how many "joys" I had.'

'Yes, yes!' cried Pollyanna absorbedly, as the boy
paused for breath.

'Well, I didn't expect to get many, but – do you
know? – I got a lot. There was somethin' about 'most
everythin' that I liked a *little*, so in it had to go. The
very first one was the book itself – that I'd got it, you
know, to write in. Then somebody give me a flower in
a pot, and Jerry found a dandy book in the subway.
After that it was really fun to hunt 'em out – I'd find
'em in such queer places, sometimes. Then one day
Jerry got hold of the little notebook, and found out
what 'twas. Then he give it its name – the Jolly Book.
And – and that's all.'

'All – *all*!' cried Pollyanna, delight and amazement
struggling for the mastery on her glowing little face.
'Why, that's the game! You're playing the Glad Game,
and don't know it – only you're playing it ever and
ever so much better than I ever could! Why, I – I
couldn't play it at all, I'm afraid, if I – I didn't have
enough to eat, and couldn't ever walk, or anything,'
she choked.

'The game? What game? I don't know anything
about any game,' frowned the boy.

Pollyanna clapped her hands.

'I know you don't – I know you don't, and that's
why it's so perfectly lovely, and so – so wonderful! But
listen. I'll tell you what the game is.'

And she told him.

'Gee!' breathed the boy appreciatively, when she
had finished. 'Now what do you think of that!'

'And here you are, playing *my* game better than anybody I ever saw, and I don't even know your name yet, nor anything!' exclaimed Pollyanna, in almost awestruck tones. 'But I want to – I want to know everything.'

'Pooh! there's nothing to know,' rejoined the boy, with a shrug. 'Besides, see, here's poor Sir Lancelot and all the rest, waiting for their dinner,' he finished.

'Dear me, so they are,' sighed Pollyanna, glancing impatiently at the fluttering and chattering creatures all about them. Recklessly she turned her bag upside-down and scattered her supplies to the four winds. 'There, now, that's done, and we can talk again,' she rejoiced. 'And there's such a lot I want to know. First, please, what *is* your name? I only know it isn't Sir James.'

The boy smiled.

'No, it isn't; but that's what Jerry 'most always calls me. Mumsey and the rest call me Jamie.'

'*Jamie!*' Pollyanna caught her breath and held it suspended. A wild hope had come to her eyes. It was followed almost instantly, however, by fearful doubt.

'Does Mumsey mean – mother?'

'Sure!'

Pollyanna relaxed visibly. Her face fell. If this Jamie had a mother, he could not, of course, be Mrs Carew's Jamie, whose mother had died long ago. Still, even as he was, he was wonderfully interesting.

'But where do you live?' she catechized eagerly. 'Is there anybody else in your family but your mother and – and Jerry? Do you always come here every day? Where is your Jolly Book? Mayn't I see it? Don't the doctors say you can ever walk again? And where was it you said you got it? – this wheel-chair, I mean.'

The boy chuckled.

'Say, how many of them questions do you expect me to answer all at once? I'll begin at the last one, anyhow, and work backward, maybe, if I don't forget what they be. I got this chair a year ago. Jerry knew one of them fellers that writes for the papers, you know, and he put it in about me – how I couldn't ever walk, and all that, and – and the Jolly Book, you see. The first thing I knew, a whole lot of men and women come one day toting this chair, and said 'twas for me. That they'd read all about me, and they wanted me to have it to remember them by.'

'My! how glad you must have been!'

'I was. It took a whole page of my Jolly Book to tell about that chair.'

'But can't you *ever* walk again?' Pollyanna's eyes were blurred with tears.

'It don't look like it. They said I couldn't.'

'Oh, but that's what they said about me, and then they sent me to Dr Ames, and I stayed 'most a year; and *he* made me walk. Maybe he could *you*!'

The boy shook his head.

'He couldn't – you see; I couldn't go to him, anyway. 'Twould cost too much. We'll just have to call it that I can't ever – walk again. But never mind.' The boy threw back his head impatiently. 'I'm trying not to *think* of that. You know what it is when – when your *think* gets to going.'

'Yes, yes, of course – and here I am talking about it!' cried Pollyanna penitently. 'I *said* you knew how to play the game better than I did, now. But go on. You haven't told me half, yet. Where do you live? And is Jerry all the brothers and sisters you've got?'

A swift change came to the boy's face. His eyes glowed.

'Yes – and he ain't mine, really. He ain't any relation, nor Mumsey ain't, neither. And only think how good they've been to me!'

'What's that?' questioned Pollyanna, instantly on the alert. 'Isn't that – that "mumsey" your mother at all?'

'No; and that's what makes –'

'And haven't you got any mother?' interrupted Pollyanna, in growing excitement.

'No; I never remember any mother, and Father died six years ago.'

'How old were you?'

'I don't know. I was little. Mumsey says she guesses maybe I was about six. That's when they took me, you see.'

'And your name is Jamie?' Pollyanna was holding her breath.

'Why, yes, I told you that.'

'And what's the other name?' Longingly, but fearfully, Pollyanna asked this question.

'I don't know.'

'*You don't know!*'

'I don't remember. I was too little, I suppose. Even the Murphys don't know. They never knew me as anything but Jamie.'

A great disappointment came to Pollyanna's face, but almost immediately a flash of thought drove the shadow away.

'Well, anyhow, if you don't know what your name is, you can't know it isn't Kent!' she exclaimed.

'Kent?' puzzled the boy.

'Yes,' began Pollyanna, all excitement. 'You see, there was a little boy named Jamie Kent that –' She stopped abruptly and bit her lip. It had occurred to Pollyanna that it would be kinder not to let this boy know yet of her hope that he might be the lost Jamie. It would be better that she make sure of it before raising any expectations, otherwise she might be bringing him sorrow rather than joy. She had not forgotten how disappointed Jimmy Bean had been when she had been obliged to tell him that the Ladies' Aid did not want him, and again when at first Mr Pendleton had not wanted him, either. She was determined that she would not make the same mistake a third time; so very promptly now she assumed an air of elaborate indifference on this most dangerous subject, as she said:

'But never mind about Jamie Kent. Tell me about yourself. I'm *so* interested!'

'There isn't anything to tell. I don't know anything nice,' hesitated the boy. 'They said Father was – was queer, and never talked. They didn't even know his name. Everybody called him "The Professor". Mumsey says he and I lived in a little back room on the top floor of the house in Lowell where they used to live. They were poor then, but they wasn't near so poor as they are now. Jerry's father was alive them days, and had a job.'

'Yes, yes, go on,' prompted Pollyanna.

'Well, Mumsey says my father was sick a lot, and he got queerer and queerer, so that they had me downstairs with them a good deal. I could walk then, a little, but my legs wasn't right. I played with Jerry, and the little girl that died. Well, when Father died there wasn't anybody to take me, and some men were goin' to put me in an orphan asylum; but Mumsey says I took on so, and Jerry took on so, that they said they'd keep me. And they did. The little girl had just died, and they said I might take her place. And they've had me ever since. And I fell and got worse, and they're awful poor now, too, besides Jerry's father dyin'. But they've kept me. Now ain't that what you call bein' pretty good to a feller?'

'Yes, oh, yes,' cried Pollyanna. 'But they'll get their reward – I know they'll get their reward!' Pollyanna was quivering with delight now. The last doubt had fled. She had found the lost Jamie. She was sure of it. But not yet must she speak. First Mrs Carew must see him. Then – *then*! Even Pollyanna's imagination failed when it came to picturing the bliss in store for Mrs Carew and Jamie at that glad reunion.

She sprang lightly to her feet in utter disregard of Sir Lancelot who had come back and was nosing in her lap for more nuts.

'I've got to go now, but I'll come again tomorrow. Maybe I'll have a lady with me that you'll like to know. You'll be here tomorrow, won't you?' she finished anxiously.

'Sure, if it's pleasant. Jerry totes me up here most every mornin'. They fixed it so he could, you know; and I bring my dinner and stay till four o'clock. Jerry's good to me – he is!'

'I know, I know,' nodded Pollyanna. 'And maybe you'll find somebody else to be good to you, too,' she carolled. With which cryptic statement and a beaming smile, she was gone.

9

Plans and Plottings

On the way home Pollyanna made joyous plans. Tomorrow, in some way or other, Mrs Carew must be persuaded to go with her for a walk in the Public Garden. Just how this was to be brought about Pollyanna did not know; but brought about it must be.

To tell Mrs Carew plainly that she had found Jamie, and wanted her to go to see him, was out of the question. There was, of course, a bare chance that this might not be her Jamie; and if it were not, and if she had thus raised in Mrs Carew false hopes, the result might be disastrous. Pollyanna knew, from what Mary had told her, that twice already Mrs Carew had been made very ill by the great disappointment of following alluring clues that had led to some boy very different from her dead sister's son. So Pollyanna knew that she could not tell Mrs Carew why she wanted her to go to walk tomorrow in the Public Garden. But there would be a way, declared Pollyanna to herself as she happily hurried homeward.

Fate, however, as it happened, once more intervened in the shape of a heavy rainstorm; and Pollyanna did not have to more than look out of doors the next morning to realize that there would be no Public Garden stroll that day. Worse yet, neither the next day nor the next saw the clouds dispelled; and Pollyanna spent all three afternoons wandering from window to window, peering up into the sky, and anxiously demanding of every one: '*Don't* you think it looks a *little* like clearing up?'

So unusual was this behaviour on the part of the cheery little girl, and so irritating was the constant questioning, that at last Mrs Carew lost her patience.

'For pity's sake, child, what is the trouble?' she cried. 'I never knew you to fret so about the weather. Where's that wonderful Glad Game of yours today?'

Pollyanna reddened and looked abashed.

'Dear me, I reckon maybe I did forget the game this time,' she admitted. 'And of course there *is* something about it I can be glad for, if I'll only hunt for it. I can be glad that – that it will *have* to stop raining some time 'cause God said He *wouldn't* send another flood. But you see, I did so want it to be pleasant today.'

'Why, especially?'

'Oh, I – I just wanted to go to walk in the Public Garden.' Pollyanna was trying hard to speak unconcernedly. 'I – I thought maybe you'd like to go with me, too.' Outwardly Pollyanna was nonchalance itself. Inwardly, however, she was a-quiver with excitement and suspense.

'*I* go to walk in the Public Garden?' queried Mrs Carew, with brows slightly uplifted. 'Thank you, no, I'm afraid not,' she smiled.

'Oh, but you – you wouldn't *refuse*!' faltered Pollyanna, in quick panic.

'I have refused.'

Pollyanna swallowed convulsively. She had grown really pale.

'But, Mrs Carew, please, *please* don't say you *won't* go, when it gets pleasant,' she begged. 'You see, for a – a special reason I wanted you to go – with me – just this once.'

Mrs Carew frowned. She opened her lips to make the 'No' more decisive; but something in Pollyanna's pleading eyes must have changed the words, for when they came they were a reluctant acquiescence.

'Well, well, child, have your own way. But if I promise to go, *you* must promise not to go near the window for an hour, and not to ask again today if I think it's going to clear up.'

'Yes'm, I will – I mean, I won't,' palpitated Pollyanna. Then, as a pale shaft of light that was almost a sunbeam came aslant through the window, she cried joyously, 'But you *do* think it *is* going to – Oh!' she broke off in dismay, and ran from the room.

Unmistakably it 'cleared up' the next morning. But, though the sun shone brightly, there was a sharp chill in the air, and by afternoon, when Pollyanna came home from school, there was a brisk wind. In spite of protests, however, she insisted that it was a beautiful day out, and that she should be perfectly miserable if Mrs Carew would not come for a walk in the Public Garden. And Mrs Carew went, though still protesting.

As might have been expected, it was a fruitless journey. Together the impatient woman and the anxious-eyed little girl hurried shiveringly up one path and down another. (Pollyanna, not finding the boy in his accustomed place, was making frantic search in every nook and corner of the Garden. To Pollyanna it seemed that she could not have it so. Here she was in the Garden, and here with her was Mrs Carew; but not anywhere to be found was Jamie – and yet not one word could she say to Mrs Carew.) At last, thoroughly chilled and exasperated, Mrs Carew insisted on going home; and despairingly Pollyanna went.

Sorry days came to Pollyanna then. What to her was perilously near a second deluge – but according to Mrs Carew was merely 'the usual fall rains' – brought a series of damp, foggy, cold, cheerless days, filled with either a dreary drizzle of rain, or, worse yet, a steady downpour. If perchance occasionally there came a day of sunshine, Pollyanna always flew to the Garden; but in vain. Jamie was never there. It was the middle of November now, and even the Garden itself was full of dreariness. The trees were bare, the benches almost empty, and not one boat was on the little pond. True, the squirrels and pigeons were there, and the sparrows were as pert as ever, but to feed them was almost more of a sorrow than a joy, for every saucy switch of Sir Lancelot's feathery tail but brought bitter memories of the lad who had given him his name – and who was not there.

'And to think I didn't find out where he lived!' mourned Pollyanna to herself over and over again, as the days passed. 'And he was Jamie – I just know he was Jamie. And now I'll have to wait and wait till spring comes, and it's warm enough for him to come here again. And then, maybe, *I* shan't be coming here by that time. Oh, dear, oh, dear – and he *was* Jamie, I know he was Jamie!'

Then, one dreary afternoon, the unexpected happened. Pollyanna, passing through the upper hallway, heard angry voices in the hall below, one of which she recognized as being Mary's, while the other – the other . . .

The other voice was saying:

'Not on yer life! It's nix on the beggin' business. Do yer get me? I wants ter see the kid, Pollyanna. I got a message for her from – from Sir James. Now beat it, will ye, and trot out the kid, if ye don't mind.'

With a glad little cry Pollyanna turned and fairly flew down the stairway.

'Oh, I'm here, I'm here, I'm right here!' she panted, stumbling forward. 'What is it? Did Jamie send you?'

In her excitement she had almost flung herself with outstretched arms upon the boy when Mary intercepted a shocked, restraining hand.

'Miss Pollyanna, Miss Pollyanna, do you mean to say you know this – this beggar-boy?'

The boy flushed angrily; but before he could speak Pollyanna interposed valiant championship.

'He isn't a beggar-boy. He belongs to one of my very best friends. Besides, he's the one that found me and brought me home that time I was lost.' Then to the boy she turned with impetuous questioning. 'What is it? Did Jamie send you?'

'Sure he did. He hit the hay a month ago, and he hain't been up since.'

'He hit – what?' puzzled Pollyanna.

'Hit the hay – went ter bed. He's sick, I mean, and he wants ter see ye. Will ye come?'

'Sick? Oh, I'm so sorry!' grieved Pollyanna. 'Of course I'll come. I'll go get my hat and coat right away.'

'Miss Pollyanna!' gasped Mary in stern disapproval.

'As if Mrs Carew would let you go – *anywhere* with a strange boy like this!'

'But he isn't a strange boy,' objected Pollyanna. 'I've known him ever so long, and I *must* go. I –'

'What in the world is the meaning of this?' demanded Mrs Carew icily from the drawing-room doorway. 'Pollyanna, who is this boy, and what is he doing here?'

Pollyanna turned with a quick cry.

'Oh, Mrs Carew, you'll let me go, won't you?'

'Go where?'

'To see my brother, ma'am,' cut in the boy hurriedly, and with an obvious effort to be very polite. 'He's sort of off his feed, ye know, and he wouldn't give me no peace till I come up – after her,' with an awkward gesture towards Pollyanna. 'He thinks a sight an' all of her.'

'I may go, mayn't I?' pleaded Pollyanna.

Mrs Carew frowned.

'Go with this boy – *you*? Certainly not, Pollyanna! I wonder you are wild enough to think of it for a moment.'

'Oh, but I want you to come, too,' began Pollyanna.

'I? Absurd, child! That is impossible. You may give this boy here a little money if you like, but –'

'Thank ye, ma'am, but I didn't come for money,' resented the boy, his eyes flashing. 'I come for – her.'

'Yes, and Mrs Carew, it's Jerry – Jerry Murphy, the boy that found me when I was lost, and brought me home,' appealed Pollyanna. '*Now* won't you let me go?'

Mrs Carew shook her head.

'It is out of the question, Pollyanna.'

'But he says Ja– the other boy is sick, and wants me!'

'I can't help that.'

'And I know him real well, Mrs Carew. I do, truly. He reads books – lovely books, all full of knights and lords and ladies, and he feeds the birds and squirrels and gives 'em names, and everything. And he can't walk, and he doesn't have enough to eat, lots of days,' panted Pollyanna; 'and he's been playing my Glad Game for a year, and didn't know it. And he plays it ever and ever so much better than I do. And I've hunted and hunted for him, ever and ever so many days. Honest and truly, Mrs Carew, I've just *got* to see him,' almost sobbed Pollyanna. 'I can't lose him again!'

An angry colour flamed into Mrs Carew's cheeks.

'Pollyanna, this is sheer nonsense. I am surprised. I am amazed at you for insisting upon doing something you know I disapprove of. I *cannot* allow you to go with this boy. Now please let me hear no more about it.'

A new expression came to Pollyanna's face. With a look half terrified, half exalted, she lifted her chin and squarely faced Mrs Carew. Tremulously, but determinedly, she spoke.

'Then I'll have to tell you. I didn't mean to – till I was sure. I wanted you to see him first. But now I've got to tell. I can't lose him again. I think, Mrs Carew, he's Jamie.'

'Jamie! Not – *my* – Jamie!' Mrs Carew's face had grown very white.

'Yes.'

'Impossible!'

'I know; but, please, his name *is* Jamie, and he doesn't know the other one. His father died when he was six years old, and he can't remember his mother. He's twelve years old, he thinks. These folks took him in when his father died, and his father was queer, and didn't tell folks his name, and –'

But Mrs Carew had stopped her with a gesture. Mrs Carew was even whiter than before, but her eyes burned with a sudden fire.

'We'll go at once,' she said. 'Mary, tell Perkins to have the car here as soon as possible. Pollyanna, get your hat and coat. Boy, wait here, please. We'll be ready to go with you immediately.' The next minute she had hurried upstairs.

In the hall the boy drew a long breath.

'Gee whiz!' he muttered softly. 'If we ain't goin' ter go in a buzz-wagon! Some class ter that! Gorry! what'll Sir James say?'

10

IN MURPHY'S ALLEY

With the opulent purr that seems to be peculiar to
luxurious limousines, Mrs Carew's car rolled down
Commonwealth Avenue and out upon Arlington Street
to Charles. Inside sat a shining-eyed little girl and a
white-faced, tense woman. Outside, to give directions
to the plainly disapproving chauffeur, sat Jerry
Murphy, inordinately proud and insufferably
important.

When the limousine came to a stop before a shabby
doorway in a narrow, dirty alley, the boy leaped to the
ground, and, with a ridiculous imitation of the liveried
pomposities he had so often watched, threw open the
door of the car and stood waiting for the ladies to
alight.

Pollyanna sprang out at once, her eyes widening
with amazement and distress as she looked about her.
Behind her came Mrs Carew, visibly shuddering as
her gaze swept the filth, the sordidness, and the ragged
children that swarmed shrieking and chattering out of
the dismal tenements, and surrounded the car in a
second.

Jerry waved his arms angrily.

'Here, you, beat it!' he yelled to the motley throng.
'This ain't no free movies! *Can* that racket and get a

move on ye. Lively, now! We gotta get by. Jamie's got comp'ny.'

Mrs Carew shuddered again, and laid a trembling hand on Jerry's shoulder.

'Not – *here*!' she recoiled.

But the boy did not hear. With shoves and pushes from sturdy fists and elbows, he was making a path for his charges; and before Mrs Carew knew quite how it was done, she found herself with the boy and Pollyanna at the foot of a rickety flight of stairs in a dim, evil-smelling hallway.

Once more she put out a shaking hand.

'Wait,' she commanded huskily. 'Remember! Don't either of you say a word about – about his being possibly the boy I'm looking for. I must see for myself first, and – question him.'

'Of course!' agreed Pollyanna.

'Sure! I'm on,' nodded the boy. 'I gotta go right off anyhow, so I won't bother ye none. Now toddle easy up these 'ere stairs. There's always holes, and most generally there's a kid or two asleep somewheres. An' the elevator ain't runnin' ter-day,' he gibed cheerfully. 'We gotta go ter the top, too!'

Mrs Carew found the 'holes' – broken boards that creaked and bent fearsomely under her shrinking feet; and she found one 'kid' – a two-year-old baby playing with an empty tin can on a string which he was banging up and down the second flight of stairs. On all sides doors were opened, now boldly, now stealthily, but always disclosing women with tousled heads or peering children with dirty faces. Somewhere a baby was wailing piteously. Somewhere else a man was cursing. Everywhere was the smell of bad whisky, stale cabbage, and unwashed humanity.

At the top of the third and last stairway the boy came to a pause before a closed door.

'I'm just a-thinkin' what Sir James'll say when he's wise ter the prize package I'm bringin' him,' he whispered in a throaty voice. 'I know what Mumsey'll do – she'll turn on the weeps in no time ter see Jamie so tickled.' The next moment he threw wide the door with a gay: 'Here we be – an' we come in a buzzwagon! Ain't that goin' some, Sir James?'

It was a tiny room, cold and cheerless and pitifully bare, but scrupulously neat. There were here no tousled heads, no peering children, no odours of whisky, cabbage, and unclean humanity. There were two beds, three broken chairs, a dry-goods-box table, and a stove with a faint glow of light that told of a fire not nearly brisk enough to heat even that tiny room. On one of the beds lay a lad with flushed cheeks and fever-bright eyes. Near him sat a thin, white-faced woman, bent and twisted with rheumatism.

Mrs Carew stepped into the room and, as if to steady herself, paused a minute with her back to the wall. Pollyanna hurried forward with a low cry just as Jerry, with an apologetic 'I gotta go now; good-bye!' dashed through the door.

'Oh, Jamie, I'm so glad I've found you,' cried Pollyanna. 'You don't know how I've looked and looked for you every day. But I'm so sorry you're sick!'

Jamie smiled radiantly and held out a thin white hand.

'I ain't sorry – I'm *glad*,' he emphasized meaningly; ''cause it's brought you to see me. Besides, I'm better now, anyway. Mumsey, this is the little girl, you know, that told me the Glad Game – and Mumsey's playing it too,' he triumphed, turning back to Pollyanna. 'First she cried 'cause her back hurts too bad to let her work; then when I was took worse she was *glad* she couldn't work, 'cause she could be here to take care of me, you know.'

At that moment Mrs Carew hurried forward, her eyes half fearfully, half longingly on the face of the lame boy in the bed.

'It's Mrs Carew. I've brought her to see you, Jamie,' introduced Pollyanna, in a tremulous voice.

The little twisted woman by the bed had struggled to her feet by this time, and was nervously offering her chair. Mrs Carew accepted it without so much as a glance. Her eyes were still on the boy in the bed.

'Your name is – Jamie?' she asked, with visible difficulty.

'Yes, ma'am.' The boy's bright eyes looked straight into hers.

'What is your other name?'

'I don't know.'

'He is not your son?' For the first time Mrs Carew turned to the twisted little woman who was still standing by the bed.

'No, madam.'

'And you don't know his name?'

'No, madam. I never knew it.'

With a despairing gesture Mrs Carew turned back to the boy.

'But think, think – don't you remember *anything* of your name but – Jamie?'

The boy shook his head. Into his eyes was coming a puzzled wonder.

'No, nothing.'

'Haven't you anything that belonged to your father, with possibly his name in it?'

'There wasn't anything worth savin' but them books,' interposed Mrs Murphy. 'Them's his. Maybe you'd like to look at 'em,' she suggested, pointing to a row of worn volumes on a shelf across the room. Then, in plainly uncontrollable curiosity, she asked: 'Was you thinkin' you knew him, ma'am?'

'I don't know,' murmured Mrs Carew, in a half-stifled voice, as she rose to her feet and crossed the room to the shelf of books.

There were not many – perhaps ten or a dozen. There was a volume of Shakespeare's plays, an *Ivanhoe*, a much-thumbed *Lady of the Lake*, a book of miscellaneous poems, a coverless *Tennyson*, a dilapidated *Little Lord Fauntleroy*, and two or three books of ancient and medieval history. But, though Mrs Carew looked carefully through every one, she found nowhere any written word. With a despairing sigh she turned back to the boy and to the woman, both of whom now were watching her with startled, questioning eyes.

'I wish you'd tell me – both of you – all you know about yourselves,' she said brokenly, dropping herself once more into the chair by the bed.

And they told her. It was much the same story that Jamie had told Pollyanna in the Public Garden. There was little that was new, nothing that was significant, in spite of the probing questions that Mrs Carew asked. At its conclusion Jamie turned eager eyes on Mrs Carew's face.

'Do you think you knew – my father?' he begged.

Mrs Carew closed her eyes and pressed her hand to her head.

'I don't – know,' she answered. 'But I think – not.'

Pollyanna gave a quick cry of keen disappointment, but as quickly she suppressed it in obedience to Mrs Carew's warning glance. With new horror, however, she surveyed the tiny room.

Jamie, turning his wondering eyes from Mrs Carew's face, suddenly awoke to his duties as host.

'Wasn't you good to come!' he said to Pollyanna gratefully. 'How's Sir Lancelot? Do you ever go to feed him now?' Then, as Pollyanna did not answer at once, he hurried on, his eyes going from her face to the somewhat battered pink in a broken-necked bottle in the window. 'Did you see my posy? Jerry found it. Somebody dropped it and he picked it up. Ain't it pretty? And it *smells* a little.'

But Pollyanna did not seem even to have heard him. She was still gazing wide-eyed about the room, clasping and unclasping her hands nervously.

'But I don't see how you can ever play the game here at all, Jamie,' she faltered. 'I didn't suppose there could be anywhere such a perfectly awful place to live,' she shuddered.

'Ho!' scoffed Jamie, valiantly. 'You'd oughter see the Pikes' downstairs. Theirs is a whole lot worse'n this. You don't know what a lot of nice things there is about this room. Why, we get the sun in that winder there for 'most two hours every day, when it shines. And if you get real near it you can see a whole lot of sky from it. If we could only *keep* the room – but you see we've got to leave, we're afraid. And that's what's worryin' us.'

'Leave!'

'Yes. We got behind on the rent – Mumsey bein' sick so, and not earnin' anythin'.' In spite of a courageously cheerful smile, Jamie's voice shook. 'Mis' Dolan downstairs – the woman what keeps my wheelchair for me, you know – is helpin' us out this week. But of course she can't do it always, and then we'll have to go – if Jerry don't strike it rich, or somethin'.'

'Oh, but can't we –' began Pollyanna.

She stopped short. Mrs Carew had risen to her feet abruptly with a hurried:

'Come, Pollyanna, we must go.' Then to the woman she turned wearily. 'You won't have to leave. I'll send you money and food at once, and I'll mention your case to one of the charity organizations in which I am interested, and they will –'

In surprise she ceased speaking. The bent little figure of the woman opposite had drawn itself almost erect. Mrs Murphy's cheeks were flushed. Her eyes showed a smouldering fire.

'Thank you, no, Mrs Carew,' she said tremulously, but proudly. 'We're poor – God knows; but we ain't charity folks.'

'Nonsense!' cried Mrs Carew sharply. 'You're letting the woman downstairs help you. This boy said so.'

'I know; but that ain't charity,' persisted the woman, still tremulously. 'Mrs Dolan is my *friend*. She knows I'd do *her* a good turn just as quick – I have done 'em for her in times past. Help from *friends* ain't charity. They *care*; and that – that makes a difference. We wa'n't always as we are now, you see; and that makes it hurt all the more – all this. Thank you; but we couldn't take – your money.'

Mrs Carew frowned angrily. It had been a most disappointing, heart-breaking, exhausting hour for her. Never a patient woman, she was exasperated now, besides being utterly tired out.

'Very well, just as you please,' she said coldly. Then, with vague irritation she added, 'But why don't you go to your landlord and insist that he make you even decently comfortable while you do stay? Surely you're entitled to something besides broken windows stuffed with rags and papers! And those stairs that I came up are positively dangerous.'

Mrs Murphy sighed in a discouraged way. Her twisted little figure had fallen back into its old hopelessness.

'We have tried to have something done, but it's never amounted to anything. We never see anybody but the agent, of course; and he says the rents are too low for the owner to put out any more money on repairs.'

'Nonsense!' snapped Mrs Carew, with all the sharpness of a nervous, distraught woman who has at last found an outlet for her exasperation. 'It's shameful! What's more, I think it's a clear case of violation of the law – those stairs are, certainly. I shall make it my business to see that he's brought to terms. What is the name of that agent, and who is the owner of this delectable establishment?'

'I don't know the name of the owner, madam; but the agent is Mr Dodge.'

'Dodge!' Mrs Carew turned sharply, an odd look on her face. 'You don't mean – Henry Dodge?'

'Yes, madam. His name is Henry, I think.'

A flood of colour swept into Mrs Carew's face, then receded, leaving it whiter than before.

'Very well, I – I'll attend to it,' she murmured, in a half-stifled voice, turning away. 'Come, Pollyanna, we must go now.'

Over at the bed Pollyanna was bidding Jamie a tearful good-bye.

'But I'll come again. I'll come real soon,' she promised brightly, as she hurried through the door after Mrs Carew.

Not until they had picked their precarious way down the three long flights of stairs and through the jabbering, gesticulating crowd of men, women, and children that surrounded the scowling Perkins and the limousine, did Pollyanna speak again. But then she scarcely waited for the irate chauffeur to slam the door upon them before she pleaded:

'Dear Mrs Carew, please, please say that it was Jamie! Oh, it would be so nice for him to be Jamie.'

'But he isn't Jamie!'

'Oh, dear! Are you sure?'

There was a moment's pause, then Mrs Carew covered her face with her hands.

'No, I'm not sure – and that's the tragedy of it,' she moaned. 'I don't think he is; I'm almost positive he isn't. But, of course, there *is* a chance – and that's what's killing me.'

'Then can't you just *think* he's Jamie,' begged Pollyanna, 'and play he was? Then you could take him home, and –' But Mrs Carew turned fiercely.

'Take that boy into my home when he *wasn't* Jamie? Never, Pollyanna! I couldn't.'

'But if you *can't* help Jamie, I should think you'd be so glad there was some one like him you *could* help,' urged Pollyanna tremulously. 'What if your Jamie was like this Jamie, all poor and sick, wouldn't you want some one to take him in and comfort him, and –'

'Don't – don't, Pollyanna,' moaned Mrs Carew, turning her head from side to side, in a frenzy of grief. 'When I think that maybe, somewhere, our Jamie is like that –' Only a choking sob finished the sentence.

'That's just what I mean – that's just what I mean!' triumphed Pollyanna excitedly. 'Don't you see? If this *is* your Jamie, of course you'll want him; and if it isn't, you couldn't be doing any harm to the other Jamie by taking this one, and you'd do a whole lot of good, for you'd make this one so happy – so happy. And then, by and by, if you should find the real Jamie, you wouldn't have lost anything, but you'd have made two little boys happy instead of one and –' But again Mrs Carew interrupted her.

'Don't, Pollyanna, don't! I want to think – I want to think.'

Tearfully Pollyanna sat back in her seat. By a very visible effort she kept still for one whole minute. Then, as if the words fairly bubbled forth of themselves, there came this:

'Oh, but what an awful, awful place that was! I just wish the man that owned it had to live in it himself – and then see what he'd have to be glad for!'

Mrs Carew sat suddenly erect. Her face showed a curious change. Almost as if in appeal she flung out her hand towards Pollyanna.

'Don't!' she cried. 'Perhaps – she didn't know, Pollyanna. Perhaps she didn't know. I'm sure she didn't know – she owned a place like that. But it will be fixed now – it will be fixed.'

'*She!* Is it a woman that owns it, and do you know her? And do you know the agent, too?'

'Yes.' Mrs Carew bit her lips. '*I* know her, and I know the agent.'

'Oh, I'm so glad,' sighed Pollyanna. 'Then it'll be all right now.'

'Well, it certainly will be – better,' avowed Mrs Carew with emphasis, as the car stopped before her own door.

Mrs Carew spoke as if she knew what she was talking about. And perhaps, indeed, she did – better than she cared to tell Pollyanna. Certainly, before she slept that night, a letter left her hands addressed to one Henry Dodge, summoning him to an immediate conference as to certain changes and repairs to be made at once in tenements she owned. There were, moreover, several scathing sentences concerning 'rag-stuffed windows', and 'rickety stairways', that caused this same Henry Dodge to scowl angrily, and to say a sharp word behind his teeth – though at the same time he paled with something very like fear.

11

A Surprise for Mrs Carew

The matter of repairs and improvements having been properly and efficiently attended to, Mrs Carew told herself that she had done her duty, and that the matter was closed. She would forget it. The boy was not Jamie – he could not be Jamie. That ignorant, sickly, crippled boy her dead sister's son? Impossible! She would cast the whole thing from her thoughts.

It was just here, however, that Mrs Carew found herself against an immovable, impassable barrier; the whole thing refused to be cast from her thoughts. Always before her eyes was the picture of that bare little room and the wistful-faced boy. Always in her ears was that heart-breaking 'What if it *were* Jamie?' And always, too, there was Pollyanna; for even though Mrs Carew might (as she did) silence the pleadings and questionings of the little girl's tongue, there was no getting away from the prayers and reproaches of the little girl's eyes.

Twice again in desperation Mrs Carew went to see the boy, telling herself each time that only another visit was needed to convince her that the boy was not the one she sought. But even though, while there in the boy's presence, she told herself that she *was* convinced, once away from it, the old, old questioning returned. At last, in still greater desperation she wrote to her sister, and told her the whole story.

I had not meant to tell you [she wrote, after she had stated the bare facts of the case], I thought it a pity to harrow you up, or to raise false hopes. I am so sure it is not he – and yet, even as I write these words, I know I am *not* sure. That is why I want you to come – why you must come. I must have you see him.

I wonder – oh, I wonder what you'll say! Of course we haven't seen our Jamie since he was four years old. He would be twelve now. This boy is twelve, I should judge. (He doesn't know his age.) He has hair and eyes not unlike our Jamie's. He is crippled, but that condition came upon him through a fall, six years ago, and was made worse through another one four years later. Anything like a complete description of his father's appearance seems impossible to obtain; but what I have learned contains nothing conclusive either for or against his being poor Doris's husband. He was called 'the Professor', was very queer, and seemed to own nothing save a few books. This might, or might not signify. John Kent was certainly always queer, and a good deal of a Bohemian in his tastes. Whether he cared for books or not I don't remember. Do you? And of course the title 'Professor' might easily have been assumed, if he wished, or it might have been merely given him by others. As for this boy – I don't know, I don't know – but I do hope *you* will!

Your distracted sister,

Ruth

Della came at once, and she went immediately to see the boy; but she did not 'know'. Like her sister, she said she did not think it was their Jamie, but at the same time there was that chance – it might be he, after all. Like Pollyanna, however, she had what she thought was a very satisfactory way out of the dilemma.

'But why don't you take him, dear?' she proposed to her sister. 'Why don't you take him and adopt him? It would be lovely for him – poor little fellow – and –' But Mrs Carew shuddered and would not even let her finish.

'No, no, I can't, I can't!' she moaned. 'I want my Jamie, my own Jamie – or no one.' And with a sigh Della gave it up and went back to her nursing.

If Mrs Carew thought that this closed the matter, however, she was again mistaken; for her days were still restless, and her nights were still either sleepless or filled with dreams of a 'may be' or a 'might be' masquerading as an 'it is so'. She was, moreover, having a difficult time with Pollyanna.

Pollyanna was puzzled. She was filled with questionings and unrest. For the first time in her life Pollyanna had come face to face with real poverty. She knew people who did not have enough to eat, who wore ragged clothing, and who lived in dark, dirty, and very tiny rooms. Her first impulse, of course, had been 'to help'. With Mrs Carew she made two visits to Jamie, and greatly did she rejoice at the changed conditions she found there after 'that man Dodge' had 'tended to things'. But this, to Pollyanna, was a mere drop in the bucket. There were yet all those other sick-looking men, unhappy-looking women, and ragged children out in the street – Jamie's neighbours. Confidently she looked to Mrs Carew for help for them, also.

'Indeed!' exclaimed Mrs Carew, when she learned what was expected of her, 'so you want the whole street to be supplied with fresh paper, paint, and new stairways, do you? Pray, is there anything else you'd like?'

'Oh, yes, lots of things,' sighed Pollyanna happily. 'You see, there are so many things they need – all of them! And what fun it will be to get them! How I wish I was rich so I could help, too; but I'm 'most as glad to be with you when you get them.'

Mrs Carew quite gasped aloud in her amazement. She lost no time – though she did lose not a little patience – in explaining that she had no intention of doing anything further in 'Murphy's Alley', and that there was no reason why she should. No one would expect her to. She had cancelled all possible obligations, and had even been really very generous, anyone would say, in what she had done for the tenement where lived Jamie and the Murphys. (That she owned the tenement building she did not think it necessary to state.) At some length she explained to Pollyanna that there were charitable institutions, both numerous and efficient, whose business it was to aid all the worthy poor, and that to these institutions she gave frequently and liberally.

Even then, however, Pollyanna was not convinced.

'But I don't see,' she argued, 'why it's any better, or even so nice, for a whole lot of folks to club together and do what everybody would like to do for themselves. I'm sure I'd much rather give Jamie a – a nice book, now, than to have some old society do it; and I *know* he'd like better to have me do it, too.'

'Very likely,' returned Mrs Carew, with some weariness and a little exasperation. 'But it is just possible that it would not be so well for Jamie as – as if that book were given by a body of people who knew what sort of one to select.'

This led her to say much, also (none of which Pollyanna in the least understood), about 'pauperizing the poor', the 'evils of indiscriminate giving', and the 'pernicious effect of unorganized charity'.

'Besides,' she added, in answer to the still perplexed expression on Pollyanna's worried little face, 'very likely if I offered to help these people they would not take it. You remember Mrs Murphy declined, at the first, to let me send food and clothing – though they accepted it readily enough from their neighbours on the first floor, it seems.'

'Yes, I know,' sighed Pollyanna, turning away. 'There's something there somehow that I don't understand. But it doesn't seem right that *we* should have such a lot of nice things, and that *they* shouldn't have anything, hardly.'

As the days passed, this feeling on the part of Pollyanna increased rather than diminished; and the questions she asked and the comments she made were anything but a relief to the state of mind in which Mrs Carew herself was. Even the test of the Glad Game, in this case, Pollyanna was finding to be very near a failure; for, as she expressed it:

'I don't see how you can find anything about this poor-people business to be glad for. Of course we can be glad for ourselves that we aren't poor like them; but whenever I'm thinking how glad I am for that, I get so sorry for them that I *can't* be glad any longer. Of course we *could* be glad there were poor folks, because we could help them. But if we *don't* help them, where's the glad part of that coming in?' And to this Pollyanna could find no one who could give her a satisfactory answer.

Especially she asked this question of Mrs Carew; and Mrs Carew, still haunted by the visions of the Jamie that was, and the Jamie that might be, grew only more restless, more wretched, and more utterly despairing. Nor was she helped any by the approach of Christmas. Nowhere was there glow of holly or flash of tinsel that did not carry its pang to her; for always to Mrs Carew it but symbolized a child's empty stocking – a stocking that might be Jamie's.

Finally, a week before Christmas, she fought what she thought was the last battle with herself. Resolutely, but with no real joy in her face, she gave terse orders to Mary, and summoned Pollyanna.

'Pollyanna,' she began, almost harshly, 'I have decided to – to take Jamie. The car will be here at once. I'm going after him now, and bring him home. You may come with me if you like.'

A great light transfigured Pollyanna's face.

'Oh, oh, oh, how glad I am!' she breathed. 'Why, I'm so glad I – I want to cry! Mrs Carew, why is it, when you're the very gladdest of anything, you always want to cry?'

'I don't know, I'm sure, Pollyanna,' rejoined Mrs Carew abstractedly. On Mrs Carew's face there was still no look of joy.

Once in the Murphy's little one-room tenement, it did not take Mrs Carew long to tell her errand. In a few short sentences she told the story of the lost Jamie, and of her first hopes that this Jamie might be he. She made no secret of her doubts that he was the one; at the same time, she said she had decided to take him home with her and give him every possible advantage. Then, a little wearily, she told what were the plans she had made for him.

At the foot of the bed Mrs Murphy listened, crying softly. Across the room Jerry Murphy, his eyes dilating, emitted an occasional low 'Gee! Can ye beat that, now?' As to Jamie – Jamie, on the bed, had listened at first with the air of one to whom suddenly a door has opened into a longed-for Paradise; but gradually, as Mrs Carew talked, a new look came to his eyes. Very slowly he closed them, and turned away his face.

When Mrs Carew ceased speaking there was a long silence before Jamie turned his head and answered. They saw then that his face was very white, and that his eyes were full of tears.

'Thank you, Mrs Carew, but – I can't go,' he said simply.

'You can't – what?' cried Mrs Carew, as if she doubted the evidence of her own ears.

'Jamie!' gasped Pollyanna.

'Oh, come, kid, what's eatin' ye?' scowled Jerry, hurriedly coming forward. 'Don't ye know a good thing when ye see it?'

'Yes; but I can't go,' said the crippled boy again.

'But, Jamie, Jamie, think, *think* what it would mean to you!' quavered Mrs Murphy at the foot of the bed.

'I am a-thinkin',' choked Jamie. 'Don't you suppose I know what I'm doin' – what I'm givin' up?' Then to Mrs Carew he turned tear-wet eyes. 'I can't,' he faltered. 'I can't let you do all that for me. If you – *cared* it would be different. But you don't care – not really. You don't *want* me – not *me*. You want the real Jamie, and I ain't the real Jamie. You don't think I am. I can see it in your face.'

'I know. But – but –' began Mrs Carew helplessly.

'And it isn't as if – as if I was like other boys, and could walk, either,' interrupted the cripple feverishly. 'You'd get tired of me in no time. And I'd see it comin'. I couldn't stand it – to be a burden like that. Of course, if you *cared* – like Mumsey here –' He threw out his hand, choked back a sob, then turned his head away again. 'I'm not the Jamie you want. I – can't – go,' he said. With the words his thin, boyish hand fell clenched till the knuckles showed white against the tattered old shawl that covered the bed.

There was a moment's breathless hush, then, very quietly, Mrs Carew got to her feet. Her face was colourless; but there was that in it that silenced the sob that rose to Pollyanna's lips.

'Come, Pollyanna,' was all she said.

'Well, if you ain't the fool limit!' babbled Jerry Murphy to the boy on the bed, as the door closed a moment later.

But the boy on the bed was crying very much as if the closing door had been the one that had led to Paradise – and that had now closed for ever.

12

From Behind a Counter

Mrs Carew was very angry. To have brought herself to the point where she was willing to take this lame boy into her home, and then to have the lad calmly refuse to come, was unbearable. Mrs Carew was not in the habit of having her invitations ignored, or her wishes scorned. Furthermore, now that she could not have the boy, she was conscious of an almost frantic terror lest he were, after all, the real Jamie. She knew then that her true reason for wanting him had been – not because she cared for him, not even because she wished to help him and make him happy – but because she hoped, by taking him, that she would ease her own mind, and for ever silence that awful eternal questioning on her part: 'What if he *were* her own Jamie?'

It certainly had not helped matters any that the boy had divined her state of mind, and had given as the reason for his refusal that she 'did not care'. To be sure, Mrs Carew now very proudly told herself that she did not indeed 'care', that he was *not* her sister's boy, and that she would 'forget all about it'.

But she did not forget all about it. However insistently she might disclaim responsibility and relationship, just as insistently responsibility and relationship thrust themselves upon her in the shape of panicky doubts; and however resolutely she turned her thoughts to other matters, just so resolutely visions of a wistful-eyed boy in a poverty-stricken room loomed always before her.

Then, too, there was Pollyanna. Clearly Pollyanna was not herself at all. In a most un-Pollyanna-like spirit she moped about the house, finding apparently no interest anywhere.

'Oh, no, I'm not sick,' she would answer, when remonstrated with, and questioned.

'But what *is* the trouble?'

'Why, nothing. It – it's only that I was thinking of Jamie, you know – how *he* hasn't got all these beautiful things – carpets, and pictures, and curtains.'

It was the same with her food. Pollyanna was actually losing her appetite; but here again she disclaimed sickness.

'Oh, no,' she would sigh mournfully. 'It's just that I don't seem hungry. Some way, just as soon as I begin to eat, I think of Jamie, and how *he* doesn't have only old doughnuts and dry rolls; and then I – I don't want anything.'

Mrs Carew, spurred by a feeling that she herself only dimly understood, and recklessly determined to bring about some change in Pollyanna at all costs, ordered a huge tree, two dozen wreaths, and quantities of holly and Christmas baubles. For the first time in many years the house was aflame and a-glitter with scarlet and tinsel. There was even to be a Christmas party, for Mrs Carew had told Pollyanna to invite half a dozen of her schoolgirl friends for the tree on Christmas Eve.

But even here Mrs Carew met with disappointment;

for, although Pollyanna was always grateful, and at times interested and even excited, she still carried frequently a sober little face. And in the end the Christmas party was more of a sorrow than a joy; for the first glimpse of the glittering tree sent her into a storm of sobs.

'Why, Pollyanna!' ejaculated Mrs Carew. 'What in the world is the matter now?'

'N-n-nothing,' wept Pollyanna. 'It's only that it's so perfectly, perfectly beautiful that I just had to cry. I was thinking how Jamie would love to see it.'

It was then that Mrs Carew's patience snapped.

'Jamie, Jamie, Jamie!' she exclaimed. 'Pollyanna, *can't* you stop talking about that boy? You know perfectly well that it is not my fault that he is not here. I asked him to come here to live. Besides, where is that Glad Game of yours? I think it would be an excellent idea if you would play it on this.'

'I *am* playing it,' quavered Pollyanna. 'And that's what I don't understand. I never knew it to act so funny. Why, before, when I've been glad about things, I've happy. But now, about Jamie – I'm so glad I've got carpets and pictures and nice things to eat, and that I can walk and run, and go to school, and all that; but the harder I'm glad for myself, the sorrier I am for him. I never knew the game to act so funny, and I don't know what ails it. Do you?'

But Mrs Carew, with a despairing gesture, merely turned away without a word.

It was the day after Christmas that something so wonderful happened that Pollyanna, for a time, almost forgot Jamie. Mrs Carew had taken her shopping, and it was while Mrs Carew was trying to decide between a duchesse-lace and a point-lace collar, that Pollyanna chanced to spy farther down the counter a face that looked vaguely familiar. For a moment she regarded it frowningly; then, with a little cry, she ran down the aisle.

'Oh, it's you – it *is* you!' she exclaimed joyously to a girl who was putting into the showcase a tray of pink bows. 'I'm so glad to see you!'

The girl behind the counter lifted her head and stared at Pollyanna in amazement. But almost immediately her dark, sombre face lighted with a smile of glad recognition.

'Well, well, if it isn't my little Public Garden kiddie!' she ejaculated.

'Yes. I'm so glad you remembered,' beamed Pollyanna. 'But you never came again. I looked for you lots of times.'

'I couldn't. I had to work. That was our last half-holiday, and – Fifty cents, madam,' she broke off in answer to a sweet-faced old lady's question as to the price of a black-and-white bow on the counter.

'Fifty cents? Hm-m!' The old lady fingered the bow, hesitated, then laid it down with a sigh. 'Hm, yes; well, it's very pretty, I'm sure, my dear,' she said, as she passed on.

Immediately behind her came two bright-faced girls who, with much giggling and bantering, picked out a jewelled creation of scarlet velvet, and a fairy-like structure of tulle and pink buds. As the girls turned chattering away Pollyanna drew an ecstatic sigh.

'Is this what you do all day? My, how glad you must be you chose this!'

'*Glad!*'

'Yes. It must be such fun – such lots of folks, you know, and all different! And you can talk to 'em. You *have* to talk to 'em – it's your business. I should love that. I think I'll do this when I grow up. It must be such fun to see what they all buy!'

'Fun! Glad!' bristled the girl behind the counter. 'Well, child, I guess if you knew half – That's a dollar, madam,' she interrupted herself hastily, in answer to a young woman's sharp question as to the price of a flaring yellow bow of beaded velvet in the showcase.

'Well, I should think 'twas time you told me,' snapped the young woman. 'I had to ask you twice.'

The girl behind the counter bit her lip.

'I didn't hear you, madam.'

'I can't help that. It is your business *to* hear. You are paid for it, aren't you? How much is that black one?'

'Fifty cents.'

'And that blue one?'

'One dollar.'

'No impudence, miss! You needn't be so short about it, or I shall report you. Let me see that tray of pink ones.'

The salesgirl's lips opened, then closed in a thin, straight line. Obediently she reached into the showcase and took out the tray of pink bows; but her eyes flashed, and her hands shook visibly as she set the tray down on the counter. The young woman whom she was serving picked up five bows, asked the price of four of them, then turned away with a brief:

'I see nothing I care for.'

'Well,' said the girl behind the counter, in a shaking

voice, to the wide-eyed Pollyanna, 'what do you think of my business now? Anything to be glad about there?'

Pollyanna giggled a little hysterically.

'My, wasn't she cross? But she was kind of funny, too – don't you think? Anyhow, you can be glad that – that they aren't *all* like *her*, can't you?'

'I suppose so,' said the girl, with a faint smile. 'But I can tell you right now, kiddie, that Glad Game of yours you was tellin' me about that day in the Garden may be all very well for you; but –' Once more she stopped with a tired 'Fifty cents, madam,' in answer to a question from the other side of the counter.

'Are you as lonesome as ever?' asked Pollyanna wistfully, when the salesgirl was at liberty again.

'Well, I can't say I've given more'n five parties, nor been to more'n seven, since I saw you,' replied the girl so bitterly that Pollyanna detected the sarcasm.

'Oh, but you did something nice at Christmas, didn't you?'

'Oh, yes. I stayed in bed all day with my feet done up in rags and read four newspapers and one magazine. Then at night I hobbled out to a restaurant where I had to blow in thirty-five cents for chicken pie instead of a quarter.'

'But what ailed your feet?'

'Blistered. Standin' on 'em – Christmas rush.'

'Oh!' shuddered Pollyanna sympathetically. 'And you didn't have any tree, or party, or anything?' she cried, distressed and shocked.

'Well, hardly!'

'Oh, dear! How I wish you could have seen mine!' sighed the little girl. 'It was just lovely, and – But oh, say!' she exclaimed joyously. 'You can see it, after all.

It isn't gone yet. Now, can't you come out tonight, or tomorrow night, and –'

'Poll*yanna*!' interrupted Mrs Carew in her chilliest accents. 'What in the world does this mean? Where have you been? I have looked everywhere for you. I even went 'way back to the suit department.'

Pollyanna turned with a happy little cry.

'Oh, Mrs Carew, I'm so glad you've come,' she rejoiced. 'This is – well, I don't know her name yet, but I know *her*, so it's all right. I met her in the Public Garden ever so long ago. And she's lonesome, and doesn't know anybody. And her father was a minister like mine, only he's alive. And she didn't have any Christmas tree, only blistered feet and chicken pie; and I want her to see mine, you know – the tree, I mean,' plunged on Pollyanna breathlessly. 'I've asked her to come out tonight, or tomorrow night. And you'll let me have it all lighted up again, won't you?'

'Well, really, Pollyanna,' began Mrs Carew, in cold disapproval. But the girl behind the counter interrupted with a voice quite as cold, and even more disapproving.

'Don't worry, madam. I've no notion of goin'.'

'Oh, but *please*,' begged Pollyanna. 'You don't know how I want you, and –'

'I notice the lady ain't doin' any askin',' interrupted the salesgirl, a little maliciously.

Mrs Carew flushed an angry red, and turned as if to go; but Pollyanna caught her arm and held it, talking meanwhile almost frenziedly to the girl behind the counter, who happened, at the moment, to be free from customers.

'Oh, but she will, she will,' Pollyanna was saying. 'She wants you to come – I know she does. Why, you don't know how good she is, and how much money she gives to – to charitable 'sociations and everything.'

'Poll*anna*!' remonstrated Mrs Carew sharply. Once more she would have gone, but this time she was held spellbound by the ringing scorn in the low, tense voice of the salesgirl.

'Oh, yes, I know! There's lots of 'em that'll give to *rescue* work. There's always plenty of helpin' hands stretched out to them that has gone wrong. And that's all right. I ain't findin' no fault with that. Only sometimes I wonder there don't some of 'em think of helpin' the girls *before* they go wrong. Why don't they give *good* girls pretty homes with books and pictures and soft carpets and music, and somebody round 'em to care? Maybe then there wouldn't be so many – Good heavens, what am I sayin'?' she broke off, under her breath. Then, with the old weariness, she turned to a young woman who had stopped before her and picked up a blue bow.

'That's fifty cents, madam,' Mrs Carew heard, as she hurried Pollyanna away.

13

A Waiting and a Winning

It was a delightful plan. Pollyanna had it entirely formulated in about five minutes; then she told Mrs Carew. Mrs Carew did not think it was a delightful plan, and she said so very distinctly.

'Oh, but I'm sure *they'll* think it is,' argued Pollyanna, in reply to Mrs Carew's objections. 'And just think how easy we can do it! The tree is just as it was – except for the presents, and we can get more of those. It won't be so very long till just New Year's Eve; and only think how glad she'll be to come! Wouldn't *you* be, if you hadn't had anything for Christmas, only blistered feet and chicken pie?'

'Dear, dear, what an impossible child you are!' frowned Mrs Carew. 'Even yet it doesn't seem to occur to you that we don't know this young person's name.'

'So we don't! And isn't it funny, when I feel that I know *her* so well?' smiled Pollyanna. 'You see, we had such a good talk in the Garden that day, and she told me all about how lonesome she was, and that she thought the lonesomest place in the world was in a crowd in a big city, because folks didn't think nor notice. Oh, there was one that noticed; but he noticed too much, she said, and he hadn't ought to notice her any – which is kind of funny, isn't it, when you come to think of it. But anyhow, he came for her there in the Garden to go somewhere with him, and she wouldn't go, and he was a real handsome gentleman, too – until he began to look so cross, just at the last. Folks aren't so pretty when they're cross, are they? Now there was a lady today looking at bows, and she said – well, lots of things that weren't nice, you know. And *she* didn't look pretty, either, after – after she began to talk. But you will let me have the tree New Year's Eve, won't you, Mrs Carew? – and invite this girl who sells bows, and Jamie? He's better, you know, now, and he *could* come. Of course Jerry would have to wheel him – but then, we'd want Jerry, anyway.'

'Oh, of course, *Jerry*!' exclaimed Mrs Carew in ironic scorn. 'But why stop with Jerry? I'm sure Jerry has hosts of friends who would love to come. And –'

'Oh, Mrs Carew, *may* I?' broke in Pollyanna, in uncontrollable delight. 'Oh, how good, *good*, GOOD you are! I've so wanted –' But Mrs Carew fairly gasped aloud in surprise and dismay.

'No, no, Pollyanna, I –' she began protestingly. But Pollyanna, entirely mistaking the meaning of her interruption, plunged in again in stout championship.

'Indeed you *are* good – just the bestest ever; and I shan't let you say you aren't. Now I reckon I'll have a party all right! There's Tommy Dolan and his sister Jennie, and the two Macdonald children, and three girls whose names I don't know that live under the Murphys, and a whole lot more, if we have room for 'em. And only think how glad they'll be when I tell 'em! Why, Mrs Carew, seems to me as if I never knew anything so perfectly lovely in all my life – and it's all your doing! Now mayn't I begin right away to invite 'em – so they'll *know* what's coming to 'em?'

And Mrs Carew, who would not have believed such a thing possible, heard herself murmuring a faint 'Yes,' which, she knew, bound her to the giving of a Christmas-tree party on New Year's Eve to a dozen children from Murphy's Alley and a young salesgirl whose name she did not know.

Perhaps in Mrs Carew's memory was still lingering a young girl's 'Sometimes I wonder there don't some of 'em think of helpin' the girls *before* they go wrong.' Perhaps in her ears was still ringing Pollyanna's story of that same girl who had found a crowd in a big city the loneliest place in the world, yet who had refused to go with the handsome man that had 'noticed too much'. Perhaps in Mrs Carew's heart was the undefined hope that somewhere in it all lay the peace she had so longed for. Perhaps it was a little of all three combined with utter helplessness in the face of Pollyanna's amazing twisting of her irritated sarcasm into the wide-sweeping hospitality of a willing hostess. Whatever it was, the thing was done; and at once Mrs Carew found herself caught into a veritable whirl of plans and plottings, the centre of which was always Pollyanna and the party.

To her sister, Mrs Carew wrote distractedly of the whole affair, closing with:

What I'm going to do I don't know; but I suppose I shall have to keep right on doing as I am doing. There is no other way. Of course, if Pollyanna once begins to preach – but she hasn't yet; so I can't, with a clear conscience, send her back to you.

Della, reading this letter at the Sanatorium, laughed aloud at the conclusion.

'"Hasn't preached yet", indeed!' she chuckled to herself. 'Bless her dear heart! And yet you, Ruth Carew, own up to giving two Christmas-tree parties within a week, and, as I happen to know, your home, which used to be shrouded in deathlike gloom, is aflame with scarlet and green from top to toe. But she hasn't preached yet – oh, no, she hasn't preached yet!'

The party was a great success. Even Mrs Carew admitted that. Jamie, in his wheel-chair, Jerry with his startling but expressive vocabulary, and the girl (whose name proved to be Sadie Dean), vied with each other in amusing the more diffident guests. Sadie Dean, much to the others' surprise – and perhaps to her own – disclosed an intimate knowledge of the most fascinating games; and these games, with Jamie's stories and Jerry's good-natured banter, kept every one in gales of laughter until supper, and the generous distribution of presents from the laden tree sent the happy guests home with tired sighs of content.

If Jamie (who with Jerry was the last to leave) looked about him a bit wistfully, no one apparently noticed it. Yet Mrs Carew, when she bade him good-night, said low in his ear, half impatiently, half embarrassedly:

'Well, Jamie, have you changed your mind – about coming?'

The boy hesitated. A faint colour stole into his cheeks. He turned and looked into her eyes wistfully, searchingly. Then very slowly he shook his head.

'If it could always be – like tonight, I – could,' he sighed. 'But it wouldn't. There'd be tomorrow, and

next week, and next month, and next year comin'; and
I'd know before next week that I hadn't oughter
come.'

If Mrs Carew had thought that the New Year's Eve
party was to end the matter of Pollyanna's efforts on
behalf of Sadie Dean, she was soon undeceived; for the
very next morning Pollyanna began to talk of her.

'And I'm so glad I found her again,' she prattled
contentedly. 'Even if I haven't been able to find the
real Jamie for you, I've found somebody else for you
to love – and of course you'll love to love her, 'cause
it's just another way of loving Jamie.'

Mrs Carew drew in her breath and gave a little gasp
of exasperation. This unfailing faith in her goodness of
heart, and unhesitating belief in her desire to 'help
everybody' was most disconcerting, and sometimes
most annoying. At the same time it was a most difficult
thing to disclaim under the circumstances, especially
with Pollyanna's happy, confident eyes full on her
face.

'But, Pollyanna,' she objected impotently, at last,
feeling very much as if she were struggling against
invisible silken cords, 'I – you – this girl really isn't
Jamie, at all, you know.'

'I know she isn't,' sympathized Pollyanna quickly.
'And of course I'm just as sorry she *isn't* Jamie as can
be. But she's somebody's Jamie – that is, I mean she
hasn't got anybody down here to love her and – and
notice, you know; and so whenever you remember
Jamie I should think you couldn't be glad enough
there was *somebody* you could help, just as you'd want
folks to help Jamie, wherever *he* is.'

Mrs Carew shivered and gave a little moan.

'But I want *my* Jamie,' she grieved.

Pollyanna nodded with understanding eyes.

'I know – the "child's presence". Mr Pendleton told me about it – only you've *got* the "woman's hand".'

'"Woman's hand"?'

'Yes – to make a home, you know. He said that it took a woman's hand or a child's presence to make a home. That was when he wanted me, and I found him Jimmy, and he adopted him instead.'

'*Jimmy?*' Mrs Carew looked up with the startled something in her eyes that always came into them at the mention of any variant of that name.

'Yes; Jimmy Bean.'

'Oh – *Bean*,' said Mrs Carew, relaxing.

'Yes. He was from an Orphans' Home, and he ran away. I found him. He said he wanted another kind of a home with a mother in it instead of a Matron. I couldn't find him the mother part, but I found him Mr Pendleton, and he adopted him. His name is Jimmy Pendleton now.'

'But it was – Bean.'

'Yes, it was Bean.'

'Oh!' said Mrs Carew, this time with a long sigh.

Mrs Carew saw a good deal of Sadie Dean during the days that followed the New Year's Eve party. She saw a good deal of Jamie, too. In one way and another Pollyanna contrived to have them frequently at the house; and this, Mrs Carew, much to her surprise and vexation, could not seem to prevent. Her consent and even her delight were taken by Pollyanna as so much a matter of course that she found herself helpless to convince the child that neither approval nor satisfaction entered into the matter at all, as far as she was concerned.

But Mrs Carew, whether she herself realized it or not, was learning many things – things she never could have learned in the old days, shut up in her rooms, with orders to Mary to admit no one. She was learning something of what it means to be a lonely young girl in a big city, with one's living to earn, and with no one to care – except one who cares too much, and too little.

'But what did you mean?' she nervously asked Sadie Dean one evening; 'what did you mean that first day in the store – what you said – about helping the girls?'

Sadie Dean coloured distressfully.

'I'm afraid I was rude,' she apologized.

'Never mind that. Tell me what you meant. I've thought of it so many times since.'

For a moment the girl was silent; then, a little bitterly, she said:

''Twas because I knew a girl once, and I was thinkin' of her. She came from my town, and she was pretty and good, but she wasn't overstrong. For a year we pulled together, sharin' the same room, boiling our eggs over the same gas-jet, and eatin' our hash and fish-balls for supper at the same cheap restaurant. There was never anything to do evenin's but to walk on the Common, or go to the movies, if we had the dime to blow in, or just stay in our room. Well, our room wasn't very pleasant. It was hot in summer, and cold in winter, and the gas-jet was so measly and so flickery that we couldn't sew or read, even if we hadn't been too fagged out to do either – which we 'most generally was. Besides, over our heads was a squeaky board that some one was always rockin' on, and under us was a feller that was learnin' to play the cornet. Did you ever hear anyone learn to play the cornet?'

'N-no, I don't think so,' murmured Mrs Carew.

'Well, you've missed a lot,' said the girl drily. Then, after a moment, she resumed her story.

'Sometimes, 'specially at Christmas and holidays, we used to walk up here on the Avenue, and other streets, huntin' for windows where the curtains were up, and we could look in. You see, we were pretty lonesome, them days 'specially, and we said it did us good to see homes with folks, and lamps on the centre-tables, and children playin' games; but we both of us knew that really it only made us feel worse than ever, because we were so hopelessly out of it all. 'Twas even harder to see the automobiles and the gay young folks in them, laughing and chatting. You see, we were young, and I suspect we wanted to laugh and chatter. We wanted a good time, too; and by and by – my chum began to have it – this good time.

'Well, to make a long story short, we broke partner-ship one day, and she went her way, and I mine. I didn't like the company she was keepin', and I said so. She wouldn't give 'em up, so we quit. I didn't see her again for 'most two years, then I got a note from her, and I went. This was just last month. She was in one of them rescue homes. It was a lovely place: soft rugs, fine pictures, plants, flowers, and books, a piano, a beautiful room, and everything possible done for her. Rich women came in their automobiles and carriages to take her driving, and she was taken to concerts and matinées. She was learnin' stenography, and they were going to help her to a position just as soon as she could take it. Everybody was wonderfully good to her, she

said, and showed they wanted to help her in every
way. But she said something else, too. She said:

'"Sadie, if they'd taken one-half the pains to show
me they cared and wanted to help long ago when I
was an honest, self-respectin', hard-workin' homesick
girl – I wouldn't have been here for them to help
now." And – well, I never forgot it. That's all. It ain't
that I'm objectin' to the rescue work – it's a fine thing,
and they ought to do it. Only I'm thinkin' there
wouldn't be quite so much of it for them to do – if
they'd just show a little of their interest earlier in the
game.'

'But I thought – there were working-girls' homes,
and – and settlement-houses that – that did that sort of
thing,' faltered Mrs Carew in a voice that few of her
friends would have recognized.

'There are. Did you ever see the inside of one of
them?'

'Why, n-no; though I – I have given money to
them.' This time Mrs Carew's voice was almost apolo-
getically pleading in tone.

Sadie Dean smiled curiously.

'Yes, I know. There are lots of good women that
have given money to them – and have never seen the
inside of one of them. Please don't understand that
I'm sayin' anythin' against the homes. I'm not. They're
good things. They're almost the only thing that's doing
anything to help; but they're only a drop in the bucket
to what is really needed. I tried one once; but there
was an air about it – somehow I felt – But there,
what's the use? Probably they aren't all like that one,
and maybe the fault was with me. If I should try to tell
you, you wouldn't understand. You'd have to live in it

– and you haven't even seen the inside of one. But I can't help wonderin' sometimes why so many of those good women never seem to put the real *heart* and *interest* into the preventin' that they do into the rescuin'. But there! I didn't mean to talk such a lot. But – you asked me.'

'Yes, I asked you,' said Mrs Carew in a half-stifled voice, as she turned away.

Not only from Sadie Dean, however, was Mrs Carew learning things never learned before, but from Jamie, also.

Jamie was there a great deal. Pollyanna liked to have him there, and he liked to be there. At first, to be sure, he had hesitated; but very soon he had quieted his doubts and yielded to his longings by telling himself (and Pollyanna) that, after all, visiting was not 'staying for keeps'.

Mrs Carew often found the boy and Pollyanna contentedly settled on the library window-seat, with the empty wheel-chair close by. Sometimes they were poring over a book. (She heard Jamie tell Pollyanna one day that he didn't think he'd mind so very much being lame if he had so many books as Mrs Carew, and that he guessed he'd be so happy he'd fly clean away if he had both books and legs.) Sometimes, the boy was telling stories, and Pollyanna was listening, wide-eyed and absorbed.

Mrs Carew wondered at Pollyanna's interest – until one day she herself stopped and listened. After that she wondered no longer – but she listened a good deal longer. Crude and incorrect as was much of the boy's language, it was always wonderfully vivid and picturesque, so that Mrs Carew found herself, hand in hand with Pollyanna, trailing down the Golden Ages at the beck of a glowing-eyed boy.

Dimly Mrs Carew was beginning to realize, too, something of what it must mean to be in spirit and ambition the centre of brave deeds and wonderful adventures, while in reality one was only a crippled boy in a wheelchair. But what Mrs Carew did not realize was the part this crippled boy was beginning to play in her own life. She did not realize how much a matter of course his presence was becoming, nor how interested she now was in finding something new 'for Jamie to see'. Neither did she realize how day by day he was coming to seem to her more and more the lost Jamie, her dead sister's child.

As February, March, and April passed, however, and May came, bringing with it the near approach of the date set for Pollyanna's homegoing, Mrs Carew did suddenly awake to the knowledge of what that homegoing was to mean to her.

She was amazed and appalled. Up to now she had, in belief, looked forward with pleasure to the departure of Pollyanna. She had said that then once again the house would be quiet, with the glaring sun shut out. Once again she would be at peace, and able to hide herself away from the annoying, tiresome world. Once again she would be free to summon to her aching consciousness all those dear memories of the lost little lad who had so long ago stepped into that vast unknown and closed the door behind him. All this she had believed would be the case when Pollyanna should go home.

But now that Pollyanna was really going home, the picture was far different. The 'quiet house with the sun shut out' had become one that promised to be 'gloomy and unbearable'. The longed-for 'peace' would be 'wretched loneliness'; and as for her being able to 'hide herself away from the annoying, tiresome world', and 'free to summon to her aching conscious- ness all those dear memories of that lost little lad' – just as if anything could blot out those other aching memories of the new Jamie (who yet might be the old Jamie) with his pitiful, pleading eyes!

Full well now Mrs Carew knew that without Polly- anna the house would be empty; but that without the lad, Jamie, it would be worse than that. To her pride this knowledge was not pleasing. To her heart it was torture – since the boy had twice said that he would not come. For a time, during those last few days of Pollyanna's stay, the struggle was a bitter one, though pride always kept the ascendancy. Then, on what Mrs Carew knew would be Jamie's last visit, her heart triumphed, and once more she asked Jamie to come and be to her the Jamie that was lost.

What she said she never could remember afterwards; but what the boy said, she never forgot. After all, it was compassed in six short words.

For what seemed a long, long minute his eyes had searched her face; then to his own had come a transfig- uring light, as he breathed:

'Oh, yes! Why, you – *care*, now!'

14

JIMMY AND THE GREEN-EYED MONSTER

This time Beldingsville did not literally welcome Pollyanna home with brass bands and bunting – perhaps
because the hour of her expected arrival was known to
but few of the townspeople. But there certainly was no
lack of joyful greetings on the part of everybody from
the moment she stepped from the railway train with
her Aunt Polly and Dr Chilton. Nor did Pollyanna
lose any time in starting on a round of fly-away minute
calls on all her old friends. Indeed, for the next few
days, according to Nancy, 'There wasn't no putting of
your finger on her anywheres, for by the time you'd
got your finger down she wa'n't there.'

And always, everywhere she went, Pollyanna met
the question: 'Well, how did you like Boston?' Perhaps
to no one did she answer this more fully than she did
to Mr Pendleton. As was usually the case when this
question was put to her, she began her reply with a
troubled frown.

'Oh, I liked it – I just loved it – some of it.'

'But not all of it?' smiled Mr Pendleton.

'No. There's parts of it – Oh, I was glad to be
there,' she explained hastily. 'I had a perfectly lovely
time, and lots of things were so queer and different,
you know – like eating dinner at night instead of

noons, when you ought to eat it. But everybody was so good to me, and I saw such a lot of wonderful things – Bunker Hill, and the Public Garden, and the 'Seeing Boston' autos, and miles of pictures and statues and store-windows and streets that didn't have any end. And folks. I never saw such a lot of folks.'

'Well, I'm sure – I thought you liked folks,' commented the man.

'I do.' Pollyanna frowned again and pondered. 'But what's the use of such a lot of them if you don't know 'em? And Mrs Carew wouldn't let me. She didn't know 'em herself. She said folks didn't, down there.'

There was a slight pause, then, with a sigh, Pollyanna resumed.

'I reckon maybe that's the part I don't like the most – that folks don't know each other. It would be such a lot nicer if they did! Why, just think, Mr Pendleton, there are lots of folks that live on dirty, narrow streets, and don't even have beans and fish-balls to eat, nor things even as good as missionary barrels to wear. Then there are other folks – Mrs Carew, and a whole lot like her – that live in perfectly beautiful houses, and have more things to eat and wear than they know what to do with. Now if *those* folks only knew the other folks –' But Mr Pendleton interrupted with a laugh.

'My dear child, did it ever occur to you that these people don't *care* to know each other?' he asked quizzically.

'Oh, but some of them do,' maintained Pollyanna, in eager defence. 'Now there's Sadie Dean – she sells bows, lovely bows in a big store – she *wants* to know people; and I introduced her to Mrs Carew, and we had her up to the house, and we had Jamie and lots of others there, too; and she was so glad to know them! And that's what made me think that if only a lot of Mrs Carew's kind could know the other kind – but of course *I* couldn't do the introducing. I didn't know many of them myself, anyway. But if they *could* know each other, so that the rich people could give the poor people part of their money –'

But again Mr Pendleton interrupted with a laugh.

'Oh, Pollyanna, Pollyanna,' he chuckled; 'I'm afraid you're getting into pretty deep water. You'll be a rabid little socialist before you know it.'

'A – what?' questioned the little girl, dubiously. 'I – I don't think I know what a socialist is. But I know what being *sociable* is – and I like folks that are that. If it's anything like that, I don't mind being one, a mite. I'd like to be one.'

'I don't doubt it, Pollyanna,' smiled the man. 'But when it comes to this scheme of yours for the wholesale distribution of wealth – you've got a problem on your hands that you might have difficulty with.'

Pollyanna drew a long sigh.

'I know,' she nodded. 'That's the way Mrs Carew talked. She says I don't understand; that 'twould – er – pauperize her and be indiscriminate and pernicious, and – Well, it was *something* like that, anyway,' bridled the little girl, aggrievedly, as the man began to laugh. 'And, anyway, I *don't* understand why some folks should have such a lot, and other folks shouldn't have anything; and I *don't* like it. And if I ever have a lot I shall just give some of it to folks who don't have any, even if it does make me pauperized and pernicious, and –' But Mr Pendleton was laughing so hard now that Pollyanna, after a moment's struggle, surrendered and laughed with him.

'Well, anyway,' she reiterated, when she had caught her breath, 'I don't understand it, all the same.'

'No, dear, I'm afraid you don't,' agreed the man, growing suddenly very grave and tender-eyed; 'nor any of the rest of us, for that matter. But, tell me,' he added, after a minute, 'who is this Jamie you've been talking so much about since you came?'

And Pollyanna told him.

In talking of Jamie Pollyanna lost her worried, baffled look. Pollyanna loved to talk of Jamie. Here was something she understood. Here was no problem that had to deal with big, fearsome-sounding words. Besides, in this particular instance – would not Mr Pendleton be especially interested in Mrs Carew's taking the boy into her home, for who better than himself could understand the need of a child's presence?

For that matter, Pollyanna talked to everybody about Jamie. She assumed that everybody would be as interested as she herself was. On most occasions she was not disappointed in the interest shown; but one day she met with a surprise. It came through Jimmy Pendleton.

'Say, look a-here,' he demanded one afternoon irritably. 'Wasn't there *anybody* else down to Boston but just that everlasting Jamie?'

'Why, Jimmy Bean, what do you mean?' cried Pollyanna.

The boy lifted his chin a little.

'I'm not Jimmy Bean. I'm Jimmy Pendleton. And I mean that I should think, from your talk, that there wasn't *anybody* down to Boston but just that loony boy who calls them birds and squirrels Lady Lancelot, and all that tommyrot.'

'Why, Jimmy Be– Pendleton!' gasped Pollyanna. Then, with some spirit: 'Jamie isn't loony! He is a very nice boy. And he knows a lot – books and stories! Why, he can *make* stories right out of his own head! Besides, it isn't "Lady Lancelot" – it's "Sir Lancelot". If you knew half as much as he does you'd know that, too!' she finished, with flashing eyes.

Jimmy Pendleton flushed miserably and looked utterly wretched. Growing more and more jealous moment by moment, still doggedly he held his ground.

'Well, anyhow,' he scoffed, 'I don't think much of his name. Jamie! Humph! – sounds sissy! And I know somebody else that said so, too.'

'Who was it?'

There was no answer.

'*Who was it?*' demanded Pollyanna, more peremptorily.

'Dad.' The boy's voice was sullen.

'Your – dad?' repeated Pollyanna, in amazement. 'Why, how could he know Jamie?'

'He didn't. 'Twasn't about that Jamie. 'Twas about me.' The boy still spoke sullenly, with his eyes turned away. Yet there was a curious softness in his voice that was always noticeable whenever he spoke of his father.

'*You!*'

'Yes. 'Twas just a little while before he died. We stopped 'most a week with a farmer. Dad helped about the hayin' – and I did, too, some. The farmer's wife was awful good to me, and pretty quick she was callin' me Jamie. I don't know why, but she just did. And one day Father heard her. He got awful mad – so mad that I remembered it always – what he said. He said Jamie wasn't no sort of a name for a boy, and that no son of his should ever be called it. He said 'twas a sissy name, and he hated it. 'Seems so I never saw him so mad as he was that night. He wouldn't stay to finish the work, but him and me took to the road again that night. I was kind of sorry 'cause I liked her – the farmer's wife, I mean. She was good to me.'

Pollyanna nodded, all sympathy and interest. It was not often that Jimmy said much of that mysterious past of his, before she had known him.

'And what happened next?' she prompted. Pollyanna had, for the moment, forgotten all about the original subject of the controversy – the name Jamie that was dubbed 'sissy'.

The boy sighed.

'We just went on till we found another place. And 'twas there Dad – died. Then they put me in the 'sylum.'

'And then you ran away and I found you that day, down by Mrs Snow's,' exulted Pollyanna softly. 'And I've known you ever since.'

'Oh, yes – and you've known me ever since,' repeated Jimmy – but in a far different voice; Jimmy had suddenly come back to the present, and to his grievance. 'But, then, I ain't *Jamie*, you know,' he finished with scornful emphasis, as he turned loftily away, leaving a distressed, bewildered Pollyanna behind him.

'Well, anyway, I can be glad he doesn't always act

like this,' sighed the little girl, as she mournfully watched the sturdy, boyish figure with its disagreeable, amazing swagger.

15

AUNT POLLY TAKES ALARM

Pollyanna had been at home about a week when the letter from Della Wetherby came to Mrs Chilton.

I wish I could make you see what your little niece has done for my sister [wrote Miss Wetherby], but I'm afraid I can't. You would have to know what she was before. You did see her, to be sure, and perhaps you saw something of the hush and gloom in which she has shrouded herself for so many years. But you can have no conception of her bitterness of heart, her lack of aim and interest, her insistence upon eternal mourning.

Then came Pollyanna. Probably I didn't tell you, but my sister regretted her promise to take the child, almost the minute it was given; and she made the stern stipulation that the moment Pollyanna began to preach, back she should come to me. Well, she hasn't preached – at least, my sister says she hasn't; and my sister ought to know. And yet – well, just let me tell you what I found when I went to see her yesterday. Perhaps nothing else could give you a better idea of what that wonderful little Pollyanna of yours has accomplished.

To begin with, as I approached the house, I saw that nearly all the shades were up; they used to be down – 'way down to the sill. The minute I stepped into the hall I heard music – *Parsifal*. The drawing-rooms were open, and the air was sweet with roses.

'Mrs Carew and Master Jamie are in the music-room,' said the maid. And there I found them – my sister and the youth she has taken into her home, listening to one of those modern contrivances that can hold an entire opera company, including the orchestra.

The boy was in a wheel-chair. He was pale, but plainly beatifically happy. My sister looked ten years younger. Her usually colourless cheeks showed a faint pink, and her eyes glowed and sparkled. A little later, after I had talked a few minutes with the boy, my sister and I went upstairs to her own rooms; and there she talked to me – of Jamie. Not of the old Jamie, as she used to, with tear-wet eyes and hopeless sighs, but of the new Jamie – and there were no sighs nor tears now. There was, instead, the eagerness of enthusiastic interest.

'Della, he's wonderful,' she began. 'Everything that is best in music, art, and literature seems to appeal to him in a perfectly marvellous fashion, only, of course, he needs development and training. That's what I'm going to see that he gets. A tutor is coming tomorrow. Of course his language is something awful; at the same time, he has read so many good books that his vocabulary is quite amazing – and you should hear the stories he can reel off! Of course in general education he is very deficient; but he's eager to learn, so that will soon be remedied. He loves music, and I shall give him what training in that he wishes. I have already put in a stock of carefully selected records. I wish you could have seen his face when he first heard that Holy Grail music. He knows all about King Arthur and his Round Table, and he prattles of knights and lords and ladies as you and I do of the members of our own family – only sometimes I don't know whether his Sir Lancelot means the ancient knight or a squirrel in the Public Garden. And, Della, I believe he can be made to walk. I'm going to have Dr Ames see him, anyway, and –'

And so on and on she talked, while I sat amazed and tongue-tied, but, oh, so happy! I tell you all this, dear Mrs Chilton, so you can see for yourself how interested she is, how eagerly she is going to watch this boy's growth and development, and how, in spite of herself, it is all going to change her attitude towards life. She *can't* do what she is doing for this boy, Jamie, and not do for herself at the same time. Never again, I believe, will she be the soured, morose woman she was before. And it's all because of Pollyanna.

Pollyanna! Dear child – and the best part of it is, she is so unconscious of the whole thing. I don't believe even my sister yet quite realizes what is taking place within her own heart and life, and certainly Pollyanna doesn't – least of all does she realize the part she played in the change.

And now, dear Mrs Chilton, how can I thank you? I know I can't; so I'm not even going to try. Yet in your heart I believe you know how grateful I am to both you and Pollyanna.

Della Wetherby

'Well, it seems to have worked a cure, all right,' smiled Dr Chilton, when his wife had finished reading the letter to him.

To his surprise she lifted a quick, remonstrative hand.

'Thomas, don't, please!' she begged.

'Why, Polly, what's the matter? Aren't you glad that – that the medicine worked?'

Mrs Chilton dropped despairingly back in her chair.

'There you go again, Thomas,' she sighed. 'Of *course* I'm glad that this misguided woman has forsaken the error of her ways and found that she can be of use to some one. And of course I'm glad that Pollyanna did it. But I am not glad to have that child continually spoken of as if she were a – a bottle of medicine, or a "cure". Don't you see?'

'Nonsense! After all, where's the harm? I've called Pollyanna a tonic ever since I knew her.'

'Harm! Thomas Chilton, that child is growing older every day. Do you want to spoil her? Thus far she has been utterly unconscious of her extraordinary power. And therein lies the secret of her success. The minute she *consciously* sets herself to reform somebody, you know as well as I do that she will be simply impossible. Consequently, heaven forbid that she ever gets it into her head that she's anything like a cure-all for poor, sick, suffering humanity.'

'Nonsense! I wouldn't worry,' laughed the doctor.

'But I do worry, Thomas.'

'But, Polly, think of what she's done,' argued the doctor. 'Think of Mrs Snow and John Pendleton, and quantities of others – why, they're not the same people at all that they used to be, any more than Mrs Carew is. And Pollyanna did do it – bless her heart!'

'I know she did,' nodded Mrs Polly Chilton emphatically. 'But I don't want Pollyanna to know she did it! Oh, of course, she knows it in a way. She knows she taught them to play the Glad Game with her, and that they are lots happier in consequence. And that's all right. It's a game – *her* game, and they're playing it together. To you I will admit that Pollyanna had preached to us one of the most powerful sermons I ever heard; but the minute *she* knows it – well, I don't want her to. That's all. And right now let me tell you that I've decided that I will go to Germany with you this fall. At first I thought I wouldn't. I didn't want to leave Pollyanna – and I'm not going to leave her now.

I'm going to take her with me.'

'Take her with us? Good! Why not?'

'I've got to. That's all. Furthermore, I should be glad to plan to stay a few years, just as you said you'd like to. I want to get Pollyanna away, quite away from Beldingsville for a while. I'd like to keep her sweet and unspoiled, if I can. And she shall not get silly notions into her head if I can help myself. Why, Thomas Chilton, do we want that child made an insufferable little prig?'

'We certainly don't,' laughed the doctor. 'But, for that matter, I don't believe anything or anybody could make her so. However, this Germany idea suits me to a T. You know I didn't want to come away when I did – if it hadn't been for Pollyanna. So the sooner we get back there the better I'm satisfied. And I'd like to stay – for a little practice, as well as study.'

'Then that's settled.' And Aunt Polly gave a satisfied sigh.

16

When Pollyanna was Expected

All Beldingsville was fairly aquiver with excitement. Not since Pollyanna Whittier came home from the Sanatorium, *walking*, had there been such a chatter of talk over backyard fences and on every street corner. Today, too, the centre of interest was Pollyanna. Once again Pollyanna was coming home – but so different a Pollyanna, and so different a homecoming!

Pollyanna was twenty now. For six years she had spent her winters in Germany, her summers leisurely travelling with Dr Chilton and his wife. Only once during that time had she been in Beldingsville, and then it was for but a short four weeks the summer she was sixteen. Now she was coming home – to stay, report said; she and her Aunt Polly.

The doctor would not be with them. Six months before, the town had been shocked and saddened by the news that the doctor had died suddenly. Beldingsville had expected then that Mrs Chilton and Pollyanna would return at once to the old home. But they had not come. Instead had come word that the widow and her niece would remain abroad for a time. The report said that, in entirely new surroundings, Mrs Chilton was trying to seek distraction and relief from her great sorrow.

Very soon, however, vague rumours, and rumours
not so vague, began to float through the town that,
financially, all was not well with Mrs Polly Chilton.
Certain railroad stocks, in which it was known that the
Harrington estate had been heavily interested, wavered
uncertainly, then tumbled into ruin and disaster. Other
investments, according to report, were in a most precarious condition. From the doctor's estate, little could
be expected. He had not been a rich man, and his
expenses had been heavy for the past six years. Beldingsville was not surprised, therefore, when, not quite
six months after the doctor's death, word came that
Mrs Chilton and Pollyanna were coming home.

Once more the old Harrington homestead, so long
closed and silent, showed up-flung windows and wide-
open doors. Once more Nancy – now Mrs Timothy
Durgin – swept and scrubbed and dusted until the old
place shone in spotless order.

'No, I hain't had no instructions ter do it; I hain't, I
hain't.' Nancy explained to curious friends and neighbours who halted at the gate, or came more boldly up
to the doorways. 'Mother Durgin's had the key,
'course, and has come in regerler to air up and see that
things was all right; and Mis' Chilton just wrote and
said she and Miss Pollyanna was comin' this week
Friday, and ter please see that the rooms and sheets
were aired, and ter leave the key under the side-door
mat on that day.

'Under the mat, indeed! Just as if I'd leave them
two poor things ter come into this house alone, and all
forlorn like that – and me only a mile away, a-sittin' in
my own parlour like as if I was a fine lady an' hadn't
no heart at all, at all! Just as if the poor things hadn't

enough ter stand without that – a-comin' into this
house an' the doctor gone – bless his kind heart! – an'
never comin' back. An' no money, too. Did ye hear
about that? An' ain't it a shame, a shame! Think of
Miss Polly – I mean, Mis' Chilton – bein' poor! My
stars and stockings, I can't sense it – I can't, I can't!'

Perhaps to no one did Nancy speak so interestedly
as she did to a tall, good-looking young fellow with
peculiarly frank eyes and a particularly winning smile,
who cantered up to the side-door on a mettlesome
thoroughbred at ten o'clock that Thursday morning.
At the same time to no one did she talk with so much
evident embarrassment, so far as the manner of address
was concerned; for her tongue stumbled and blundered
out a 'Master Jimmy – er – Mr Bean – I mean, Mr
Pendleton, Master Jimmy!' with a nervous precipita-
tion that sent the young man himself into a merry peal
of laughter.

'Never mind, Nancy! Let it go at whatever comes
handiest,' he chuckled. 'I've found out what I wanted
to know; Mrs Chilton and her niece really are expected
tomorrow.'

'Yes, sir, they be, sir,' curtsied Nancy, '– more's the
pity! Not but that I shall be glad enough ter see 'em,
you understand, but it's the *way* they're a-comin'.'

'Yes, I know. I understand,' nodded the youth
gravely, his eyes sweeping the fine old house before
him. 'Well, I suppose that part can't be helped. But
I'm glad you're doing – just what you are doing. That
will help a whole lot,' he finished with a bright smile,
as he wheeled about and rode rapidly down the
driveway.

Back on the steps Nancy wagged her head wisely.

'I ain't surprised, Master Jimmy,' she declared aloud, her admiring eyes following the handsome figures of horse and man. 'I ain't surprised that you ain't lettin' no grass grow under your feet 'bout inquirin' for Miss Pollyanna. I said long ago 'twould come some time, an' it's bound to – what with your growin' so handsome and tall. An' I hope 'twill; I do, I do. It'll be just like a book, what with her a-findin' you an' gettin' you into that grand home with Mr Pendleton. My, but who'd ever take you now for that little Jimmy Bean that used to be! I never did see such a change in anybody – I didn't, I didn't!' she answered, with one last look at the rapidly disappearing figures far down the road.

Something of the same thought must have been in the mind of John Pendleton some time later that same morning, for, from the veranda of his big grey house on Pendleton Hill, John Pendleton was watching the rapid approach of that same horse and rider; and in his eyes was an expression very like the one that had been in Mrs Nancy Durgin's. On his lips, too, was an admiring 'Jove! what a handsome pair!' as the two dashed by on the way to the stable.

Five minutes later the youth came round the corner of the house and slowly ascended the veranda steps.

'Well, my boy, is it true? Are they coming?' asked the man, with visible eagerness.

'Yes.'

'When?'

'Tomorrow.' The young fellow dropped himself into a chair.

At the crisp terseness of the answer, John Pendleton frowned. He threw a quick look into the young man's face. For a moment he hesitated; then, a little abruptly, he asked:

'Why, son, what's the matter?'

'Matter? Nothing, sir.'

'Nonsense! I know better. You left here an hour ago so eager to be off that wild horses could not have held you. Now you sit humped up in that chair and look as if wild horses couldn't drag you out of it. If I didn't know better I'd think you weren't glad that our friends are coming.'

He paused, evidently for a reply. But he did not get it.

'Why, Jim, *aren't* you glad they're coming?'

The young fellow laughed and stirred restlessly.

'Why, yes, of course.'

'Humph! You act like it.'

The youth laughed again. A boyish red flamed into his face.

'Well, it's only that I was thinking – of Pollyanna.'

'Pollyanna! Why, man alive, you've done nothing but prattle of Pollyanna ever since you came home from Boston and found she was expected. I thought you were dying to see Pollyanna.'

The other leaned forward with curious intentness.

'That's exactly it! See? You said it a minute ago. It's just as if yesterday wild horses couldn't keep me from seeing Pollyanna; and now, today when I know she's coming – they couldn't drag me to see her.'

'Why, *Jim*!'

At the shocked incredulity on John Pendleton's face the younger man fell back in his chair with an embarrassed laugh.

'Yes, I know. It sounds nutty, and I don't expect I

can make you understand. But, somehow, I don't think – I ever wanted Pollyanna to grow up. She was such a dear, just as she was. I like to think of her as I saw her last, her earnest, freckled little face, her yellow pigtails, her tearful: "Oh, yes, I'm glad I'm going; but I think I shall be a little gladder when I come back." That's the last time I saw her. You know we were in Egypt that time she was here four years ago.'

'I know. I see exactly what you mean, too. I think I felt the same way – till I saw her last winter in Rome.'

The other turned eagerly.

'Sure enough, you have seen her! Tell me about her.'

A shrewd twinkle came into John Pendleton's eyes.

'Oh, but I thought you didn't want to know Pollyanna – grown up.'

With a grimace the young fellow tossed this aside.

'Is she pretty?'

'Oh, ye young men!' shrugged John Pendleton, in mock despair. 'Always the first question – "Is she pretty?"'

'Well, is she?' insisted the youth.

'I'll let you judge for yourself. If you – On second thoughts, though, I believe I won't. You might be too disappointed. Pollyanna isn't pretty, so far as regular features, curls, and dimples go. In fact, to my certain knowledge the great cross in Pollyanna's life thus far is that she is so sure she isn't pretty. Long ago she told me that black curls were one of the things she was going to have when she got to heaven; and last year in Rome she said something else. It wasn't much, perhaps, so far as words went, but I detected the longing beneath. She said she did wish that some time some

one would write a novel with a heroine who had
straight hair and a freckle on her nose; but that she
supposed she ought to be glad girls in books didn't
have to have them.'

'That sounds like the old Pollyanna.'

'Oh, you'll still find her – Pollyanna,' smiled the
man quizzically. 'Besides, *I* think she's pretty. Her
eyes are lovely. She is the picture of health. She
carries herself with all the joyous springiness of youth,
and her whole face lights up so wonderfully when she
talks that you quite forget whether her features are
regular or not.'

'Does she still – play the game?'

John Pendleton smiled fondly.

'I imagine she plays it, but she doesn't say much
about it now, I fancy. Anyhow, she didn't to me, the
two or three times I saw her.'

There was a short silence; then, a little slowly,
young Pendleton said:

'I think that was one of the things that was worrying
me. That game has been so much to so many people.
It has meant so much everywhere, all through the
town! I couldn't bear to think of her giving it up and
not playing it. At the same time I couldn't fancy a
grown-up Pollyanna perpetually admonishing people
to be glad for something. Someway, I – well, as I said,
I – I just didn't want Pollyanna to grow up, anyhow.'

'Well, I wouldn't worry,' shrugged the elder man,
with a peculiar smile. 'Always, with Pollyanna, you
know, it was the "clearing-up shower", both literally
and figuratively; and I think you'll find she lives up to
the same principle now – though perhaps not quite in
the same way. Poor child, I fear she'll need some kind

of game to make existence endurable, for a while, at least.'

'Do you mean because Mrs Chilton has lost her money? Are they so very poor, then?'

'I suspect they are. In fact, they are in rather bad shape, so far as money matters go, as I happen to know. Mrs Chilton's own fortune has shrunk unbeliev- ably, and poor Tom's estate is very small, and hope- lessly full of bad debts – professional services never paid for, and that never will be paid for. Tom could never say no when his help was needed, and all the dead beats in town knew it and imposed on him accordingly. Expenses have been heavy with him lately. Besides, he expected great things when he should have completed this special work in Germany. Naturally he supposed his wife and Pollyanna were more than amply provided for through the Harrington estate; so he had no worry in that direction.'

'Hm-m; I see, I see. Too bad, too bad!'

'But that isn't all. It was about two months after Tom's death that I saw Mrs Chilton and Pollyanna in Rome, and Mrs Chilton then was in a terrible state. In addition to her sorrow, she had just begun to get an inkling of the trouble with her finances, and she was nearly frantic. She refused to come home. She declared she never wanted to see Beldingsville, or anybody in it, again. You see, she has always been a peculiarly proud woman, and it was all affecting her in a rather curious way. Pollyanna said that her aunt seemed pos- sessed with the idea that Beldingsville had not ap- proved of her marrying Dr Chilton in the first place, at her age; and now that he was dead, she felt that they were utterly out of sympathy in any grief that she might show. She resented keenly, too, the fact that they must now know that she was poor as well as widowed. In short, she had worked herself into an utterly morbid, wretched state, as unreasonable as it was terrible. Poor little Pollyanna! It was a marvel to me how she stood it. All is, if Mrs Chilton kept it up, and continues to keep it up, that child will be a wreck. That's why I said Pollyanna would need some kind of a game if ever anybody did.'

'The pity of it! – to think of that happening to Pollyanna!' exclaimed the young man, in a voice that was not quite steady.

'Yes; and you can see all is not right by the way they are coming today – so quietly, with not a word to anybody. That was Polly Chilton's doing, I'll warrant. She didn't *want* to be met by anybody. I understand she wrote to no one but her Old Tom's wife, Mrs Durgin, who had the keys.'

'Yes, so Nancy told me – good old soul! She'd got the whole house open, and had contrived somehow to make it look as if it wasn't a tomb of dead hopes and lost pleasures. Of course the grounds looked fairly well, for Old Tom has kept them up, after a fashion. But it made my heart ache – the whole thing.'

There was a long silence, then, curtly, John Pendleton suggested:

'They ought to be met.'

'They will be met.'

'Are *you* going to the station?'

'I am.'

'Then you know what train they're coming on.'

'Oh, no. Neither does Nancy.'

'Then how will you manage?'

'I'm going to begin in the morning and go to every train till they come,' laughed the young man, a bit grimly. 'Timothy's going too, with the family carriage. After all, there aren't many trains, anyway, that they can come on, you know.'

'Hm-m, I know,' said John Pendleton. 'Jim, I admire your nerve, but not your judgment. I'm glad you're going to follow your nerve and not your judgment, however – and I wish you good luck.'

'Thank you, sir,' smiled the young man dolefully. 'I need 'em – your good wishes – all right, all right, as Nancy says.'

17

WHEN POLLYANNA CAME

As the train neared Beldingsville Pollyanna watched her aunt anxiously. All day Mrs Chilton had been growing more and more restless, more and more gloomy; and Pollyanna was fearful of the time when the familiar home station should be reached.

As Pollyanna looked at her aunt, her heart ached. She was thinking that she would not have believed it possible that any one could have changed and aged so greatly in six short months. Mrs Chilton's eyes were lustreless, her cheeks pallid and shrunken, and her forehead crossed and recrossed by fretful lines. Her mouth drooped at the corners, and her hair was combed tightly back in the unbecoming fashion that had been hers when Pollyanna first had seen her, years before. All the softness and sweetness that seemed to have come to her with her marriage had dropped from her like a cloak, leaving uppermost the old hardness and sourness that had been hers when she was Miss Polly Harrington, unloved, and unloving.

'Pollyanna!' Mrs Chilton's voice was incisive.

Pollyanna started guiltily. She had an uncomfortable feeling that her aunt might have read her thoughts.

'Yes, Auntie.'

'Where is that black bag – the little one?'

'Right here.'

'Well, I wish you'd get out my black veil. We're nearly there.'

'But it's so hot and thick, Auntie!'

'Pollyanna, I asked for that black veil. If you'd please learn to do what I ask without arguing about it, it would be a great deal easier for me. I want that veil. Do you suppose I'm going to give all Beldingsville a chance to see how I "take it"?'

'Oh, Auntie, they'd never be there in *that* spirit,' protested Pollyanna, hurriedly rummaging in the black bag for the much-wanted veil. 'Besides, there won't be anybody there, anyway, to meet us. We didn't tell anyone we were coming, you know.'

'Yes, I know. We didn't *tell* anyone to meet us. But we instructed Mrs Durgin to have the rooms aired and the key under the mat for today. Do you suppose Mary Durgin has kept that information to herself? Not much! Half the town knows we're coming today, and a dozen or more will "happen around" the station about train time. I know them! They want to see what Polly Harrington *poor* looks like. They –'

'Oh, Auntie, Auntie,' begged Pollyanna, with tears in her eyes.

'If I wasn't so alone. If – the doctor were only here, and –' She stopped speaking and turned away her head. Her mouth worked convulsively. 'Where is – that veil?' she choked huskily.

'Yes, dear. Here it is – right here,' comforted Pollyanna, whose only aim now, plainly, was to get the veil into her aunt's hands with all haste. 'And here we are now almost there. Oh, Auntie, I do wish you'd had Old Tom or Timothy meet us!'

'And ride home in state, as if we could *afford* to keep such horses and carriages? And when we know we shall have to sell them tomorrow? No, I thank you, Pollyanna. I prefer to use the public carriage, under those circumstances.'

'I know, but –' The train came to a jolting, jarring stop, and only a fluttering sigh finished Pollyanna's sentence.

As the two women stepped to the platform, Mrs Chilton, in her black veil, looked neither to the right nor the left. Pollyanna, however, was nodding and smiling tearfully in half a dozen directions before she had taken twice as many steps. Then, suddenly, she found herself looking into a familiar, yet strangely unfamiliar, face.

'Why, it isn't – it *is* – Jimmy!' she beamed, reaching forth a cordial hand. 'That is, I suppose I should say "*Mr Pendleton*",' she corrected herself with a shy smile that said plainly: 'Now that you've grown so tall and fine!'

'I'd like to see you try it,' challenged the youth, with a very Jimmy-like tilt to his chin. He turned then to speak to Mrs Chilton; but the lady, with her head half averted, was hurrying on a little in advance.

He turned back to Pollyanna, his eyes troubled and sympathetic.

'If you'd please come this way – both of you,' he urged hurriedly. 'Timothy is here with the carriage.'

'Oh, how good of him,' cried Pollyanna, but with an anxious glance at the sombre, veiled figure ahead. Timidly she touched her aunt's arm. 'Auntie dear, Timothy's here. He's come with the carriage. He's over this side. And – this is Jimmy Bean, Auntie. You remember Jimmy Bean!'

In her nervousness and embarrassment Pollyanna did not notice that she had given the young man the old name of his boyhood. Mrs Chilton, however, evidently did notice it. With palpable reluctance she turned and inclined her head ever so slightly.

'Mr – Pendleton is very kind, I am sure; but – I am sorry that he or Timothy took quite so much trouble,' she said frigidly.

'No trouble – no trouble at all, I assure you,' laughed the young man, trying to hide his embarrassment. 'Now if you'll just let me have your checks, so I can see to your baggage.'

'Thank you,' began Mrs Chilton, 'but I am very sure we can –'

But Pollyanna, with a relieved little 'Thank you!' had already passed over the checks; and dignity demanded that Mrs Chilton say no more.

The drive home was a silent one. Timothy, vaguely hurt at the reception he had met with at the hands of his former mistress, sat up in front stiff and straight, with tense lips. Mrs Chilton, after a weary 'Well, well, child, just as you please; I suppose we shall have to ride home in it now!' had subsided into stern gloom. Pollyanna, however, was neither stern, nor tense, nor gloomy. With eager, though tearful, eyes she greeted each loved landmark as they came to it. Only once did she speak, and that was to say:

'Isn't Jimmy fine? How he has improved! And hasn't he the nicest eyes and smile?'

She waited hopefully, but as there was no reply to this, she contented herself with a cheerful: 'Well, I think he has, anyhow.'

Timothy had been both too aggrieved and too afraid to tell Mrs Chilton what to expect at home; so the wide-flung doors and flower-adorned rooms with Nancy curtsying on the porch were a complete surprise to Mrs Chilton and Pollyanna.

'Why, Nancy, how perfectly lovely!' cried Pollyanna, springing lightly to the ground. 'Auntie, here's Nancy to welcome us. And only see how charming she's made everything look!'

Pollyanna's voice was determinedly cheerful, though it shook audibly. This homecoming without the dear doctor whom she had loved so well was not easy for her; and if hard for her, she knew something of what it must be for her aunt. She knew, too, that the one thing her aunt was dreading was a breakdown before Nancy, than which nothing could be worse in her eyes. Behind the heavy black veil the eyes were brimming and the lips were trembling, Pollyanna knew. She knew, too, that to hide these facts her aunt would probably seize the first opportunity for fault-finding, and make her anger a cloak to hide the fact that her heart was breaking. Pollyanna was not surprised, therefore, to hear her aunt's few cold words of greeting to Nancy followed by a sharp: 'Of course all this was very kind, Nancy; but, really, I would have much preferred that you had not done it.'

All the joy fled from Nancy's face. She looked hurt and frightened.

'Oh, but Miss Polly – I mean, Mis' Chilton,' she entreated; 'it seemed as if I couldn't let you –'

'There, there, never mind, Nancy,' interrupted Mrs Chilton. 'I – I don't want to talk about it.' And, with her head proudly high, she swept out of the room. A minute later they heard the door of her bedroom shut upstairs.

Nancy turned in dismay.

'Oh, Miss Pollyanna, what is it? What have I done? I thought she'd *like* it. I meant it all right!'

'Of course you did,' wept Pollyanna, fumbling in her bag for her handkerchief. 'And 'twas lovely to have you do it, too – just lovely.'

'But *she* didn't like it.'

'Yes, she did. But she didn't want to show she liked it. She was afraid if she did she'd show – other things, and – Oh, Nancy, Nancy, I'm so glad just to c-cry!' And Pollyanna was sobbing on Nancy's shoulder.

'There, there, dear; so she shall, so she shall,' soothed Nancy, patting the heaving shoulders with one hand, and trying, with the other, to make the corner of her apron serve as a handkerchief to wipe her own tears away.

'You see, I mustn't – cry – before – *her*,' faltered Pollyanna; 'and it *was* hard – coming here – the first time, you know, and all. And I *knew* how she was feeling.'

'Of course, of course, poor lamb,' crooned Nancy. 'And to think the first thing *I* should have done was somethin' ter vex her, and –'

'Oh, but she wasn't vexed at that,' corrected Pollyanna agitatedly. 'It's just her way, Nancy. You see, she doesn't like to show how badly she feels about – about the doctor. And she's so afraid she *will* show it that she – she just takes anything for an excuse to – to talk about. She does it to me too, just the same. So I know all about it. See?'

'Oh, yes, I see, I do, I do,' Nancy's lips snapped together a little severely, and her sympathetic pats, for the minute, were even more loving, if possible. 'Poor lamb! I'm glad I come, anyhow, for your sake.'

'Yes, so I am,' breathed Pollyanna, gently drawing herself away and wiping her eyes. 'There, I feel better. And I do thank you ever so much, Nancy, and I appreciate it. Now don't let us keep you when it's time for you to go.'

'Ho! I'm thinking I'll stay for a spell,' sniffed Nancy.

'Stay! Why, Nancy, I thought you were married. Aren't you Timothy's wife?'

'Sure! But he won't mind – for you. He'd *want* me to stay – for you.'

'Oh, but, Nancy, we couldn't let you,' demurred Pollyanna. 'We can't have anybody – now, you know. I'm going to do the work. Until we know just how things are, we shall live very economically, Aunt Polly says.'

'Ho! as if I'd take money from –' began Nancy, in bridling wrath; but at the expression on the other's face she stopped, and let her words dwindle off in a mumbling protest, as she hurried from the room to look after her creamed chicken on the stove.

Not until supper was over, and everything put in order, did Mrs Timothy Durgin consent to drive away with her husband; then she went with evident reluctance, and with many pleadings to be allowed to come 'just ter help out a bit' at any time.

After Nancy had gone Pollyanna came into the living-room where Mrs Chilton was sitting alone, her hand over her eyes.

'Well, dearie, shall I light up?' suggested Pollyanna, brightly.

'Oh, I suppose so.'

'Wasn't Nancy a dear to fix us all up so nice?'

No answer.

'Where in the world she found all these flowers I can't imagine. She has them in every room down here, and in both bedrooms, too.'

Still no answer.

Pollyanna gave a half-stifled sigh and threw a wistful glance into her aunt's averted face. After a moment she began again hopefully.

'I saw Old Tom in the garden. Poor man, his rheumatism is worse than ever. He was bent nearly double. He inquired very particularly for you and –'

Mrs Chilton turned with a sharp interruption.

'Pollyanna, what are we going to do?'

'Do? Why, the best we can, of course, dearie.'

Mrs Chilton gave an impatient gesture.

'Come, come, Pollyanna, do be serious for once. You'll find it is serious, fast enough. *What* are we going to *do*? As you know, my income has almost entirely stopped. Of course, some of the things are worth something, I suppose; but Mr Hart says very few of them will pay anything at present. We have something in the bank, and a little coming in, of course. And we have this house. But of what earthly use is the house? We can't eat it, or wear it. It's too big for us, the way we shall have to live; and we couldn't sell it for half what it's really worth, unless we *happened* to find just the person that wanted it.'

'Sell it! Oh, Auntie, you wouldn't – this beautiful house full of lovely things!'

'I may have to, Pollyanna. We have to eat – unfortunately.'

'I know it; and I'm always *so* hungry,' mourned Pollyanna, with a rueful laugh. 'Still, I suppose I ought to be glad my appetite is so good.'

'Very likely. You'd find something to be glad about, of course. But what shall we do, child? I do wish you'd be serious for a minute.'

A quick change came to Pollyanna's face.

'I am serious, Aunt Polly. I've been thinking. I – I wish I could earn some money.'

'Oh, child, child, to think of my ever living to hear you say that!' moaned the woman; '– a daughter of the Harringtons having to earn her bread!'

'Oh, but that isn't the way to look at it,' laughed Pollyanna. 'You ought to be glad if a daughter of the Harringtons is *smart* enough to earn her bread! That isn't any disgrace, Aunt Polly.'

'Perhaps not; but it isn't very pleasant to one's pride, after the position we've always occupied in Beldingsville, Pollyanna.'

Pollyanna did not seem to have heard. Her eyes were musingly fixed on space.

'If only I had some talent! If only I could do something better than anybody else in the world,' she sighed at last. 'I can sing a little, play a little, embroider a little, and darn a little; but I can't do any of them well – not well enough to be paid for it.'

'I think I'd like best to cook,' she resumed, after a minute's silence, 'and keep house. You know I loved that in Germany winters, when Gretchen used to bother us so much by not coming when we wanted her. But I don't exactly want to go into other people's kitchens to do it.'

'As if I'd let you! Pollyanna!' shuddered Mrs Chilton again.

'And, of course, to just work in our own kitchen here doesn't bring in anything,' bemoaned Pollyanna, '– not any money, I mean. And it's money we need.'

'It most emphatically is,' sighed Aunt Polly.

There was a long silence, broken at last by Pollyanna.

'To think that after all you've done for me, Auntie – to think that now, if I only could, I'd have such a splendid chance to help! And yet – I can't do it. Oh, why wasn't I born with something that's worth money?'

'There, there, child, don't, don't! Of course, if the doctor –' The words choked into silence.

Pollyanna looked up quickly, and sprang to her feet.

'Dear, dear, this will never do!' she exclaimed, with a complete change of manner. 'Don't you fret, Auntie. What'll you wager that I don't develop the most marvellous talent going, one of these days? Besides, *I* think it's real exciting – all this. There's so much uncertainty in it. There's a lot of fun in wanting things – and then watching for them to come. Just living along and *knowing* you're going to have everything you want is so – so humdrum, you know,' she finished, with a gay little laugh.

Mrs Chilton, however, did not laugh. She only sighed and said:

'Dear me, Pollyanna, what a child you are!'

18

A MATTER OF ADJUSTMENT

The first few days at Beldingsville were not easy either for Mrs Chilton or for Pollyanna. They were days of adjustment; and days of adjustment are seldom easy.

From travel and excitement it was not easy to put one's mind to the consideration of the price of butter and the delinquencies of the butcher. From having all one's time for one's own, if was not easy to find always the next task clamouring to be done. Friends and neighbours called, too, and although Pollyanna welcomed them with glad cordiality, Mrs Chilton, when possible, excused herself; and always she said bitterly to Pollyanna:

'Curiosity, I suppose, to see how Polly Harrington likes being poor.'

Of the doctor Mrs Chilton seldom spoke, yet Pollyanna knew very well that almost never was he absent from her thoughts; and that more than half her taciturnity was but her usual cloak for a deeper emotion which she did not care to show.

Jimmy Pendleton Pollyanna saw several times during that first month. He came first with John Pendleton for a somewhat stiff and ceremonious call – not that it was either stiff or ceremonious until after Aunt Polly came into the room; then it was both. For some reason Aunt Polly had not excused herself on this occasion. After that Jimmy had come by himself, once with flowers, once with a book for Aunt Polly, twice with no excuse at all. Pollyanna welcomed him with frank pleasure always. Aunt Polly, after that first time, did not see him at all.

To the most of their friends and acquaintances Pollyanna said little about the change in their circumstances. To Jimmy, however, she talked freely, and always her constant cry was: 'If only I could do something to bring in some money!'

'I'm getting to be the most mercenary little creature you ever saw,' she laughed dolefully. 'I've got so I measure everything with a dollar bill, and I actually *think* in quarters and dimes. You see, Aunt Polly does feel so poor!'

'It's a shame!' stormed Jimmy.

'I know. But, honestly, I think she feels a little poorer than she needs to – she's brooded over it so. But I do wish I could help!'

Jimmy looked down at the wistful, eager face with its luminous eyes, and his own eyes softened.

'What do you *want* to do – if you could do it?' he asked.

'Oh, I want to cook and keep house,' smiled Pollyanna, with a pensive sigh. 'I just love to beat eggs and sugar, and hear the soda gurgle its little tune in the cup of sour milk. I'm happy if I've got a day's baking before me. But there isn't any money in that – except in somebody else's kitchen, of course. And I – I don't exactly love it well enough for that!'

'I should say not!' ejaculated the young fellow.

Once more he glanced down at the expressive face

so near him. This time a queer look came to the corners of his mouth. He pursed his lips, then spoke, a slow red mounting to his forehead.

'Well, of course you might – marry. Have you thought of that – Miss Pollyanna?'

Pollyanna gave a merry laugh. Voice and manner were unmistakably those of a girl quite untouched by even the most far-reaching of Cupid's darts.

'Oh, no, I shall never marry,' she said blithely. 'In the first place I'm not pretty, you know; and in the second place, I'm going to live with Aunt Polly and take care of her.'

'Not pretty, eh?' smiled Pendleton quizzically. 'Did it ever – er – occur to you that there might be a difference of opinion on that, Pollyanna?'

Pollyanna shook her head.

'There couldn't be. I've got a mirror, you see,' she objected, with a merry glance.

It sounded like coquetry. In any other girl it would have been coquetry, Pendleton decided. But, looking into the face before him now, Pendleton knew that it was not coquetry. He knew, too, suddenly, why Pollyanna had seemed so different from any girl he had ever known. Something of her old literal way of looking at things still clung to her.

'Why aren't you pretty?' he asked.

Even as he uttered the question, and sure as he was of his estimate of Pollyanna's character, Pendleton quite held his breath at his temerity. He could not help thinking of how quickly any other girl he knew would have resented that implied acceptance of her claim to no beauty. But Pollyanna's first words showed him that even this lurking fear of his was quite groundless.

'Why, I just am not,' she laughed, a little ruefully. 'I wasn't made that way. Maybe you don't remember, but long ago, when I was a little girl, it always seemed to me that one of the nicest things heaven was going to give me when I got there was black curls.'

'And is that your chief desire now?'

'N-no, maybe not,' hesitated Pollyanna. 'But I still think I'd like them. Besides, my eyelashes aren't long enough, and my nose isn't Grecian, or Roman, or any of those delightfully desirable ones that belong to a "type". It's just *nose*. And my face is too long, or too short, I've forgotten which; but I measured it once with one of those "correct-for-beauty" tests, and it wasn't right, anyhow. And they said the width of the face should be equal to five eyes, and the width of the eyes equal to – to something else. I've forgotten that, too – only that mine wasn't.'

'What a lugubrious picture!' laughed Pendleton. Then, with his gaze admiringly regarding the girl's animated face and expressive eyes, he asked:

'Did you ever look in the mirror when you were *talking*, Pollyanna?'

'Why, no, of course not!'

'Well, you'd better try it some time.'

'What a funny idea! Imagine my doing it,' laughed the girl. 'What shall I say? Like this? "Now, you, Pollyanna, what if your eyelashes aren't long, and your nose is just a nose, be glad you've got *some* eyelashes and *some* nose!"'

Pendleton joined in her laugh, but an odd expression came to his face.

'Then you still play – the game,' he said, a little diffidently.

Pollyanna turned soft eyes of wonder full upon him.

'Why, of course! Why, Jimmy, I don't believe I could have lived – the last six months – if it hadn't been for that blessed game.' Her voice shook a little.

'I haven't heard you say much about it,' he commented.

She changed colour.

'I know. I think I'm afraid – of saying too much – to outsiders, who don't care, you know. It wouldn't sound quite the same from me now, at twenty, as it did when I was ten. I realize that, of course. Folks don't like to be preached at, you know,' she finished, with a whimsical smile.

'I know,' nodded the young fellow gravely. 'But I wonder sometimes, Pollyanna, if you really understand yourself what that game is, and what it has done for those who are playing it.'

'I know – what it has done for myself.' Her voice was low, and her eyes were turned away.

'You see, it really works, if you play it,' he mused aloud, after a short silence. 'Somebody said once that it would revolutionize the world if everybody would really play it. And I believe it would.'

'Yes; but some folks don't want to be revolutionized,' smiled Pollyanna. 'I ran across a man in Germany last year. He had lost his money, and was in hard luck generally. Dear, dear, but he was gloomy! Somebody in my presence tried to cheer him up one day by saying, "Come, come, things might be worse, you know!" Dear, dear, but you should have heard that man then!

'"If there is anything on earth that makes me mad clear through," he snarled, "it is to be told that things might be worse, and to be thankful for what I've got left. These people who go around with an everlasting grin on their faces carolling forth that they are thankful that they can breathe, or eat, or walk, or lie down, I have no use for. I don't *want* to breathe, or eat, or walk, or lie down – if things are as they are now with me. And when I'm told that I ought to be thankful for some such tommyrot as that, it makes me just want to go out and shoot somebody." Imagine what *I'd* have gotten if I'd have introduced the Glad Game to that man!' laughed Pollyanna.

'I don't care. He needed it,' answered Jimmy.

'Of course he did – but he wouldn't have thanked me for giving it to him.'

'I suppose not. But, listen! As he was, under his present philosophy and scheme of living, he made himself and everybody else wretched, didn't he? Well, just suppose he was playing the game. While he was trying to hunt up something to be glad about in everything that had happened to him, he *couldn't* be at the same time grumbling and growling about how bad things were; so that much would be gained. He'd be a whole lot easier to live with, both for himself and for his friends. Meanwhile, just thinking of the doughnut instead of the hole couldn't make things any worse for him, and it might make things better; for it wouldn't give him such a gone feeling in the pit of his stomach, and his digestion would be better. I tell you, troubles are poor things to hug. They've got too many prickers.'

Pollyanna smiled appreciatively.

'That makes me think of what I told a poor old lady once. She was one of my Ladies' Aiders out West, and was one of the kind of people that really *enjoys* being miserable and telling over her causes for unhappiness. I was perhaps ten years old, and was trying to teach her the game. I reckon I wasn't having very good success, and evidently I at last dimly realized the reason, for I said to her triumphantly, "Well, anyhow, you can be glad you've got such a lot of things to make you miserable, for you love to be miserable so well!"'

'Well, if that wasn't a good one on her,' chuckled Jimmy.

Pollyanna raised her eyebrows.

'I'm afraid she didn't enjoy it any more than the man in Germany would have if I'd told him the same thing.'

'But they ought to be told, and you ought to tell –' Pendleton stopped short with so queer an expression on his face that Pollyanna looked at him in surprise.

'Why, Jimmy, what is it?'

'Oh, nothing. I was only thinking,' he answered, puckering his lips. 'Here I am urging you to do the very thing I was afraid you *would* do before I saw you, you know. That is, I was afraid before I saw you that – that –' He floundered into a helpless pause, looking very red indeed.

'Well, Jimmy Pendleton,' bridled the girl, 'you needn't think you can stop there, sir. Now just what do you mean by all that, please?'

'Oh, er – n-nothing much.'

'I'm waiting,' murmured Pollyanna. Voice and manner were calm and confident, though the eyes twinkled mischievously.

The young fellow hesitated, glanced at her smiling face, and capitulated.

'Oh, well, have it your own way,' he shrugged. 'It's only that I was worrying – a little – about that game, for fear you *would* talk it just as you used to, you know, and –' But a merry peal of laughter interrupted him.

'There, what did I tell you? Even you were worried, it seems, lest I should be at twenty just what I was at ten!'

'N-no, I didn't mean – Pollyanna, honestly, I thought – of course I knew –' But Pollyanna only put her hands to her ears and went off into another peal of laughter.

19

Two Letters

It was towards the latter part of June that the letter came to Pollyanna from Della Wetherby.

I am writing to ask you a favour [Miss Wetherby wrote]. I am hoping you can tell me of some quiet private family in Beldingsville that will be willing to take my sister to board for the summer. There would be three of them, Mrs Carew, her secretary, and her adopted son, Jamie. (You remember Jamie, don't you?) They do not like to go to an ordinary hotel or boarding-house. My sister is very tired, and the doctor has advised her to go into the country for a complete rest and change. He suggested Vermont or New Hampshire. We immediately thought of Beldingsville and you; and we wondered if you couldn't recommend just the right place to us. I told Ruth I would write you. They would like to go right away, early in July, if possible. Would it be asking too much to request you to let us know as soon as you conveniently can if you do know of a place? Please address me here. My sister is with us here at the Sanatorium for a few weeks' treatment.

Hoping for a favourable reply, I am,

Most cordially yours,

Della Wetherby

For the first few minutes after the letter was finished, Pollyanna sat with frowning brow, mentally searching the homes of Beldingsville for a possible

boarding-house for her old friends. Then a sudden
something gave her thoughts a new turn, and with a
joyous exclamation she hurried to her aunt in the
living-room.

'Auntie, Auntie,' she panted; 'I've got the loveliest
idea. I told you something would happen, and that I'd
develop that wonderful talent some time. Well, I have.
I have right now. Listen! I've had a letter from Miss
Wetherby, Mrs Carew's sister – where I stayed that
winter in Boston, you know – and they want to come
into the country to board for the summer, and Miss
Wetherby's written to see if I didn't know a place for
them. They don't want a hotel or an ordinary
boarding-house, you see. And at first I didn't know of
one; but now I do. I do, Aunt Polly! Just guess where
'tis.'

'Dear me, child,' ejaculated Mrs Chilton, 'how you
do run on! I should think you were a dozen years old
instead of a woman grown. Now what are you talking
about?'

'About a boarding-place for Mrs Carew and Jamie.
I've found it,' babbled Pollyanna.

'Indeed! Well, what of it? Of what possible interest
can that be to me, child?' murmured Mrs Chilton,
drearily.

'Because it's *here*. I'm going to have them here,
Auntie.'

'Pollyanna!' Mrs Chilton was sitting erect in horror.

'Now, Auntie, please don't say no – please don't,'
begged Pollyanna eagerly. 'Don't you see? This is my
chance, the chance I've been waiting for; and it's just
dropped right into my hands. We can do it lovely. We
have plenty of room, and you know I *can* cook and

keep house. And now there'd be money in it, for they'd pay well, I know; and they'd love to come, I'm sure. There'd be three of them – there's a secretary with them.'

'But, Pollyanna, I can't! Turn this house into a boarding-house? – the Harrington homestead a common boarding-house? Oh, Pollyanna, I can't, I can't!'

'But it wouldn't be a common boarding-house, dear. 'Twill be an uncommon one. Besides, they're our friends. It would be like having our friends come to see us; only they'd be *paying* guests, so meanwhile we'd be earning money – money that we *need*, Auntie, money that we need,' she emphasized significantly.

A spasm of hurt pride crossed Polly Chilton's face. With a low moan she fell back in her chair.

'But how could you do it?' she asked at last faintly. 'You couldn't do the work part alone, child!'

'Oh, no, of course not,' chirped Pollyanna. (Pollyanna was on sure ground now. She knew her point was won.) 'But I could do the cooking and the overseeing, and I'm sure I could get one of Nancy's younger sisters to help about the rest. Mrs Durgin would do the laundry part just as she does now.'

'But, Pollyanna, I'm not well at all – you know I'm not. I couldn't do much.'

'Of course not. There's no reason why you should,' scorned Pollyanna loftily. 'Oh, Auntie, won't it be splendid? Why, it seems too good to be true – money just dropped into my hands like that!'

'Dropped into your hands, indeed! You still have some things to learn in this world, Pollyanna, and one is that summer boarders don't drop money into anybody's hands without looking very sharply to it that they get ample return. By the time you fetch and carry and bake and brew until you are ready to sink, and by the time you nearly kill yourself trying to serve everything to order from fresh-laid eggs to the weather, you will believe what I tell you.'

'All right, I'll remember,' laughed Pollyanna. 'But I'm not doing any worrying now; and I'm going to hurry and write Miss Wetherby at once so I can give it to Jimmy Bean to mail when he comes out this afternoon.'

Mrs Chilton stirred restlessly.

'Pollyanna, I do wish you'd call that young man by his proper name. That "Bean" gives me the shivers. His name is Pendleton now, as I understand it.'

'So it is,' agreed Pollyanna, 'but I do forget it half the time. I even call him that to his face, sometimes, and of course that's dreadful, when he really is adopted, and all. But you see I'm so excited,' she finished, as she danced from the room.

She had the letter all ready for Jimmy when he called at four o'clock. She was still quivering with excitement, and she lost no time in telling her visitor what it was all about.

'And I'm crazy to see them, besides,' she cried when she had told him of her plans. 'I've never seen either of them since that winter. You know I told you – didn't I tell you? – about Jamie.'

'Oh, yes, you told me.' There was a touch of constraint in the young man's voice.

'Well, isn't it splendid, if they can come?'

'Why, I don't know as I should call it exactly splendid,' he parried.

'Not splendid that I've got such a chance to help

Aunt Polly out, for even this little while? Why, Jimmy, of course it's splendid.'

'Well, it strikes me that it's going to be rather *hard* – for you,' bridled Jimmy, with more than a shade of irritation.

'Yes, of course, in some ways. But I shall be so glad for the money coming in that I'll think of that all the time. You see,' she sighed, 'how mercenary I am, Jimmy.'

For a long minute there was no reply; then, a little abruptly, the young man asked:

'Let's see, how old is this Jamie now?'

Pollyanna glanced up with a merry smile.

'Oh, I remember – you never did like his name, "Jamie",' she twinkled. 'Never mind; he's adopted now, legally, I believe, and has taken the name of Carew. So you can call him that.'

'But that isn't telling me how old he is,' reminded Jimmy stiffly.

'Nobody knows, exactly, I suppose. You know he couldn't tell; but I imagine he's about your age. I wonder how he is now. I've asked all about it in this letter, anyway.'

'Oh, you have!' Pendleton looked down at the letter in his hand and flipped it a little spitefully. He was thinking that he would like to drop it, to tear it up, to give it to somebody, to throw it away, to do anything with it – but mail it.

Jimmy knew perfectly well that he was jealous, that he always had been jealous of this youth with the name so like and yet so unlike his own. Not that he was in love with Pollyanna, he assured himself wrathfully. He was not that, of course. It was just that he did not care to have this strange youth with the sissy name come to Beldingsville and be always around to spoil all their good times. He almost said as much to Pollyanna, but something stayed the words on his lips; and after a time he took his leave, carrying the letter with him.

That Jimmy did not drop the letter, tear it up, give it to anybody, or throw it away, was evidenced a few days later, for Pollyanna received a prompt and delighted reply from Miss Wetherby; and when Jimmy came next time he heard it read – or rather he heard part of it, for Pollyanna prefaced the reading by saying:

'Of course the first part is just where she says how glad they are to come, and all that. I won't read that. But the rest I thought you'd like to hear, because you've heard me talk so much about them. Besides, you'll know them yourself pretty soon, of course. I'm depending a whole lot on you, Jimmy, to help me make it pleasant for them.'

'Oh, are you!'

'Now don't be sarcastic, just because you don't like Jamie's name,' reproved Pollyanna, with mock severity. 'You'll like *him*, I'm sure, when you know him; and you'll *love* Mrs Carew.'

'Will I, indeed?' retorted Jimmy huffily. 'Well, that *is* a serious prospect. Let us hope, if I do, the lady will be so gracious as to reciprocate.'

'Of course,' dimpled Pollyanna. 'Now listen, and I'll read to you about her. This letter is from her sister, Della – Miss Wetherby, you know, at the Sanatorium.'

'All right. Go ahead!' directed Jimmy, with a somewhat too evident attempt at polite interest. And Pollyanna, still smiling mischievously, began to read:

You ask me to tell you everything about everybody. That is a large commission, but I'll do the best I can. To begin with, I think you'll find my sister quite changed. The new interests that have come into her life during the last six years have done wonders for her. Just now she is a bit thin and tired from overwork, but a good rest will soon remedy that, and you'll see how young and blooming and happy she looks. Please notice I said *happy*. That won't mean so much to you as it does to me, of course, for you were too young to realize quite how unhappy she was when you first knew her that winter in Boston. Life was such a dreary, hopeless thing to her then; and now it is so full of interest and joy.

First she has Jamie, and when you see them together you won't need to be told what he is to her. To be sure, we are no nearer knowing whether he is the *real* Jamie, or not, but my sister loves him like an own son now, and has legally adopted him, as I presume you know.

Then she has her girls. Do you remember Sadie Dean, the salesgirl? Well, from getting interested in her, and trying to help her to a happier living, my sister has broadened her efforts little by little, until she has scores of girls now who regard her as their own best and particular good angel. She has started a Home for Working Girls along new lines. Half a dozen wealthy and influential men and women are associated with her, of course, but she is head and shoulders of the whole thing, and never hesitates to give *herself* to each and every one of the girls. You can imagine what that means in nerve strain. Her chief support and right-hand man is her secretary, this same Sadie Dean. You'll find *her* changed, too, yet she is the same old Sadie.

As for Jamie – poor Jamie! The great sorrow of his life is that he knows now he can never walk. For a time we all had hopes. He was here at the Sanatorium under Dr Ames for a year, and he improved to such an extent that he can go now with crutches. But the poor boy will always be a cripple – so far as his feet are concerned, but never as regards anything else. Some way, after you know Jamie, you seldom think of him as a cripple, his *soul* is so free. I can't explain it, but you'll know what I mean when you see him; and he has retained, to a marvellous degree, his old boyish enthusiasm and joy of living. There is just one thing – and only one, I believe – that would utterly quench that bright spirit and cast him into utter despair; and that is to find that he is not Jamie Kent, our nephew. So long has he brooded over this, and so ardently has he wished it, that he has come actually to believe that he *is* the real Jamie; but if he isn't I hope he will never find it out.

'There, that's all she says about them,' announced Pollyanna, folding up the closely written sheets in her hands. 'But isn't that interesting?'

'Indeed it is!' There was a ring of genuineness in Jimmy's voice now. Jimmy was thinking suddenly of what his own good legs meant to him. He even, for the moment, was willing that this poor crippled youth should have a *part* of Pollyanna's thoughts and attentions, if he were not so presuming as to claim too much of them, of course! 'By George! it is tough for the poor chap, and no mistake.'

'Tough! You don't know anything about it, Jimmy Bean,' choked Pollyanna: 'but *I* do. *I* couldn't walk once. *I know!*'

'Yes, of course, of course,' frowned the youth, moving restively in his seat. Jimmy, looking into Pollyanna's sympathetic face and brimming eyes, was suddenly not so sure, after all, that he *was* willing to have this Jamie come to town – if just to *think* of him made Pollyanna look like that!

20

THE PAYING GUESTS

The few intervening days before the expected arrival of 'those dreadful people', as Aunt Polly termed her niece's paying guests, were busy ones indeed for Polly-anna – but they were happy ones, too, as Pollyanna refused to be weary, or discouraged, or dismayed, no matter how puzzling were the daily problems she had to meet.

Summoning Nancy, and Nancy's younger sister, Betty, to her aid, Pollyanna systematically went through the house, room by room, and arranged for the comfort and convenience of her expected boarders. Mrs Chilton could do but little to assist. In the first place she was not well. In the second place her mental attitude towards the whole idea was not conducive to aid or comfort, for at her side stalked always the Harrington pride of name and race, and on her lips was the constant moan:

'Oh, Pollyanna, Pollyanna, to think of the Har-rington homestead ever coming to this!'

'It isn't, dearie,' Pollyanna at last soothed laugh-ingly. 'It's the Carews that are *coming to the Harrington homestead*!'

But Mrs Chilton was not to be so lightly diverted, and responded only with a scornful glance and a deeper sigh, so Pollyanna was forced to leave her to travel alone her road of determined gloom.

Upon the appointed day, Pollyanna with Timothy (who owned the Harrington horses now) went to the station to meet the afternoon train. Up to this hour there had been nothing but confidence and joyous anticipation in Pollyanna's heart. But with the whistle of the engine there came to her a veritable panic of doubt, shyness, and dismay. She realized suddenly what she, Pollyanna, almost alone and unaided, was about to do. She remembered Mrs Carew's wealth, position, and fastidious tastes. She recollected, too, that this would be a new, tall, young man Jamie, quite unlike the boy she had known.

For one awful moment she thought only of getting away – somewhere, anywhere.

'Timothy, I – I feel sick. I'm not well. I – tell 'em – er – not to come,' she faltered, poising as if for flight.

'Ma'am!' exclaimed the startled Timothy.

One glance into Timothy's amazed face was enough. Pollyanna laughed and threw back her shoulders alertly.

'Nothing. Never mind! I didn't mean it, of course, Timothy. Quick – see! They're almost here,' she panted. And Pollyanna hurried forward, quite herself once more.

She knew them at once. Even had there been any doubt in her mind, the crutches in the hands of the tall, brown-eyed young man would have piloted her straight to her goal.

There were a brief few minutes of eager handclasps and incoherent exclamations, then, somehow, she found herself in the carriage with Mrs Carew at her side, and Jamie and Sadie Dean in front. She had a chance, then, for the first time, really to see her friends, and to note the changes the six years had wrought.

In regard to Mrs Carew, her first feeling was one of surprise. She had forgotten that Mrs Carew was so lovely. She had forgotten that the eyelashes were so long, that the eyes they shaded were so beautiful. She even caught herself thinking enviously of how exactly that perfect face must tally, figure by figure, with that dread beauty-test table. But more than anything else she rejoiced in the absence of the old fretful lines of gloom and bitterness.

Then she turned to Jamie. Here again she was surprised, and for much the same reason. Jamie too had grown handsome. To herself Pollyanna declared that he was really distinguished-looking. His dark eyes, rather pale face, and dark, waving hair she thought most attractive. Then she caught a glimpse of the crutches at his side, and a spasm of aching sympathy contracted her throat.

From Jamie Pollyanna turned to Sadie Dean. Sadie, so far as features went, looked much as she had when Pollyanna first saw her in the Public Garden; but Pollyanna did not need a second glance to know that Sadie, so far as hair, dress, temper, speech, and disposition were concerned, was a very different Sadie indeed.

Then Jamie spoke.

'How good you were to let us come,' he said to Pollyanna. 'Do you know what I thought of when you wrote that we could come?'

'Why, n-no, of course not,' stammered Pollyanna. Pollyanna was still seeing the crutches at Jamie's side, and her throat was still tightened from that aching sympathy.

'Well, I thought of the little maid in the Public Garden with her bag of peanuts for Sir Lancelot and Lady Guinevere, and I knew that you were just putting us in their places, for if you had a bag of peanuts, and we had none, you wouldn't be happy until you'd shared it with us.'

'A bag of peanuts, indeed!' laughed Pollyanna.

'Oh, of course in this case your bag of peanuts happened to be airy country rooms, and cow's milk, and real eggs from a real hen's nest,' returned Jamie whimsically; 'but it amounts to the same thing. And maybe I'd better warn you – you remember how greedy Sir Lancelot was; well –' He paused meaningly.

'All right, I'll take the risk,' dimpled Pollyanna, thinking how glad she was that Aunt Polly was not present to hear her worst predictions so nearly fulfilled thus early. 'Poor Sir Lancelot! I wonder if anybody feeds him now, or if he's there at all.'

'Well, if he's there, he's fed,' interposed Mrs Carew merrily. 'This ridiculous boy still goes down there at least once a week with his pockets bulging with peanuts and I don't know what all. He can be traced any time by the trail of small grains he leaves behind him; and, half the time, when I order my cereal for breakfast it isn't forthcoming, because, forsooth, "Master Jamie has fed it to the pigeons, ma'am!"'

'Yes, but let me tell you,' plunged in Jamie enthusiastically. And the next minute Pollyanna found herself listening with all the old fascination to a story of a couple of squirrels in a sunlit garden. Later she saw what Della Wetherby had meant in her letter, for when the house was reached, it came as a distinct shock to her to see Jamie pick up his crutches and swing himself out of the carriage with their aid. She knew then that already in ten short minutes he had made her forget that he was lame.

To Pollyanna's great relief that first dreaded meeting between Aunt Polly and the Carew party passed off much better than she had feared. The newcomers were so frankly delighted with the old house and everything in it, that it was an utter impossibility for the mistress and the owner of it all to continue her stiff attitude of disapproving resignation to their presence. Besides, as was plainly evident before an hour had passed, the personal charm and magnetism of Jamie had pierced even Aunt Polly's armour of distrust; and Pollyanna knew that at least one of her own most dreaded problems was a problem no longer, for already Aunt Polly was beginning to play the stately yet gracious hostess to these, her guests.

Notwithstanding her relief at Aunt Polly's change of attitude, however, Pollyanna did not find that all was smooth sailing, by any means. There was work, and plenty of it, that must be done. Nancy's sister, Betty, was pleasant and willing, but she was not Nancy, as Pollyanna soon found. She needed training, and training took time. Pollyanna worried, too, for fear everything should not be quite right. To Pollyanna, those days, a dusty chair was a crime and a fallen cake a tragedy.

Gradually, however, after incessant arguments and pleadings on the part of Mrs Carew and Jamie, Pollyanna came to take her tasks more easily, and to realize that the real crime and tragedy in her friends' eyes was, not the dusty chair nor the fallen cake, but the frown of worry and anxiety on her own face.

'Just as if it wasn't enough for you to *let* us come,' Jamie declared, 'without just killing yourself with work to get us something to eat.'

'Besides, we ought not to eat so much anyway,' Mrs Carew laughed, 'or else we shall get "digestion", as one of my girls calls it when her food disagrees with her.'

It was wonderful after all how easily the three new members of the family fitted into the daily life. Before twenty-four hours had passed, Mrs Carew had gotten Mrs Chilton to asking really interested questions about the new Home for Working Girls, and Sadie Dean and Jamie were quarrelling over the chance to help with the pea-shelling or the flower-picking.

The Carews had been at the Harrington homestead nearly a week when one evening John Pendleton and Jimmy called. Pollyanna had been hoping they would come soon. She had, indeed, urged it very strongly before the Carews came. She made the introductions now with visible pride.

'You are such good friends of mine, I want you to know each other, and be good friends together,' she explained.

That Jimmy and Mr Pendleton should be clearly impressed with the charm and beauty of Mrs Carew did not surprise Pollyanna in the least; but the look that came into Mrs Carew's face at sight of Jimmy did surprise her very much. It was almost a look of recognition.

'Why, Mr Pendleton, haven't I met you before?' Mrs Carew cried.

Jimmy's frank eyes met Mrs Carew's gaze squarely, admiringly.

'I think not,' he smiled back at her. 'I'm sure I never have met you. I should have remembered it – if *I* had met *you*,' he bowed.

So unmistakable was his significant emphasis that everybody laughed, and John Pendleton chuckled:

'Well done, son – for a youth of your tender years. I couldn't have done half so well myself.'

Mrs Carew flushed slightly and joined in the laugh.

'No, but really,' she urged; 'joking aside, there certainly is a strangely familiar something in your face. I think I must have *seen* you somewhere, if I haven't actually met you.'

'And maybe you have,' cried Pollyanna, 'in Boston. Jimmy goes to Tech there winters, you know. Jimmy's going to build bridges and dams, you see – when he grows up, I mean,' she finished with a merry glance at the big six-foot fellow still standing before Mrs Carew.

Everybody laughed again – that is, everybody but Jamie; and only Sadie Dean noticed that Jamie, instead of laughing, closed his eyes as if at the sight of something that hurt. And only Sadie Dean knew how – and why – the subject was so quickly changed, for it was Sadie herself who changed it. It was Sadie too who, when the opportunity came, saw to it that books and flowers and beasts and birds – things that Jamie knew and understood – were talked about as well as dams and bridges which (as Sadie knew) Jamie could never build. That Sadie did all this, however, was not realized by anybody, least of all by Jamie, the one who most of all was concerned.

When the call was over and the Pendletons had gone, Mrs Carew referred again to the curiously haunting feeling that somewhere she had seen young Pendleton before.

'I have, I know I have – somewhere,' she declared musingly. 'Of course it may have been in Boston; but –' She let the sentence remain unfinished; then, after a minute, she added, 'He's a fine young fellow, anyway. I like him.'

'I'm so glad! I do too,' nodded Pollyanna. 'I've always liked Jimmy.'

'You've known him some time, then?' queried Jamie, a little wistfully.

'Oh, yes. I knew him years ago when I was a little girl, you know. He was Jimmy Bean then.'

'Jimmy *Bean*! Why, isn't he Mr Pendleton's son?' asked Mrs Carew, in surprise.

'No, only by adoption.'

'Adoption!' exclaimed Jamie. 'Then *he* isn't a real son any more than I am.' There was a curious note of almost joy in the lad's voice.

'No. Mr Pendleton hasn't any children. He never married. He – he was going to, once, but he – he didn't.' Pollyanna blushed and spoke with sudden diffidence. Pollyanna had never forgotten that it was her mother who, in the long ago, had said no to this same John Pendleton, and who had thus been responsible for the man's long, lonely years of bachelorhood.

Mrs Carew and Jamie, however, being unaware of this and seeing now only the blush on Pollyanna's cheek and the diffidence in her manner, drew suddenly the same conclusion.

'Is it possible,' they asked themselves, 'that this

man, John Pendleton, ever had a love affair with Pollyanna, child that she is?'

Naturally they did not say this aloud; so, naturally, there was no answer possible. Naturally, too, perhaps, the thought, though unspoken, was still not forgotten, but was tucked away in a corner of their minds for future reference – if need arose.

21

SUMMER DAYS

Before the Carews came Pollyanna had told Jimmy that she was depending on him to help her entertain them. Jimmy had not expressed himself then as being overwhelmingly desirous to serve her in this way; but before the Carews had been in town a fortnight he had shown himself as not only willing but anxious – judging by the frequency and length of his calls, and the lavishness of his offers of the Pendleton horses and motor-cars.

Between him and Mrs Carew there sprang up at once a warm friendship based on what seemed to be a peculiarly strong attraction for each other. They walked and talked together, and even made sundry plans for the Home for Working Girls, to be carried out the following winter when Jimmy should be in Boston. Jamie too came in for a good measure of attention, nor was Sadie Dean forgotten. Sadie, as Mrs Carew plainly showed, was to be regarded as if she were quite one of the family; and Mrs Carew was careful to see that she had full share in any plans for merrymaking.

Nor did Jimmy always come alone with his offers for entertainment. More and more frequently John Pendleton appeared with him. Rides and drives and picnics were planned and carried out, and long delightful afternoons were spent over books and fancywork on the Harrington veranda.

Pollyanna was delighted. Not only were her paying guests being kept from any possibilities of *ennui* and homesickness, but her good friends, the Carews, were becoming delightfully acquainted with her other good friends, the Pendletons. So, like a mother hen with a brood of chickens, she hovered over the veranda meetings, and did everything in her power to keep the group together and happy.

Neither the Carews nor the Pendletons, however, were at all satisfied to have Pollyanna merely an onlooker in their pastimes, and very strenuously they urged her to join them. They would not take no for an answer, indeed, and Pollyanna very frequently found the way opened for her.

'Just as if we were going to have you poked up in this hot kitchen frosting cake!' Jamie scolded one day, after he had penetrated the fastness of her domain. 'It is a perfectly glorious morning, and we're all going over to the Gorge and take our luncheon. And *you* are going with us.'

'But, Jamie, I can't – indeed I can't,' refused Pollyanna.

'Why not? You won't have dinner to get for us, for we shan't be here to eat it.'

'But there's the – the luncheon.'

'Wrong again. We'll have the luncheon with us, so you *can't* stay home to get that. Now what's to hinder your going along *with* the luncheon, eh?'

'Why, Jamie, I – I can't. There's the cake to frost –'

'Don't want it frosted.'

'And the dusting –'

'Don't want it dusted.'

'And the ordering to do for tomorrow.'

'Give us crackers and milk. We'd lots rather have you and crackers and milk than a turkey dinner and not you.'

'But I can't begin to tell you the things I've got to do today.'

'Don't want you to begin to tell me,' retorted Jamie cheerfully. 'I want you to stop telling me. Come, put on your bonnet. I saw Betty in the dining-room, and she says she'll put our luncheon up. Now hurry.'

'Why, Jamie, you ridiculous boy, I can't go,' laughed Pollyanna, holding feebly back, as he tugged at her dress-sleeve. 'I can't go to that picnic with you!'

But she went. She went not only then, but again and again. She could not help going, indeed, for she found arrayed against her not only Jamie, but Jimmy and Mr Pendleton, to say nothing of Mrs Carew and Sadie Dean, and even Aunt Polly herself.

'And of course I *am* glad to go,' she would sigh happily, when some dreary bit of work was taken out of her hands in spite of all protesting. 'But, surely, never before were there any boarders like mine – teasing for crackers and milk and cold things; and never before was there a boarding mistress like me – running around the country after this fashion!'

The climax came when one day John Pendleton (and Aunt Polly never ceased to exclaim because it *was* John Pendleton) suggested that they all go on a two weeks' camping trip to a little lake up among the mountains forty miles from Beldingsville.

The idea was received with enthusiastic approbation

by everybody except Aunt Polly. Aunt Polly said, privately, to Pollyanna, that it was all very good and well and desirable that John Pendleton should have gotten out of the sour, morose aloofness that had been his state for so many years, but that it did not necessarily follow that it was equally desirable that he should be trying to turn himself into a twenty-year-old boy again; and that was what, in her opinion, he seemed to be doing now! Publicly she contented herself with saying coldly that *she* certainly should not go on any insane camping trip to sleep on damp ground and eat bugs and spiders, under the guise of 'fun', nor did she think it a sensible thing for anybody over forty to do.

If John Pendleton felt any wound from this shaft, he made no sign. Certainly there was no diminution of apparent interest and enthusiasm on his part, and the plans for the camping expedition came on apace, for it was unanimously decided that, even if Aunt Polly would not go, that was no reason why the rest should not.

'And Mrs Carew will be all the chaperon we need, anyhow,' Jimmy had declared airily.

For a week, therefore, little was talked of but tents, food supplies, cameras, and fishing tackle, and little was done that was not a preparation in some way for the trip.

'And let's make it the real thing,' proposed Jimmy, eagerly, '– yes, even to Mrs Chilton's bugs and spiders,' he added, with a merry smile straight into that lady's severely disapproving eyes. 'None of your log-cabin-central-dining-room idea for us! We want real camp-fires with potatoes baked in the ashes and we want to sit around and tell stories and roast corn on a stick.'

'And we want to swim and row and fish,' chimed in Pollyanna. 'And –' She stopped suddenly, her eyes on Jamie's face. 'That is, of course,' she corrected quickly, 'we wouldn't want to – to do those things all the time. There'd be a lot of *quiet* things we'd want to do, too – read and talk, you know.'

Jamie's eyes darkened. His face grew a little white. His lips parted, but before any words came Sadie Dean was speaking.

'Oh, but on camping trips and picnics, you know, we *expect* to do outdoor stunts,' she interposed feverishly; 'and I'm sure we *want* to. Last summer we were down in Maine, and you should have seen the fish Mr Carew caught. It was – You tell it,' she begged, turning to Jamie.

Jamie laughed and shook his head.

'They'd never believe it,' he objected; '– a fish story like that!'

'Try us,' challenged Pollyanna.

Jamie still shook his head – but the colour had come back to his face, and his eyes were no longer sombre as if with pain. Pollyanna, glancing at Sadie Dean, vaguely wondered why she suddenly settled back in her seat with so very evident an air of relief.

At last the appointed day came, and the start was made in John Pendleton's big new touring-car with Jimmy at the wheel. A whir, a throbbing rumble, a chorus of good-byes, and they were off, with one long shriek of the siren under Jimmy's mischievous fingers.

In after-days Pollyanna often went back in her

thoughts to that first night in camp. The experience was so new and so wonderful in so many ways.

It was four o'clock when their forty-mile automobile journey came to an end. Since half-past three their big car had been ponderously picking its way over an old logging-road not designed for six-cylinder automobiles. For the car itself, and for the hand at the wheel, this part of the trip was a most wearing one; but for the merry passengers, who had no responsibility concerning hidden holes and muddy curves, it was nothing but a delight growing more poignant with every new vista through the green arches, and with every echoing laugh that dodged the low-hanging branches.

The site for the camp was one known to John Pendleton years before, and he greeted it now with a satisfied delight that was not unmingled with relief.

'Oh, how perfectly lovely!' chorused the others.

'Glad you like it! I thought it would be about right,' nodded John Pendleton. 'Still, I was a little anxious after all, for these places do change, you know, most remarkably sometimes. And of course this has grown up to bushes a little – but not so but what we can easily clear it.'

Everybody fell to work then, clearing the ground, putting up the two little tents, unloading the automobile, building the camp-fire, and arranging the 'kitchen and pantry'.

It was then that Pollyanna began especially to notice Jamie, and to fear for him. She realized suddenly that the hummocks and hollows and pine-littered knolls were not like a carpeted floor for a pair of crutches, and she saw that Jamie was realizing it too. She saw, also, that in spite of his infirmity, he was trying to take his share in the work; and the sight troubled her. Twice she hurried forward and intercepted him, taking from his arms the box he was trying to carry.

'Here, let me take that,' she begged. 'You've done enough.' And the second time she added, 'Do go and sit down somewhere to rest, Jamie. You look so tired!'

If she had been watching closely she would have seen the quick colour sweep to his forehead. But she was not watching, so she did not see it. She did see, however, to her intense surprise, Sadie Dean hurry forward a moment later, her arms full of boxes, and heard her cry:

'Oh, Mr Carew, please, if you *would* give me a lift with these!'

The next moment, Jamie, once more struggling with the problem of managing a bundle of boxes and two crutches, was hastening towards the tents.

With a quick word of protest on her tongue, Pollyanna turned to Sadie Dean. But the protest died unspoken, for Sadie, her finger to her lips, was hurrying straight towards her.

'I know you didn't think,' she stammered in a low voice, as she reached Pollyanna's side. 'But, don't you see? – it *hurts* him – to have you think he can't do things like other folks. There, look! See how happy he is now.'

Pollyanna looked, and she saw. She saw Jamie, his whole self alert, deftly balance his weight on one crutch and swing his burden to the ground. She saw the happy light on his face, and she heard him say nonchalantly:

'Here's another contribution from Miss Dean. She asked me to bring this over.'

'Why, yes, I see,' breathed Pollyanna, turning to Sadie Dean. But Sadie Dean had gone.

Pollyanna watched Jamie a good deal after that, though she was careful not to let him, or anyone else, see that she was watching him. And as she watched, her heart ached. Twice she saw him essay a task and fail: once with a box too heavy for him to lift; once with a folding-table too unwieldy for him to carry with his crutches. And each time she saw his quick glance about him to see if others noticed. She saw, too, that unmistakably he was getting very tired, and that his face, in spite of its gay smile, was looking white and drawn, as if he were in pain.

'I should think we might have known more,' stormed Pollyanna hotly to herself, her eyes blinded with tears. 'I should think we might have known more than to have let him come to a place like this. Camping, indeed! – and with a pair of crutches! Why couldn't we have remembered before we started?'

An hour later, round the camp-fire after supper, Pollyanna had her answer to this question; for, with the glowing fire before her, and the soft, fragrant dark all about her, she once more fell under the spell of the witchery that fell from Jamie's lips; and she once more forgot – Jamie's crutches.

22

COMRADES

They were a merry party – the six of them – and a congenial one. There seemed to be no end to the new delights that came with every new day, not the least of which was the new charm of companionship that seemed to be a part of this new life they were living.

As Jamie said one night, when they were all sitting about the fire:

'You see, we seem to know each other so much better up here in the woods – better in a week than we would in a year in town.'

'I know it. I wonder why,' murmured Mrs Carew, her eyes dreamily following the leaping blaze.

'I think it's something in the air,' sighed Pollyanna happily. 'There's something about the sky and the woods and the lake so – so – well, there just is; that's all.'

'I think you mean, because the world is shut out,' cried Sadie Dean, with a curious little break in her voice. (Sadie had not joined in the laugh that followed Pollyanna's limping conclusion.) 'Up here everything is so real and true that we, too, can be our real true selves – not what the world *says* we are because we are rich, or poor, or great, or humble; but what we really are, *ourselves*.'

'Ho!' scoffed Jimmy airily. 'All that sounds very fine; but the real common-sense reason is because we don't have any Mrs Tom and Dick and Harry sitting on their side-porches and commenting on every time we stir, and wondering among themselves where we are going, why are we going there, and how long we're intending to stay!'

'Oh, Jimmy, how you do take the poetry out of things,' reproached Pollyanna laughingly.

'But that's my business,' flashed Jimmy. 'How do you suppose I'm going to build dams and bridges if I don't see something besides poetry in the waterfall?'

'You can't, Pendleton! And it's the bridge – that counts – every time,' declared Jamie, in a voice that brought a sudden hush to the group about the fire. It was only for a moment, however, for almost at once Sadie Dean broke the silence with a gay:

'Pooh! I'd rather have the waterfall every time, without *any* bridge around – to spoil the view!'

Everybody laughed – and it was as if a tension somewhere snapped. Then Mrs Carew rose to her feet.

'Come, come, children, your stern chaperon says it's bed-time!' And with a merry chorus of good-nights the party broke up.

And so the days passed. To Pollyanna they were wonderful days, and still the most wonderful part was the charm of close companionship – a companionship that, while differing as to details with each one, was yet delightful with all.

With Sadie Dean she talked of the new Home, and of what a marvellous work Mrs Carew was doing.

They talked, too, of the old days when Sadie was selling bows behind the counter, and of what Mrs Carew had done for her. Pollyanna heard, also, something of the old father and mother 'back home', and of the joy that Sadie, in her new position, had been able to bring into their lives.

'And after all, it's really *you* that began it, you know,' she said one day to Pollyanna. But Pollyanna only shook her head at this with an emphatic:

'Nonsense! It was all Mrs Carew.'

With Mrs Carew herself Pollyanna talked also of the Home, and of her plans for the girls. And once, in the hush of a twilight walk, Mrs Carew spoke of herself and of her changed outlook on life. And she, like Sadie Dean, said brokenly, 'After all, it's really you that began it, Pollyanna.' But Pollyanna, as in Sadie Dean's case, would have none of this; and she began to talk of Jamie, and of what *he* had done.

'Jamie's a dear,' Mrs Carew answered affectionately. 'And I love him like an own son. He couldn't be dearer to me if he were really my sister's boy.'

'Then you don't think he is?'

'I don't know. We've never learned anything conclusive. Sometimes I'm sure he is. Then again I doubt it. I think *he* really believes he is – bless his heart! At all events, one thing is sure: he has good blood in him from somewhere. Jamie's no ordinary waif of the streets, you know, with his talents; and the wonderful way he has responded to teaching and training proves it.'

'Of course,' nodded Pollyanna. 'And as long as you love him so well, it doesn't really matter, anyway, does it, whether he's the real Jamie or not?'

Mrs Carew hesitated. Into her eyes crept the old sombreness of heartache.

'Not so far as he is concerned,' she sighed, at last. 'It's only that sometimes I get to thinking: if he isn't our Jamie, where is – Jamie Kent? Is he well? Is he happy? Has he anyone to love him? When I get to thinking like that, Pollyanna, I'm nearly wild. I'd give – everything I have in the world, it seems to me, to really *know* that this boy is Jamie Kent.'

Pollyanna used to think of this conversation sometimes, in her after-talks with Jamie. Jamie was so sure of himself.

'It's just somehow that I *feel* it's so,' he said once to Pollyanna. 'I believe I am Jamie Kent. I've believed it quite a while. I'm afraid I've believed it so long now, that – that I just couldn't bear it, to find out I wasn't he. Mrs Carew has done so much for me; just think if, after all, I were only a stranger!'

'But she – loves you, Jamie.'

'I know she does – and that would only hurt all the more – don't you see? – because it would be hurting her. *She* wants me to be the real Jamie. I know she does. Now if I could only *do* something for her – make her proud of me in some way! If I could only do something to support myself, even, like a man. But what can I do, with – these?' He spoke bitterly, and laid his hand on the crutches at his side.

Pollyanna was shocked and distressed. It was the first time she had heard Jamie speak of his infirmity since the old boyhood days. Frantically she cast about in her mind for just the right thing to say; but before she had even thought of anything, Jamie's face had undergone a complete change.

'But, there, forget it! I didn't mean to say it,' he cried gaily. 'And 'twas rank heresy to the game, wasn't it? I'm sure I'm *glad* I've got the crutches. They're a whole lot nicer than the wheel-chair!'

'And the Jolly Book – do you keep it now?' asked Pollyanna, in a voice that trembled a little.

'Sure! I've got a whole library of jolly books now,' he retorted. 'They're all in leather, dark red, except the first one. That is the same little old notebook that Jerry gave me.'

'Jerry! And I've been meaning all the time to ask for him,' cried Pollyanna. 'Where is he?'

'In Boston; and his vocabulary is just as picturesque as ever, only he has to tone it down at times. Jerry's still in the newspaper business – but he's *getting* the news, not selling it. Reporting, you know. I *have* been able to help him and Mumsey. And don't you suppose I was glad? Mumsey's in a sanatorium for her rheumatism.'

'And is she better?'

'Very much. She's coming out pretty soon, and going to housekeeping with Jerry. Jerry's been making up some of his lost schooling during these past few years. He's let me help him – but only as a loan. He's been very particular to stipulate that.'

'Of course,' nodded Pollyanna, in approval. 'He'd want it that way, I'm sure. I should. It isn't nice to be under obligations that you can't pay. I know how it is. That's why I so wish I could help Aunt Polly out – after all she's done for me.'

'But you are helping her this summer.'

Pollyanna lifted her eyebrows.

'Yes, I'm keeping summer boarders. I look it, don't

I?' she challenged, with a flourish of her hands to-wards her surroundings. 'Surely, never was a boarding-house mistress's task quite like mine! And you should have heard Aunt Polly's dire predictions of what summer boarders would be,' she chuckled irrepressibly.

'What was that?'

Pollyanna shook her head decidedly.

'Couldn't possibly tell you. That's a dead secret. But –' She stopped and sighed, her face growing wistful again. 'This isn't going to last, you know. It can't. Summer boarders don't. I've got to do some-thing winters. I've been thinking. I believe – I'll write stories.'

Jamie turned with a start.

'You'll – what?' he demanded.

'Write stories – to sell, you know. You needn't look so surprised! Lots of folk do that. I knew two girls in Germany who did.'

'Did you ever try it?' Jamie still spoke a little queerly.

'N-no; not yet,' admitted Pollyanna. Then, defen-sively, in answer to the expression on his face, she bridled: 'I *told* you I was keeping summer boarders now. I can't do both at once.'

'Of course not!'

She threw him a reproachful glance.

'You don't think I can ever do it?'

'I didn't say so.'

'No; but you look it. I don't see why I can't. It isn't like singing. You don't have to have a voice for it. And it isn't like an instrument that you have to learn how to play.'

'I think it is – a little – like that.' Jamie's voice was low. His eyes were turned away.

'How? What do you mean? Why, Jamie, just a pencil and paper, so – that isn't like learning to play the piano or violin!'

There was a moment's silence. Then came the answer, still in that low, diffident voice; still with the eyes turned away.

'The instrument that you play on, Pollyanna, will be the great heart of the world; and to me that seems the most wonderful instrument of all – to learn. Under your touch, if you are skilful, it will respond with smiles or tears, as you will.'

Pollyanna drew a tremulous sigh. Her eyes grew wet.

'Oh, Jamie, how beautifully you do put things – always! I never thought of it that way. But it's so, isn't it? How I would love to do it! Maybe I couldn't do – all that. But I've read stories in the magazines, lots of them. Seems as if I could write some like those, anyway. I *love* to tell stories. I'm always repeating those you tell, and I always laugh and cry, too, just as I do when *you* tell them.'

Jamie turned quickly.

'*Do* they make you laugh and cry, Pollyanna – really?' There was a curious eagerness in his voice.

'Of course they do, and you know it, Jamie. And they used to long ago, too, in the Public Garden. Nobody can tell stories like you, Jamie. *You* ought to be the one writing stories; not I. And, say, Jamie, why don't you? You could do it lovely, I know!'

There was no answer. Jamie, apparently, did not hear; perhaps because he called at that instant to a chipmunk that was scurrying through the bushes near by.

It was not always with Jamie, nor yet with Mrs Carew and Sadie Dean, that Pollyanna had delightful walks and talks, however; very often it was with Jimmy, or John Pendleton.

Pollyanna was sure now that she had never before known John Pendleton. The old taciturn moroseness seemed entirely gone since they came to camp. He rode and swam and fished and tramped with fully as much enthusiasm as did Jimmy himself, and with almost as much vigour. Around the camp-fire at night he quite rivalled Jamie with his story-telling of adventures, both laughable and thrilling, that had befallen him in his foreign travels.

'In the "Desert of Sarah", Nancy used to call it,' laughed Pollyanna one night, as she joined the rest in begging for a story.

Better than all this, however, in Pollyanna's opinion, were the times when John Pendleton, with her alone, talked of her mother as he used to know her and love her, in the days long gone. That he did so talk with her was a joy to Pollyanna, but a great surprise, too; for never in the past had John Pendleton talked so freely of the girl whom he had so loved – hopelessly. Perhaps John Pendleton himself felt some of the surprise, for once he said to Pollyanna, musingly:

'I wonder why I'm talking to you like this.'

'Oh, but I love to have you,' breathed Pollyanna.

'Yes, I know – but I wouldn't think I would do it. It must be, though, that it's because you are so like her, as I knew her. You are very like your mother, my dear.'

'Why, I thought my mother was *beautiful*!' cried Pollyanna, in unconcealed amazement.

John Pendleton smiled quizzically.

'She was, my dear.'

Pollyanna looked still more amazed.

'Then I don't see how I *can* be like her!'

The man laughed outright.

'Pollyanna, if some girls had said that, I – well, never mind what I'd say. You little witch! – you poor, homely little Pollyanna!'

Pollyanna flashed a genuinely distressed reproof straight into the man's merry eyes.

'Please, Mr Pendleton, don't look like that, and don't tease me – about *that*. I'd so *love* to be beautiful – though of course it sounds silly to say it. And I *have* a mirror, you know.'

'Then I advise you to look in it – when you're talking some time,' observed the man sententiously.

Pollyanna's eyes flew wide open.

'Why, that's just what Jimmy said,' she cried.

'Did he, indeed – the young rascal!' retorted John Pendleton drily. Then, with one of the curiously abrupt changes of manner peculiar to him, he said, very low: 'You have your mother's eyes and smile, Pollyanna; and to me you are – beautiful.'

And Pollyanna, her eyes blinded with sudden hot tears, was silenced.

Dear as were these talks, however, they still were not quite like the talks with Jimmy, to Pollyanna. For that matter, she and Jimmy did not need to *talk* to be happy. Jimmy was always so comfortable, and comforting; whether they talked or not did not matter. Jimmy always understood. There was no pulling on her heartstrings for sympathy, with Jimmy – Jimmy was delightfully big, and strong, and happy. Jimmy was not sorrowing for a long-lost nephew, nor pining for the loss of a boyhood sweetheart. Jimmy did not have to swing himself painfully about on a pair of crutches – all of which was so hard to see, and know, and think of. With Jimmy one could be just glad, and happy, and free. Jimmy was such a dear! He always rested one so – did Jimmy!

23

'Tied to Two Sticks'

It was on the last day at camp that it happened. To Pollyanna it seemed such a pity that it should have happened at all, for it was the first cloud to bring a shadow of regret and unhappiness to her heart during the whole trip, and she found herself futilely sighing:

'I wish we'd gone home day before yesterday; then it wouldn't have happened.'

But they had not gone home 'day before yesterday', and it had happened; and this was the manner of it.

Early in the morning of that last day they had all started on a two-mile tramp to the Basin.

'We'll have one more bang-up fish dinner before we go,' Jimmy had said, And the rest had joyfully agreed.

With luncheon and fishing tackle, therefore, they had made an early start. Laughing and calling gaily to each other they followed the narrow path through the woods, led by Jimmy, who best knew the way.

At first, close behind Jimmy had walked Pollyanna; but gradually she had fallen back with Jamie, who was last in the line; Pollyanna had thought she detected on Jamie's face the expression which she had come to know was there only when he was attempting something that taxed almost to the breaking-point his skill and powers of endurance. She knew that nothing would so offend him as to have her openly notice this state of affairs. At the same time, she also knew that from her, more willingly than from anyone else, would he accept an occasional steadying hand over a troublesome log or stone. Therefore, at the first opportunity to make the change without apparent design, she had dropped back step by step until she had reached her goal, Jamie. She had been rewarded instantly in the way Jamie's face brightened, and in the easy assurance with which he met and conquered a fallen tree-trunk across their path, under the pleasant fiction (carefully fostered by Pollyanna) of 'helping her across'.

Once out of the woods, their way led along an old stone wall for a time, with wide reaches of sunny, sloping pastures on each side, and a more distant picturesque farmhouse. It was in the adjoining pasture that Pollyanna saw the golden-rod which she immediately coveted.

'Jamie, wait! I'm going to get it,' she exclaimed eagerly. 'It'll make such a beautiful bouquet for our picnic table!' And nimbly she scrambled over the high stone wall and dropped herself down on the other side.

It was strange how tantalizing was that golden-rod. Always just ahead she saw another bunch, and yet another, each a little finer than the one within her reach. With joyous exclamations and gay little calls back to the waiting Jamie, Pollyanna – looking particularly attractive in her scarlet sweater – skipped from bunch to bunch, adding to her store. She had both hands full when there came the hideous bellow of an angry bull, the agonized shout from Jamie, and the sound of hoofs thundering down the hillside.

What happened next was never clear to her. She

knew she dropped her golden-rod and ran – ran as she
never ran before, ran as she thought she never could
run – back towards the wall and Jamie. She knew that
behind her the hoof-beats were gaining, gaining,
always gaining. Dimly, hopelessly, far ahead of her,
she saw Jamie's agonized face, and heard his hoarse
cries. Then, from somewhere, came a new voice –
Jimmy's – shouting a cheery call of courage.

Still on and on she ran blindly, hearing nearer and
nearer the thud of those pounding hoofs. Once she
stumbled and almost fell. Then, dizzily she righted
herself and plunged forward. She felt her strength
quite gone when suddenly, close to her, she heard
Jimmy's cheery call again. The next minute she felt
herself snatched off her feet and held close to a great
sobbing something that dimly she realized was Jimmy's
heart. It was all a hurried blur then of cries, hot,
panting breaths, and pounding hoofs thundering
nearer, ever nearer. Then, just as she knew those hoofs
to be almost upon her, she felt herself flung, still in
Jimmy's arms, sharply to one side, and yet not so far
but that she still could feel the hot breath of the
maddened animal as he dashed by. Almost at once
then she found herself on the other side of the wall,
with Jimmy bending over her, imploring her to tell
him she was not dead.

With a hysterical laugh that was yet half a sob,
she struggled out of his arms and stood upon her
feet.

'Dead? No, indeed – thanks to you, Jimmy. I'm all
right. I'm all right. Oh, how glad, glad, glad I was to
hear your voice! Oh, that was splendid! How did you
do it?' she panted.

'Pooh! That was nothing. I just –' An inarticulate choking cry brought his words to a sudden halt. He turned to find Jamie face down on the ground, a little distance away. Pollyanna was already hurrying towards him.

'Jamie, Jamie, what is the matter?' she cried. 'Did you fall? Are you hurt?'

There was no answer.

'What is it, old fellow? *Are* you hurt?' demanded Jimmy.

Still there was no answer. Then, suddenly, Jamie pulled himself half upright and turned. They saw his face, then, and fell back, shocked and amazed.

'Hurt? Am I hurt?' he choked huskily, flinging out both his hands. 'Don't you suppose it hurts to see a thing like that and not be able to do anything? To be tied, helpless, to a pair of sticks? I tell you there's no hurt in all the world to equal it!'

'But – but – Jamie,' faltered Pollyanna.

'Don't!' interrupted the cripple, almost harshly. He had struggled to his feet now. 'Don't say – anything. I didn't mean to make a scene – like this,' he finished brokenly, as he turned and swung back along the narrow path that led to the camp.

For a minute, as if transfixed, the two behind him watched him go.

'Well, by – Jove!' breathed Jimmy, then, in a voice that shook a little, 'That was – tough on him!'

'And I didn't think, and *praised* you, right before him,' half sobbed Pollyanna. 'And his hands – did you see them? They were – *bleeding* where the nails had cut right into the flesh,' she finished, as she turned and stumbled blindly up the path.

'But, Pollyanna, w-where are you going?' cried Jimmy.

'I'm going to Jamie, of course! Do you think I'd leave him like that? Come, we must get him to come back.'

And Jimmy, with a sigh that was not all for Jamie, went.

24

Jimmy Wakes Up

Outwardly the camping trip was pronounced a great success; but inwardly . . .

Pollyanna wondered sometimes if it were all herself, or if there really were a peculiar, indefinable constraint in everybody with everybody else. Certainly she felt it, and she thought she saw evidences that the others felt it, too. As for the cause of it all – unhesitatingly she attributed it to that last day at camp with its unfortunate trip to the Basin.

To be sure, she and Jimmy had easily caught up with Jamie, and had, after considerable coaxing, persuaded him to turn about and go on to the Basin with them. But, in spite of everybody's very evident efforts to act as if nothing out of the ordinary had happened, nobody really succeeded in doing so. Pollyanna, Jamie, and Jimmy overdid their gaiety a bit, perhaps; and the others, while not knowing exactly what had happened, very evidently felt that something was not quite right, though they plainly tried to hide the fact that they did feel so. Naturally, in this state of affairs, restful happiness was out of the question. Even the anticipated fish dinner was flavourless; and early in the afternoon the start was made back to the camp.

Once home again, Pollyanna had hoped that the

unhappy episode of the angry bull would be forgotten. But she could not forget it, so in all fairness she could not blame the others if they could not. Always she thought of it now when she looked at Jamie. She saw again the agony on his face, the crimson stain on the palms of his hands. Her heart ached for him, and because it did so ache, his mere presence had come to be a pain to her. Remorsefully she confessed to herself that she did not like to be with Jamie now, nor to talk with him – but that did not mean that she was not often with him. She was with him, indeed, much oftener than before, for so remorseful was she, and so fearful was she that he would detect her unhappy frame of mind, that she lost no opportunity of responding to his overtures of comradeship; and sometimes she deliberately sought him out. This last she did not often have to do, however, for more and more frequently these days Jamie seemed to be turning to her for companionship.

The reason for this, Pollyanna believed, was to be found in this same incident of the bull and the rescue. Not that Jamie ever referred to it directly. He never did that. He was, too, even gayer than usual; but Pollyanna thought she detected sometimes a bitterness underneath it all that was never there before. Certainly she could not help seeing that at times he seemed almost to want to avoid the others, and that he actually sighed, as if with relief, when he found himself alone with her. She thought she knew why this was so, after he said to her, as he did say one day, while they were watching the others play tennis:

'You see, after all, Pollyanna, there isn't anyone who can quite understand as you can.'

'Understand?' Pollyanna had not known what he meant at first. They had been watching the players for five minutes without a word between them.

'Yes; for *you*, once – couldn't walk – yourself.'

'Oh-h, yes, I know,' faltered Pollyanna; and she knew that her great distress must have shown in her face, for so quickly and so blithely did he change the subject, after a laughing:

'Come, come, Pollyanna, why don't you tell me to play the game? I would if I were in your place. Forget it, please. I was a brute to make you look like that!'

And Pollyanna smiled, and said: 'No, no – no, indeed!' But she did not 'forget it'. She could not. And it all made her only the more anxious to be with Jamie and help him all she could.

'As if *now* I'd ever let him see that I was ever anything but *glad* when he was with me!' she thought fervently, as she hurried forward a minute later to take her turn in the game.

Pollyanna, however, was not the only one in the party who felt a new awkwardness and constraint. Jimmy Pendleton felt it, though he, too, tried not to show it.

Jimmy was not happy these days. From a care-free youth whose visions were of wonderful spans across hitherto unbridgeable chasms, he had come to be an anxious-eyed young man whose visions were of a feared rival bearing away the girl he loved.

Jimmy knew very well now that he was in love with Pollyanna. He suspected that he had been in love with her for some time. He stood aghast, indeed, to find himself so shaken and powerless before this thing that had come to him. He knew that even his beloved bridges were as nothing when weighed against the smile in a girl's eyes and the word on a girl's lips. He realized that the most wonderful span in the world to him would be the thing that could help him to cross the chasm of fear and doubt that he felt lay between him and Pollyanna – doubt because of Pollyanna; fear because of Jamie.

Not until he had seen Pollyanna in jeopardy that day in the pasture had he realized how empty would be the world – his world – without her. Not until his wild dash for safety with Pollyanna in his arms had he realized how precious she was to him. For a moment, indeed, with his arms about her, and hers clinging about his neck, he had felt that she was indeed his; and even in that supreme moment of danger he knew the thrill of supreme bliss. Then, a little later, he had seen Jamie's face, and Jamie's hands. To him they could mean but one thing; Jamie too loved Pollyanna, and Jamie had to stand by, helpless – 'tied to two sticks'. That was what he had said. Jimmy believed that, had he himself been obliged to stand by helpless, 'tied to two sticks', while another rescued the girl that he loved, *he* would have looked like that.

Jimmy had gone back to camp that day with his thoughts in a turmoil of fear and rebellion. He wondered if Pollyanna cared for Jamie; that was where the fear came in. But even if she did care, a little, must he stand aside, weakly, and let Jamie, without a struggle, make her learn to care more? That was where the rebellion came in. Indeed no, he would not do it, decided Jimmy. It should be a fair fight between them.

Then, all by himself as he was, Jimmy flushed hot

to the roots of his hair. Would it be a 'fair' fight? Could any fight between him and Jamie be a 'fair' fight? Jimmy felt suddenly as he had felt years before when, as a lad, he had challenged a new boy to fight for an apple they both claimed, then, at the first blow, had discovered that the new boy had a crippled arm. He had purposely lost then, of course, and had let the crippled boy win. But he told himself fiercely now that this case was different. It was no apple that was at stake. It was his life's happiness. It might even be Pollyanna's life's happiness, too. Perhaps she did not care for Jamie at all, but would care for her old friend, Jimmy, if he but once showed her he wanted her to care. And he would show her. He would . . .

Once again Jimmy blushed hotly. But he frowned, too, angrily; if only he *could* forget how Jamie had looked when he had uttered that moaning 'tied to two sticks'! If only . . . but what was the use? It was *not* a fair fight, and he knew it. He knew, too, right there and then, that his decision would be just what it afterwards proved to be: he would watch and wait. He would give Jamie his chance; and if Pollyanna showed that she cared, he would take himself off and away out of their lives; and they should never know, either of them, how bitterly he was suffering. He would go back to his bridges – as if any bridge, though it led to the moon itself, could compare for a moment with Pollyanna! But he would do it. He must do it.

It was all very fine and heroic, and Jimmy felt so exalted he was a-tingle with something that was almost happiness when he finally dropped off to sleep that night. But martyrdom in theory and practice differs woefully, as would-be martyrs have found out from time immemorial. It was all very well to decide alone and in the dark that he would give Jamie his chance; but it was quite another matter really to do it when it involved nothing less than the leaving of Pollyanna and Jamie together almost every time he saw them. Then, too, he was very much worried at Pollyanna's apparent attitude towards the lame youth. It looked very much to Jimmy as if she did indeed care for him, so watchful was she of his comfort, so apparently eager to be with him. Then, as if to settle any possible doubt in Jimmy's mind, there came the day when Sadie Dean had something to say on the subject.

They were all out in the tennis court. Sadie was sitting alone when Jimmy strolled up to her.

'You next with Pollyanna, isn't it?' he queried.

She shook her head.

'Pollyanna isn't playing any more this morning.'

'Isn't playing!' frowned Jimmy, who had been counting on his own game with Pollyanna. 'Why not?'

For a brief minute Sadie Dean did not answer; then with very evident difficulty she said:

'Pollyanna told me last night that she thought we were playing tennis too much; that it wasn't kind to – Mr Carew, as long as he can't play.'

'I know; but –' Jimmy stopped helplessly, the frown ploughing a deeper furrow into his forehead. The next instant he fairly started with surprise at the tense something in Sadie Dean's voice, as she said:

'But he doesn't want her to stop. He doesn't want any one of us to make any difference – for him. It's that that hurts him so. She doesn't understand. She doesn't understand! But I do. She thinks she does, though!'

Something in words or manner sent a sudden pang to Jimmy's heart. He threw a sharp look into her face. A question flew to his lips. For a moment he held it back; then, trying to hide his earnestness with a bantering smile, he let it come.

'Why, Miss Dean, you don't mean to convey the idea that – that there's any *special* interest in each other – between those two, do you?'

She gave him a scornful glance.

'Where have your eyes been? She worships him! I mean – they worship each other,' she corrected hastily.

Jimmy, with an inarticulate ejaculation, turned and walked away abruptly. He could not trust himself to remain longer. He did not wish to talk any more, just then, to Sadie Dean. So abruptly, indeed, did he turn, that he did not notice that Sadie Dean too turned hurriedly, and busied herself looking in the grass at her feet, as if she had lost something. Very evidently Sadie Dean also did not wish to talk any more just then.

Jimmy Pendleton told himself that it was not true at all; that it was all falderal, what Sadie Dean had said. Yet nevertheless, true or not true, he could not forget it. It coloured all his thoughts thereafter, and loomed before his eyes like a shadow whenever he saw Pollyanna and Jamie together. He watched their faces covertly. He listened to the tones of their voices. He came then, in time, to think it was, after all, true: that they did worship each other; and his heart, in consequence, grew like lead within him. True to his promise to himself, however, he turned resolutely away. The die was cast, he told himself. Pollyanna was not to be for him.

Restless days for Jimmy followed. To stay away from the Harrington homestead entirely he did not dare, lest his secret be suspected. To be with Pollyanna at all now was torture. Even to be with Sadie Dean was unpleasant, for he could not forget that it was Sadie Dean who had finally opened his eyes. Jamie, certainly, was no haven of refuge, under the circumstances; and that left only Mrs Carew. Mrs Carew, however, was a host in herself, and Jimmy found his only comfort these days in her society. Gay or grave, she always seemed to know how to fit his mood exactly; and it was wonderful how much she knew about bridges – the kind of bridges he was going to build. She was so wise, too, and so sympathetic, knowing always just the right word to say. He even one day almost told her about 'the Packet'; but John Pendleton interrupted them at just the wrong moment, so the story was not told. John Pendleton was always interrupting them at just the wrong moment, Jimmy thought vexedly, sometimes. Then, when he remembered what John Pendleton had done for him, he was ashamed.

The Packet was a thing that dated back to Jimmy's boyhood, and had never been mentioned to anyone save to John Pendleton, and that only once, at the time of his adoption. The Packet was nothing but rather a large white envelope, worn with time, and plump with mystery behind a huge red seal. It had been given him by his father, and it bore the following instructions in his father's hand:

'To my boy Jimmy. Not to be opened until his thirtieth birthday except in case of his death, when it shall be opened at once.'

There were times when Jimmy speculated a good deal as to the contents of that envelope. There were other times when he forgot its existence. In the old days, at the Orphans' Home, his chief terror had been that it should be discovered and taken away from him. In those days he wore it always hidden in the lining of his coat. Of late years, at John Pendleton's suggestion, it had been tucked away in the Pendleton safe.

'For there's no knowing how valuable it may be,' John Pendleton had said, with a smile. 'And, anyway, your father evidently wanted you to have it, and we wouldn't want to run the risk of losing it.'

'No, I wouldn't want to lose it, of course,' Jimmy had smiled back, a little soberly. 'But I'm not counting on its being real valuable, sir. Poor Dad didn't have anything that was very valuable about him, as I remember.'

It was this Packet that Jimmy came so near mentioning to Mrs Carew one day – if only John Pendleton had not interrupted them.

'Still, maybe it's just as well I didn't tell her about it,' Jimmy reflected afterwards on his way home. 'She might have thought Dad had something in his life that wasn't – right. And I wouldn't have wanted her to think that of Dad.'

25

THE GAME AND POLLYANNA

Before the middle of September the Carews and Sadie Dean said good-bye and went back to Boston. Much as she knew she would miss them, Pollyanna drew an actual sigh of relief as the train bearing them away rolled out of the Beldingsville station. Pollyanna would not have admitted having this feeling of relief to anyone else, and even to herself she apologized in her thoughts.

'It isn't that I don't love them dearly, every one of them,' she sighed, watching the train disappear around the curve of down the track. 'It's only that – that I'm so sorry for poor Jamie all the time; and – and – I *am* tired. I shall be glad, for a while, just to go back to the old quiet days with Jimmy.'

Pollyanna, however, did not go back to the old quiet days with Jimmy. The days that immediately followed the going of the Carews were quiet, certainly, but they were not passed 'with Jimmy'. Jimmy rarely came near the house now, and when he did call he was not the old Jimmy that she used to know. He was moody, restless, and silent, or else very gay and talkative in a nervous fashion that was most puzzling and annoying. Before long, too, he himself went to Boston; and then of course she did not see him at all.

Pollyanna was surprised then to see how much she missed him. Even to know that he was in town, and that there was a chance that he might come over, was better than the dreary emptiness of certain absence; and even his puzzling moods of alternating gloominess and gaiety were preferable to this utter silence of nothingness. Then, one day, suddenly she pulled herself up with hot cheeks and shamed eyes.

'Well, Pollyanna Whittier,' she upbraided herself sharply, 'one would think you were in *love* with Jimmy Bean Pendleton! Can't you think of *anything* but him?'

Whereupon, forthwith, she bestirred herself to be very gay and lively indeed, and to put this Jimmy Bean Pendleton out of her thoughts. As it happened, Aunt Polly, though unwittingly, helped her to this.

With the going of the Carews had gone also their chief source of immediate income, and Aunt Polly was beginning to worry again, audibly, about the state of their finances.

'I don't know, really, Pollyanna, what *is* going to become of us,' she would moan frequently. 'Of course we are a little ahead now from this summer's work, and we have a small sum from the estate right along; but I never know how soon that's going to stop, like all the rest. If only we could do something to bring in some ready cash!'

It was after one of these moaning lamentations one day that Pollyanna's eyes chanced to fall on a prize-story contest offer. It was a most alluring one. The prizes were large and numerous. The conditions were set forth in glowing terms. To read it, one would think that to win out were the easiest thing in the world. It contained even a special appeal that might have been framed for Pollyanna herself.

This is for you – you who read this [it ran]. What if you never have written a story before! That is no sign you cannot write one. Try it. That's all. Wouldn't *you* like three thousand dollars? Two thousand? One thousand? Five hundred, or even one hundred? Then why not go after it?

'The very thing!' cried Pollyanna, clapping her hands. 'I'm so glad I saw it! And it *says* I can do it, too. I thought I could, if I'd just try. I'll go tell Auntie, so she needn't worry any more.'

Pollyanna was on her feet and half-way to the door when a second thought brought her steps to a pause.

'Come to think of it, I reckon I won't, after all. It'll be all the nicer to surprise her; and if I *should* get the first one –'

Pollyanna went to sleep that night planning what she *could* do with that three thousand dollars.

Pollyanna began her story the next day. That is, she, with a very important air, got out a quantity of paper, sharpened up a half a dozen pencils, and established herself at the big old-fashioned Harrington desk in the living-room. After biting restlessly at the ends of two of her pencils, she wrote down three words on the fair white page before her. Then she drew a long sigh, threw aside the second ruined pencil, and picked up a slender green one with a beautiful point. This point she eyed with a meditative frown.

'Oh, dear! I wonder *where* they get their titles,' she despaired. 'Maybe, though, I ought to decide on the story first, and then make a title to fit. Anyhow, *I'm* going to do it.' And forthwith she drew a black line through the three words and poised the pencil for a fresh start.

The start was not made at once, however. Even when it was made, it must have been a false one, for at the end of half an hour the whole page was nothing but a jumble of scratched-out lines, with only a few words here and there left to tell the tale.

At this juncture Aunt Polly came into the room. She turned tired eyes upon her niece.

'Well, Pollyanna, what *are* you up to now?' she demanded.

Pollyanna laughed and coloured guiltily.

'Nothing much, Auntie. Anyhow, it doesn't look as if it were much – yet,' she admitted, with a rueful smile. 'Besides, it's a secret, and I'm not going to tell it yet.'

'Very well; suit yourself,' sighed Aunt Polly. 'But I can tell you right now that if you're trying to make anything different out of those mortgage papers Mr Hart left, it's useless. I've been all over them myself twice.'

'No, dear, it isn't the papers. It's a whole heap nicer than any papers ever could be,' crowed Pollyanna triumphantly, turning back to her work. In Pollyanna's eyes suddenly had risen a glowing vision of what it might be, with that three thousand dollars once hers.

For still another half-hour Pollyanna wrote and scratched, and chewed her pencils; then, with her courage dulled, but not destroyed, she gathered up her papers and pencils and left the room.

'I reckon maybe I'll do better by myself upstairs,' she was thinking as she hurried through the hall. 'I *thought* I ought to do it at a desk – being literary work, so – but, anyhow, the desk didn't help me any this morning. I'll try the window-seat in my room.'

The window-seat, however, proved to be no more inspiring, judging by the scratched and re-scratched pages that fell from Pollyanna's hands; and at the end of another half-hour Pollyanna discovered suddenly that it was time to get dinner.

'Well, I'm glad 'tis, anyhow,' she sighed to herself. 'I'd a lot rather get dinner than do this. Not but that I *want* to do this, of course; only I'd no idea 'twas such an awful job – just a story, so!'

During the following month Pollyanna worked faithfully, doggedly, but she soon found that 'just a story, so' was indeed no small matter to accomplish. Pollyanna, however, was not one to set her hand to the plough and look back. Besides, there was that three-thousand-dollar prize, or even any of the others, if she should not happen to win the first one! Of course even one hundred dollars was something! So day after day she wrote and erased, and rewrote, until finally the story, such as it was, lay completed before her. Then, with some misgivings, it must be confessed, she took the manuscript to Milly Snow to be typewritten.

'It reads all right – that is, it makes sense,' mused Pollyanna doubtfully, as she hurried along towards the Snow cottage; 'and it's a real nice story about a perfectly lovely girl. But there's something somewhere that isn't quite right about it, I'm afraid. Anyhow, I don't believe I'd better count too much on the first prize; then I won't be too much disappointed when I get one of the littler ones.'

Pollyanna always thought of Jimmy when she went

to the Snows', for it was at the side of the road near their cottage that she had first seen him as a forlorn little runaway lad from the Orphans' Home years before. She thought of him again today, with a little catch of her breath. Then, with the proud lifting of her head that always came now with the second thought of Jimmy, she hurried up the Snows' door-steps and rang the bell.

As was usually the case, the Snows had nothing but the warmest of welcomes for Pollyanna; and also as usual it was not long before they were talking of the game: in no home in Beldingsville was the Glad Game more ardently played than in the Snows'.

'Well, and how are you getting along?' asked Polly-anna, when she had finished the business part of her call.

'Splendidly!' beamed Milly Snow. 'This is the third job I've got this week. Oh, Miss Pollyanna, I'm so glad you had made me take up typewriting for you see I *can* do that right at home! And it's all owing to you.'

'Nonsense!' disclaimed Pollyanna merrily.

'But it is. In the first place, I couldn't have done it anyway if it hadn't been for the game – making Mother so much better, you know, that I had some time to myself. And then, at the very first, you suggested typewriting, and helped me to buy a machine. I should like to know if that doesn't come pretty near owing it all to you!'

But once again Pollyanna objected. This time she was interrupted by Mrs Snow from her wheel-chair by the window. And so earnestly and gravely did Mrs Snow speak that Pollyanna, in spite of herself, could but hear what she had to say.

'Listen, child, I don't think you know quite what you've done. But I wish you could! There's a little look in your eyes, my dear, today, that I don't like to see there. You are plagued and worried over something, I know. I can see it. And I don't wonder: your uncle's death, your aunt's condition, everything – I won't say more about that. But there's something I do want to say, my dear, and you must let me say it, for I can't bear to see that shadow in your eyes without trying to drive it away by telling you what you've done for me, for this whole town, and for countless other people everywhere.'

'*Mrs Snow!*' protested Pollyanna, in genuine distress.

'Oh, I mean it, and I know what I'm talking about,' nodded the invalid triumphantly. 'To begin with, look at me. Didn't you find me a fretful, whining creature who never by any chance wanted what she had until she found what she didn't have? And didn't you open my eyes by bringing me three kinds of things so I'd *have* to have what I wanted, for once?'

'Oh, Mrs Snow, was I really ever quite so – impertinent as that?' murmured Pollyanna, with a painful blush.

'It wasn't impertinent,' objected Mrs Snow stoutly. 'You didn't *mean* it as impertinence – and that made all the difference in the world. You didn't preach, either, my dear. If you had, you'd never have got me to playing the game, nor anybody else, I fancy. But you did get me to playing it – and see what it's done for me, and for Milly! Here I am so much better that I can sit in a wheel-chair and go anywhere on this floor in it. That means a whole lot when it comes to waiting on yourself, and giving those around you a chance to breathe – meaning Milly, in this case. And the doctor says it's all owing to the game. Then there's others, quantities of others, right in this town, that I'm hearing of all the time. Nellie Mahoney broke her wrist and was so glad it wasn't her leg that she didn't mind the wrist at all. Old Mrs Tibbits had lost her hearing, but she's so glad 'tisn't her eyesight that she's actually happy. Do you remember cross-eyed Joe that they used to call Cross Joe, because of his temper? Nothing went to suit him either, any more than it did me. Well, somebody's taught him the game, they say, and made a different man of him. And listen, dear. It's not only this town, but other places. I had a letter yesterday from my cousin in Massachusetts and she told me all about Mrs Tom Payson that used to live here. Do you remember them? They lived on the way up Pendleton Hill.'

'Yes, oh, yes, I remember them,' cried Pollyanna.

'Well, they left here that winter you were in the Sanatorium and went to Massachusetts where my sister lives. She knows them well. She says Mrs Payson told her all about you, and how your Glad Game actually saved them from a divorce. And now not only do they play it themselves, but they've got quite a lot of others playing it down there, and *they're* getting still others. So you see, dear, there's no telling where that Glad Game of yours is going to stop. I wanted you to know. I thought it might help – even you to play the game sometimes; for don't think I don't understand, dearie, that it *is* hard for you to play your own game – sometimes.'

Pollyanna rose to her feet. She smiled, but her eyes

glistened with tears, as she held out her hand in goodbye.

'Thank you, Mrs Snow,' she said unsteadily. 'It *is* hard – sometimes; and maybe I *did* need a little help about my own game. But, anyhow, now' – her eyes flashed with their old merriment – 'if any time I think I can't play the game myself I can remember that I can still always be *glad* there are some folks playing it!'

Pollyanna walked home a little soberly that afternoon. Touched as she was by what Mrs Snow had said, there was yet an undercurrent of sadness in it all. She was thinking of Aunt Polly – Aunt Polly who played the game now so seldom; and she was wondering if she herself always played it, when she might.

'Maybe I haven't been careful, always, to hunt up the glad side of the things Aunt Polly says,' she thought with undefined guiltiness; 'and maybe if I played the game better myself, Aunt Polly would play it – a little. Anyhow I'm going to try. If I don't look out, all these other people will be playing my own game better than I am myself!'

26

John Pendleton

It was just a week before Christmas that Pollyanna sent her story (now neatly typewritten) in for the contest. The prize-winners would not be announced until April, the magazine notice said, so Pollyanna settled herself for the long wait with characteristic, philosophical patience.

'I don't know, anyhow, but I'm glad 'tis so long,' she told herself, 'for all winter I can have the fun of thinking it *may* be the first one instead of one of the others, that I'll get. I might just as well *think* I'm going to get it, then if I do get it, I won't have been unhappy any. While if I don't get it – I won't have had all these weeks of unhappiness beforehand, anyway; and I can be glad for one of the smaller ones, then.' That she might not get *any* prize was not in Pollyanna's calculations at all. The story, so beautifully typed by Milly Snow, looked almost as good as printed already – to Pollyanna.

Christmas was not a happy time at the Harrington homestead that year, in spite of Pollyanna's strenuous efforts to make it so. Aunt Polly refused absolutely to allow any sort of celebration of the day, and made her attitude so unmistakably plain that Pollyanna could not give even the simplest of presents.

Christmas evening John Pendleton called. Mrs Chilton excused herself, but Pollyanna, utterly worn out from a long day with her aunt, welcomed him joyously. But even here she found a fly in the amber of her content; for John Pendleton had brought with him a letter from Jimmy, and the letter was full of nothing but the plans he and Mrs Carew were making for a wonderful Christmas celebration at the Home for Working Girls; and Pollyanna, ashamed though she was to own it to herself, was not in a mood to hear about Christmas celebrations just then – least of all Jimmy's.

John Pendleton, however, was not ready to let the subject drop, even when the letter had been read.

'Great doings – those!' he exclaimed, as he folded the letter.

'Yes, indeed; fine!' murmured Pollyanna, trying to speak with due enthusiasm.

'And it's tonight, too, isn't it? I'd like to drop in on them about now.'

'Yes,' murmured Pollyanna again, with still more careful enthusiasm.

'Mrs Carew knew what she was about when she got Jimmy to help her, I fancy,' chuckled the man. 'But I'm wondering how Jimmy likes it – playing Santa Claus to half a hundred young women at once!'

'Why, he finds it delightful, of course!' Pollyanna lifted her chin ever so slightly.

'Maybe. Still, it's a little different from learning to build bridges, you must confess.'

'Oh, yes.'

'But I'll risk Jimmy, and I'll risk wagering that

those girls never had a better time than he'll give them tonight, too.'

'Y-yes, of course,' stammered Pollyanna, trying to keep the hated tremulousness out of her voice, and trying very hard *not* to compare her own dreary evening in Beldingsville with nobody but John Pendleton, to that of those fifty girls in Boston – with Jimmy.

There was a brief pause, during which John Pendleton gazed dreamily at the dancing fire on the hearth.

'She's a wonderful woman – Mrs Carew is,' he said at last.

'She is, indeed!' This time the enthusiasm in Pollyanna's voice was all pure gold.

'Jimmy's written me before something of what she's done for those girls,' went on the man, still gazing into the fire. 'In just the last letter before this he wrote a lot about it, and about her. He said he always admired her, but never so much as now, when he can see what she really is.'

'She's a dear – that's what Mrs Carew is,' declared Pollyanna warmly. 'She's a dear in every way, and I love her.'

John Pendleton stirred suddenly. He turned to Pollyanna with an oddly whimsical look in his eyes.

'I know you do, my dear. For that matter, there may be others, too – that love her.'

Pollyanna's heart skipped a beat. A sudden thought came to her with stunning, blinding force. *Jimmy!* Could John Pendleton be meaning that Jimmy cared *that way* – for Mrs Carew?

'You mean –?' she faltered. She could not finish.

With a nervous twitch peculiar to him, John Pendleton got to his feet.

'I mean – the girls, of course,' he answered lightly, still with that whimsical smile. 'Don't you suppose those fifty girls – love her 'most to death?'

Pollyanna said, 'Yes, of course,' and murmured something else appropriate, in answer to John Pendleton's next remark. But her thoughts were in a tumult, and she let the man do most of the talking for the rest of the evening.

Nor did John Pendleton seem averse to this. Restlessly he took a turn or two about the room, then sat down in his old place. And when he spoke, it was on his old subject, Mrs Carew.

'Queer – about that Jamie of hers, isn't it? I wonder if he *is* her nephew.'

As Pollyanna did not answer, the man went on, after a moment's silence.

'He's a fine fellow, anyway. I like him. There's something fine and genuine about him. She's bound up in him. That's plain to be seen, whether he's really her kin or not.'

There was another pause, then, in a slightly altered voice, John Pendleton said:

'Still it's queer, too, when you come to think of it, that she never – married again. She is certainly now – a very beautiful woman. Don't you think so?'

'Yes – yes, indeed she is,' plunged in Pollyanna, with precipitate haste; 'a – a very beautiful woman.'

There was a little break at the last in Pollyanna's voice. Pollyanna, just then, had caught sight of her own face in the mirror opposite – and Pollyanna to herself was never 'a very beautiful woman'.

On and on rambled John Pendleton, musingly, contentedly, his eyes on the fire. Whether he was answered or not seemed not to disturb him. Whether he was even listened to or not, he seemed hardly to know. He wanted, apparently, only to talk; but at last he got to his feet reluctantly and said good-night.

For a weary half-hour Pollyanna had been longing for him to go, that she might be alone; but after he had gone she wished he were back. She had found suddenly that she did not want to be alone – with her thoughts.

It was wonderfully clear to Pollyanna now. There was no doubt of it. Jimmy cared for Mrs Carew. That was why he was so moody and restless after she left. That was why he had come so seldom to see her, Pollyanna, his old friend. That was why –

Countless little circumstances of the past summer flocked to Pollyanna's memory now, mute witnesses that would not be denied.

And why should he not care for her? Mrs Carew was certainly beautiful and charming. True, she was older than Jimmy; but young men had married women far older than she, many times. And if they loved each other . . .

Pollyanna cried herself to sleep that night.

In the morning, bravely she tried to face the thing. She even tried, with a tearful smile, to put it to the test of the Glad Game. She was reminded then of something Nancy had said to her years before: 'If there *is* a set o' folks in the world that wouldn't have no use for that 'ere Glad Game o' your'n, it'd be a pair o' quarrellin' lovers!'

'Not that we're "quarrelling", or even "lovers",' thought Pollyanna blushingly; 'but just the same I can be glad *he's* glad, and glad *she's* glad, too, only –' Even to herself Pollyanna could not finish this sentence.

Being so sure now that Jimmy and Mrs Carew cared for each other, Pollyanna became peculiarly sensitive to everything that tended to strengthen that belief. And being ever on the watch for it, she found it, as was to be expected. First in Mrs Carew's letters.

I am seeing a lot of your friend, young Pendleton [Mrs Carew wrote one day]; and I'm liking him more and more. I do wish, however – just for curiosity's sake – that I could trace to its source that elusive feeling that I've seen him before somewhere.

Frequently, after this, she mentioned him casually; and, to Pollyanna, in the very casualness of these references lay their sharpest sting; for it showed so unmistakably that Jimmy and Jimmy's presence were now to Mrs Carew a matter of course. From other sources, too, Pollyanna found fuel for the fire of her suspicions. More and more frequently John Pendleton 'dropped in' with his stories of Jimmy, and of what Jimmy was doing; and always here there was mention of Mrs Carew. Poor Pollyanna wondered, indeed, sometimes, if John Pendleton could not talk of anything but Mrs Carew and Jimmy, so constantly was one or the other of those names on his lips.

There were Sadie Dean's letters, too, and they told of Jimmy, and of what he was doing to help Mrs Carew. Even Jamie, who wrote occasionally, had his mite to add, for he wrote one evening:

It's ten o'clock. I'm sitting here alone waiting for Mrs Carew to come home. She and Pendleton have been to one of their usual socials down to the Home.

From Jimmy himself Pollyanna heard very rarely; and for that she told herself mournfully that she *could* be *glad*.

'For if he can't write about *anything* but Mrs Carew and those girls, I'm glad he doesn't write very often!' she sighed.

27

The Day Pollyanna Did Not Play

And so one by one the winter days passed. January and February slipped away in snow and sleet, and March came in with a gale that whistled and moaned around the old house, and set loose blinds to swinging and loose gates to creaking in a way that was most trying to nerves already stretched to the breaking-point.

Pollyanna was not finding it very easy these days to play the game, but she was playing it faithfully, valiantly. Aunt Polly was not playing it at all – which certainly did not make it any the easier for Pollyanna to play it. Aunt Polly was blue and discouraged. She was not well, too, and she had plainly abandoned herself to utter gloom.

Pollyanna still was counting on the prize contest. She had dropped from the first prize to one of the smaller ones, however; Pollyanna had been writing more stories, and the regularity with which they came back from their pilgrimages to magazine editors was beginning to shake her faith in her success as an author.

'Oh, well, I can be glad that Aunt Polly doesn't know anything about it, anyway,' declared Pollyanna to herself bravely, as she twisted in her fingers the 'declined with thanks' slip that had just towed in one more shipwrecked story. 'She *can't* worry about this – she doesn't know about it!'

All of Pollyanna's life these days revolved around Aunt Polly, and it is doubtful if even Aunt Polly herself realized how exacting she had become, and how entirely her niece was giving up her life to her.

It was on a particularly gloomy day in March that matters came, in a way, to a climax. Pollyanna, upon arising, had looked at the sky with a sigh – Aunt Polly was always more difficult on cloudy days. With a gay little song, however, that still sounded a bit forced – Pollyanna descended to the kitchen and began to prepare breakfast.

'I reckon I'll make corn muffins,' she told the stove confidentially; 'then maybe Aunt Polly won't mind – other things so much.'

Half an hour later she tapped at her aunt's door.

'Up so soon? Oh, that's fine! And you've done your hair yourself!'

'I couldn't sleep. I had to get up,' sighed Aunt Polly wearily. 'I had to do my hair, too. *You* weren't here.'

'But I didn't suppose you were ready for me, Auntie,' explained Pollyanna hurriedly. 'Never mind, though. You'll be glad I wasn't when you find what I've been doing.'

'Well, I shan't – not this morning,' frowned Aunt Polly perversely. 'Nobody could be glad this morning. Look at the rain! That makes the third rainy day this week.'

'That's so – but you know the sun never seems quite so perfectly lovely as it does after a lot of rain like this,' smiled Pollyanna, deftly arranging a bit of lace and ribbon at her aunt's throat. 'Now come. Breakfast's all ready. Just you wait till you see what I've got for you.'

Aunt Polly, however, was not to be diverted, even by corn muffins, this morning. Nothing was right, nothing was even endurable, as she felt; and Pollyanna's patience was sorely taxed before the meal was over. To make matters worse, the roof over the east attic window was found to be leaking, and an unpleasant letter came in the mail. Pollyanna, true to her creed, laughingly declared that, for her part, she was glad they had a roof – to leak; and that, as for the letter, she'd been expecting it for a week, anyway, and she was actually glad she wouldn't have to worry any more for fear it would come. It *couldn't* come now, because it *had* come; and 'twas over with.

All this, together with sundry other hindrances and annoyances, delayed the usual morning work until far into the afternoon – something that was always particularly displeasing to methodical Aunt Polly, who ordered her own life, preferably, by the tick of the clock.

'But it's half-past three, Pollyanna, already! Did you know it?' she fretted at last. 'And you haven't made the beds yet.'

'No, dearie, but I will. Don't worry.'

'But did you hear what I said? Look at the clock, child. It's after three o'clock!'

'So 'tis, but never mind, Aunt Polly. We can be glad 'tisn't after four.'

Aunt Polly sniffed her disdain.

'I suppose *you* can,' she observed tartly.

Pollyanna laughed.

'Well, you see, Auntie, clocks *are* accommodating things, when you stop to think about it. I found that out long ago at the Sanatorium. When I was doing something that I liked, and I didn't *want* the time to go fast, I'd just look at the hour hand, and I'd feel as if I had lots of time – it went so slow. Then, other days, when I had to keep something that hurt on for an hour, maybe, I'd watch the little second hand; and you see then I felt as if Old Time was just humping himself to help me out by going as fast as ever he could. Now I'm watching the hour hand today, 'cause I don't want Time to go fast. See?' she twinkled mischievously, as she hurried from the room, before Aunt Polly had time to answer.

It was certainly a hard day, and by night Pollyanna looked pale and worn out. This, too, was a source of worriment to Aunt Polly.

'Dear me, child, you look tired to death!' she fumed. '*What* we're going to do I don't know. I suppose *you'll* be sick next!'

'Nonsense, Auntie! I'm not sick a bit,' declared Pollyanna, dropping herself with a sigh on to the couch. 'But I *am* tired. My! how good this couch feels! I'm glad I'm tired, after all – it's so nice to rest.'

Aunt Polly turned with an impatient gesture.

'Glad – glad – glad! Of course you're glad, Pollyanna. You're always glad for everything. I never saw such a girl. Oh, yes, I know it's the game,' she went on, in answer to the look that came to Pollyanna's face. 'And it's a very good game, too; but I think you carry it altogether too far. This eternal doctrine of "it might be worse" has got on my nerves, Pollyanna. Honestly, it would be a real relief if you *wouldn't* be glad for something, some time!'

'Why, Auntie!' Pollyanna pulled herself half erect.

'Well, it would. You just try it some time, and see.'

'But, Auntie, I –' Pollyanna stopped and eyed her aunt reflectively. An odd look came to her eyes; a slow smile curved her lips. Mrs Chilton, who had turned back to her work, paid no heed; and, after a minute, Pollyanna lay back on the couch, without finishing her sentence, the curious smile still on her lips.

It was raining again when Pollyanna got up the next morning, and a north-east wind was still whistling down the chimney. Pollyanna at the window drew an involuntary sigh; but almost at once her face changed.

'Oh, well, I'm glad –' She clapped her hands to her lips. 'Dear me,' she chuckled softly, her eyes dancing, 'I shall forget – I know I shall; and that'll spoil it all! I must just remember not to be glad for anything – not *anything* today.'

Pollyanna did not make corn muffins that morning. She started the breakfast, then went to her aunt's room.

Mrs Chilton was still in bed.

'I see it rains as usual,' she observed, by way of greeting.

'Yes, it's horrid – perfectly horrid,' scolded Pollyanna. 'It's rained 'most every day this week, too. I hate such weather.'

Aunt Polly turned with a faint surprise in her eyes; but Pollyanna was looking the other way.

'Are you going to get up now?' she asked a little wearily.

'Why, y-yes,' murmured Aunt Polly, still with the

faint surprise in her eyes. 'What's the matter, Pollyanna? Are you specially tired?'

'Yes, I am tired this morning. I didn't sleep well,
either. I hate not to sleep. Things always plague so in
the night, when you wake up.'

'I guess I know that,' fretted Aunt Polly. 'I didn't
sleep a wink after two o'clock myself. And there's that
roof! How are we going to have it fixed, pray, if it
never stops raining? Have you been up to empty the
pans?'

'Oh, yes – and took up some more. There's a new
leak now, farther over.'

'A new one! Why, it'll all be leaking yet!'

Pollyanna opened her lips. She had almost said,
'Well, we can be glad to have it fixed all at once, then,'
when she suddenly remembered, and substituted, in a
tired voice:

'Very likely it will, Auntie. It looks like it now, fast
enough. Anyway, it's made fuss enough for a whole
roof already, and I'm sick of it!' With which statement,
Pollyanna, her face carefully averted, turned and
trailed listlessly out of the room.

'It's so funny and so – so hard, I'm afraid I'm
making a mess of it,' she whispered to herself
anxiously, as she hurried downstairs to the kitchen.

Behind her, Aunt Polly, in the bedroom, gazed after
her with eyes that were again faintly puzzled.

Aunt Polly had occasion a good many times before
six o'clock that night to gaze at Pollyanna with surprise
and questioning eyes. Nothing was right with Pollyanna. The fire would not burn, the wind blew one
particular blind loose three times, and still a third leak
was discovered in the roof. The mail brought to Polly-

anna a letter that made her cry (though no amount of questioning on Aunt Polly's part would persuade her to tell why). Even the dinner went wrong, and innumerable things happened in the afternoon to call out fretful, discouraged remarks.

Not until the day was more than half gone did a look of shrewd suspicion suddenly fight for supremacy with the puzzled questioning in Aunt Polly's eyes. If Pollyanna saw this she made no sign. Certainly there was no abatement in her fretfulness and discontent. Long before six o'clock, however, the suspicion in Aunt Polly's eyes became conviction, and drove to ignominious defeat the puzzled questioning. But, curiously enough then, a new look came to take its place, a look that was actually a twinkle of amusement.

At last, after a particularly doleful complaint on Pollyanna's part, Aunt Polly threw up her hands with a gesture of half-laughing despair.

'That'll do, that'll do, child! I'll give up. I'll confess myself beaten at my own game. You can be – *glad* for that, if you like,' she finished, with a grim smile.

'I know, Auntie, but you said –' began Pollyanna demurely.

'Yes, yes, but I never will again,' interrupted Aunt Polly, with emphasis. 'Mercy, what a day this has been! I never want to live through another like it.' She hesitated, flushed a little, then went on with evident difficulty: 'Furthermore, I – I want you to know that – that I understand I haven't played the game myself – very well, lately; but, after this, I'm going to – to try – *Where's* my handkerchief?' she finished sharply, fumbling in the folds of her dress.

Pollyanna sprang to her feet and crossed instantly to her aunt's side.

'Oh, but Aunt Polly, I didn't mean – It was just a – a joke,' she quavered in quick distress. 'I never thought of your taking it *that* way.'

'Of course you didn't,' snapped Aunt Polly, with all the asperity of a stern, repressed woman who abhors scenes and sentiment, and who is mortally afraid she will show that her heart has been touched. 'Don't you suppose I know you didn't mean it that way? Do you think, if I thought you *had* been trying to teach me a lesson that I'd – I'd –' But Pollyanna's strong young arms had her in a close embrace, and she could not finish the sentence.

28

JIMMY AND JAMIE

Pollyanna was not the only one that was finding that winter a hard one. In Boston, Jimmy Pendleton, in spite of his strenuous efforts to occupy his time and thoughts, was discovering that nothing quite erased from his vision a certain pair of laughing blue eyes, and nothing quite obliterated from his memory a certain well-loved, merry voice.

Jimmy told himself that if it were not for Mrs Carew, and the fact that he could be of some use to her, life would not be worth the living. Even at Mrs Carew's it was not all joy, for always there was Jamie; and Jamie brought thoughts of Pollyanna – unhappy thoughts.

Being thoroughly convinced that Jamie and Pollyanna cared for each other, and also being equally convinced that he himself was in honour bound to step one side and give the handicapped Jamie full right of way, it never occurred to him to question further. Of Pollyanna he did not like to talk or to hear. He knew that both Jamie and Mrs Carew heard from her; and when they spoke of her, he forced himself to listen, in spite of his heartache. But he always changed the subject as soon as possible, and he limited his own letters to her to the briefest and most infrequent epistles possible. For, to Jimmy, a Pollyanna that was not his was nothing but a source of pain and wretchedness; and he had been so glad when the time came for him to leave Beldingsville and take up his studies again in Boston: to be so near Pollyanna, and yet so far from her, he had found to be nothing but torture.

In Boston, with all the feverishness of a restless mind that seeks distraction from itself, he had thrown himself into the carrying out of Mrs Carew's plans for her beloved working girls, and such time as could be spared from his own duties he had devoted to this work, much to Mrs Carew's delight and gratitude.

And so for Jimmy the winter had passed and spring had come – a joyous, blossoming spring full of soft breezes, gentle showers, and tender green buds expanding into riotous bloom and fragrance. To Jimmy, however, it was anything but a joyous spring, for in his heart was still nothing but a gloomy winter of discontent.

'If only they'd settle things and announce the engagement, once and for all,' murmured Jimmy to himself, more and more frequently these days. 'If only I could know *something* for sure, I think I could stand it better!'

Then one day late in April, he had his wish – a part of it; he learned 'something for sure'.

It was ten o'clock on a Saturday morning, and Mary, at Mrs Carew's, had ushered him into the music-room with a well-trained: 'I'll tell Mrs Carew you're here, sir. She's expecting you, I think.'

In the music-room Jimmy had found himself brought to a dismayed halt by the sight of Jamie at the piano, his arms outflung upon the rack, and his head bowed upon them. Pendleton had half turned to beat a soft retreat when the man at the piano lifted his head, bringing into view two flushed cheeks and a pair of fever-bright eyes.

'Why, Carew,' stammered Pendleton, aghast, 'has anything – er – happened?'

'Happened! Happened!' ejaculated the lame youth, flinging out both his hands, in each of which, as Pendleton now saw, was an open letter. 'Everything has happened! Wouldn't you think it had if all your life you'd been in prison, and suddenly you saw the gates flung wide open? Wouldn't you think it had if all in a minute you could ask the girl you loved to be your wife? Wouldn't you think it had if – But, listen! You think I'm crazy, but I'm not. Though maybe I am, after all, crazy with joy. I'd like to tell you. May I? I've got to tell somebody!'

Pendleton lifted his head. It was as if, unconsciously, he was bracing himself for a blow. He had grown a little white; but his voice was quite steady when he answered.

'Sure you may, old fellow. I'd be – glad to hear it.'

Carew, however, had scarcely waited for assent. He was rushing on, still a bit incoherently.

'It's not much to you, of course. You have two feet and your freedom. You have your ambitions and your bridges. But I – to me it's everything. It's a chance to live a man's life and do a man's work, perhaps – even if it isn't dams and bridges. It's something! – and it's something I've proved now I *can do*! Listen. In that letter there is the announcement that a little story of mine has won the first prize – three thousand dollars, in a contest. In that other letter there, a big publishing-house accepts with flattering enthusiasm my first book manuscript for publication. And they both came today – this morning. Do you wonder I am crazy glad?'

'No! No, indeed! I congratulate you, Carew, with all my heart,' cried Jimmy warmly.

'Thank you – and you may congratulate me. Think what it means to me. Think what it means if, by and by, I can be independent, like a man. Think what it means if I can, some day, make Mrs Carew proud and glad that she gave the crippled lad a place in her home and heart. Think what it means for me to be able to tell the girl I love that I *do* love her.'

'Yes – yes, indeed, old boy!' Jimmy spoke firmly, though he had grown very white now.

'Of course, maybe I ought not to do that last, even now,' resumed Jamie, a swift cloud shadowing the shining brightness of his countenance. 'I'm still tied to – these.' He tapped the crutches by his side. 'I can't forget, of course, that day in the woods last summer, when I saw Pollyanna – I realize that always I'll have to run the chance of seeing the girl I love in danger, and not being able to rescue her.'

'Oh, but, Carew –' began the other hastily.

Carew lifted a peremptory hand.

'I know what you'd say. But don't say it. You can't understand. *You* aren't tied to two sticks. You did the rescuing, not I. It came to me then how it would be, always, with me and – Sadie. I'd have to stand aside and see others –'

'*Sadie!*' cut in Jimmy sharply.

'Yes; Sadie Dean. You act surprised. Didn't you know? Haven't you suspected – how I felt towards

Sadie?' cried Jamie. 'Have I kept it so well to myself, then? I tried to, but –' He finished with a faint smile and a half-despairing gesture.

'Well, you certainly kept it all right, old fellow – from me, anyhow,' cried Jimmy gaily. The colour had come back to Jimmy's face in a rich flood, and his eyes had grown suddenly very bright indeed. 'So it's Sadie Dean. Good! I congratulate you again, I do, I do, as Nancy says.' Jimmy was quite babbling with joy and excitement now, so great and wonderful had been the reaction within him at the discovery that it was Sadie, not Pollyanna, whom Jamie loved. Jamie flushed and shook his head a bit sadly.

'No congratulations – yet. You see, I haven't spoken to – her. But I think she must know. I supposed everybody knew. Pray, whom did you think it was, if not – Sadie?'

Jimmy hesitated. Then, a little precipitately, he let it out.

'Why, I thought of – Pollyanna.'

Jamie smiled and pursed his lips.

'Pollyanna's a charming girl, and I love her – but not that way, any more than she does me. Besides, I fancy somebody else would have something to say about that; eh?'

Jimmy coloured like a happy, conscious boy.

'Do you?' he challenged, trying to make his voice properly impersonal.

'Of course! John Pendleton.'

'*John Pendleton!*' Jimmy wheeled sharply.

'What about John Pendleton?' queried a new voice; and Mrs Carew came forward with a smile.

Jimmy, around whose ears for the second time

within five minutes the world had crashed into fragments, barely collected himself enough for a low word of greeting. But Jamie, unabashed, turned with a triumphant air of assurance.

'Nothing; only I just said that I believed John Pendleton would have something to say about Pollyanna's loving anybody – but him.'

'*Pollyanna! John Pendleton!*' Mrs Carew sat down suddenly in the chair nearest her. If the two men before her had not been so deeply absorbed in their own affairs they might have noticed that the smile had vanished from Mrs Carew's lips, and that an odd look as of almost fear had come to her eyes.

'Certainly,' maintained Jamie. 'Were you both blind last summer? Wasn't he with her a lot?'

'Why, I thought he was with – all of us,' murmured Mrs Carew, a little faintly.

'Not as he was with Pollyanna,' insisted Jamie. 'Besides, have you forgotten that day when we were talking about John Pendleton's marrying, and Pollyanna blushed and stammered and said finally that he *had* thought of marrying – once. Well, I wondered then if there wasn't *something* between them. Don't you remember?'

'Y-yes, I think I do – now that you speak of it,' murmured Mrs Carew again. 'But I had – forgotten it.'

'Oh, but I can explain that,' cut in Jimmy, wetting his dry lips. 'John Pendleton *did* have a love affair once, but it was with Pollyanna's mother.'

'Pollyanna's mother!' exclaimed two voices in surprise.

'Yes. He loved her years ago, but she did not care

for him at all, I understand. She had another lover – a
minister, and she married him instead – Pollyanna's
father.'

'Oh-h!' breathed Mrs Carew, leaning forward suddenly in her chair. 'And is that why he's – never
married?'

'Yes,' avouched Jimmy. 'So you see there's really
nothing to that idea at all – that he cares for Pollyanna.
It was her mother.'

'On the contrary, I think it makes a whole lot to that
idea,' declared Jamie, wagging his head wisely. 'I think
it makes my case all the stronger. Listen. He once
loved the mother. He couldn't have her. What more
absolutely natural than that he should love the daughter now – and win her?'

'Oh, Jamie, you incorrigible spinner of tales!' reproached Mrs Carew, with a nervous laugh. 'This is
no tenpenny novel. It's real life. She's too young for
him. He ought to marry a woman, not a girl – that is,
if he marries anyone, I mean,' she stammeringly corrected, a sudden flood of colour in her face.

'Perhaps; but what if it happens to be a *girl* that he
loves?' argued Jamie stubbornly. 'And, really, just
stop to think. Have we had a single letter from her that
hasn't told of his being there? And you *know* how *he's*
always talking of Pollyanna in *his* letters.'

Mrs Carew got suddenly to her feet.

'Yes, I know,' she murmured, with an odd little
gesture, as if throwing something distasteful aside.
'But –' She did not finish her sentence, and a moment
later she had left the room.

When she came back in five minutes she found,
much to her surprise, that Jimmy had gone.

256 POLLYANNA GROWS UP

'Why, I thought he was going with us on the girls' picnic!' she exclaimed.

'So did I,' frowned Jamie. 'But the first thing I knew he was explaining or apologizing or something about unexpectedly having to leave town, and he'd come to tell you he couldn't go with us. Anyhow, the next thing I knew he'd gone. You see' – Jamie's eyes were glowing again – 'I don't think I knew quite what he did say, anyway. I had something else to think of.' And he jubilantly spread before her the two letters which all the time he had still kept in his hands.

'Oh, Jamie!' breathed Mrs Carew, when she had read the letters through. 'How proud I am of you!' Then suddenly her eyes filled with tears at the look of ineffable joy that illumined Jamie's face.

29

JIMMY AND JOHN

It was a very determined, square-jawed young man that alighted at the Beldingsville station late that Saturday night. And it was an even more determined, square-jawed young man that, before ten o'clock the next morning, stalked through the Sunday-quiet village streets and climbed the hill to the Harrington homestead. Catching sight of a loved and familiar flaxen coil of hair on a well-poised little head just disappearing into the summer-house, the young man ignored the conventional front steps and doorbell, crossed the lawn, and strode through the garden paths until he came face to face with the owner of the flaxen coil of hair.

'Jimmy!' gasped Pollyanna, falling back with startled eyes. 'Why, where did you – come from?'

'Boston. Last night. I had to see you, Pollyanna.'

'To – see – m–me?' Pollyanna was plainly fencing for time to regain her composure. Jimmy looked so big and strong and *dear* there in the door of the summer-house that she feared her eyes had been surprised into a tell-tale admiration, if not more.

'Yes, Pollyanna; I wanted – that is, I thought – I mean, I feared – Oh, hang it all, Pollyanna, I can't beat about the bush like this. I'll have to come straight to the point. It's just this. I stood aside before, but I won't now. It isn't a case any longer of fairness. He isn't crippled like Jamie. He's got feet and hands and a head like mine, and if he wins he'll have to win in a fair fight. *I've* got some rights!'

Pollyanna stared frankly.

'Jimmy Bean Pendleton, whatever in the world are you talking about?' she demanded.

The young man laughed shamefacedly.

'No wonder you don't know. It wasn't very lucid, was it? But I don't think I've been really lucid myself since yesterday – when I found out from Jamie himself.'

'Found out – from Jamie!'

'Yes. It was the prize that started it. You see, he'd just got one, and –'

'Oh, I know about that,' interrupted Pollyanna eagerly. 'And wasn't it splendid? Just think – the first one – three thousand dollars! I wrote him a letter last night. Why, when I saw his name, and realized it was Jamie – *our Jamie* – I was so excited I forgot all about looking for *my* name, and even when I couldn't find mine at all, and knew that I hadn't got any – I mean, I was so excited and pleased for Jamie that I – I forgot – er – everything else,' corrected Pollyanna, throwing a dismayed glance into Jimmy's face, and feverishly trying to cover up the partial admission she had made.

Jimmy, however, was too intent on his own problem to notice hers. 'Yes, yes, 'twas fine, of course. I'm glad he got it. But, Pollyanna, it was what he said *afterwards* that I mean. You see, until then I'd thought that – that he cared – that you cared – for each other, I mean; and –'

'You thought that Jamie and I cared for each other!' exclaimed Pollyanna, into whose face now was stealing a soft, shy colour. 'Why, Jimmy, it's Sadie Dean. 'Twas always Sadie Dean. He used to talk of her to me by the hour. I think she likes him, too.'

'Good! I hope she does; but, you see, I didn't know. I thought 'twas Jamie – and you. And I thought that because he was – was a cripple, you know, that it wouldn't be fair if I – if I stayed around and tried to win you myself.'

Pollyanna stooped suddenly, and picked up a leaf at her feet. When she rose, her face was turned quite away.

'A fellow can't – can't feel square, you know, running a race with a chap that – that's handicapped from the start. So I – I just stayed away and gave him his chance; though it 'most broke my heart to do it, little girl. It just did! Then yesterday morning I found out. But I found out something else, too. Jamie says there is – is somebody else in the case. But I can't stand aside for him, Pollyanna. I can't – even in spite of all he's done for me. John Pendleton is a man, and he's got two whole feet for the race. He's got to take his chances. If you care for him – if you really care for him –'

But Pollyanna had turned, wild-eyed.

'*John Pendleton!* Jimmy, what do you mean? What are you saying about John Pendleton?'

A great joy transfigured Jimmy's face. He held out both his hands.

'Then you don't – you don't! I can see it in your eyes that you don't – care!'

Pollyanna shrank back. She was white and trembling.

'Jimmy, what do you mean? What do you mean?' she begged piteously.

'I mean – you don't care for Uncle John, that way. Don't you understand? Jamie thinks you do care, and that anyway he cares for you. And then I began to see it – that maybe he did. He's always talking about you; and, of course, there was your mother –'

Pollyanna gave a low moan and covered her face with her hands. Jimmy came close and laid a caressing arm about her shoulders; but again Pollyanna shrank from him.

'Pollyanna, little girl, don't! You'll break my heart,' he begged. 'Don't you care for me – *any*? Is it that, and you don't want to tell me?'

She dropped her hands and faced him. Her eyes had the hunted look of some wild thing at bay.

'Jimmy, do *you* think – he cares for me – that way?' she entreated, just above a whisper.

Jimmy gave his head an impatient shake.

'Never mind that, Pollyanna – now. I don't know, of course. How should I? But, dearest, that isn't the question. It's you. If *you* don't care for him, and if you'll only give me a chance – half a chance to let me make you care for me –' He caught her hand, and tried to draw her to him.

'No, no, Jimmy, I mustn't! I can't!' With both her little palms she pushed him from her.

'Pollyanna, you don't mean you *do* care for him?' Jimmy's face whitened.

'No; no, indeed – not that way,' faltered Pollyanna. 'But – don't you see? – if he cares for me, I'll have to – to learn to, some way.'

'*Pollyanna!*'

'Don't. Don't look at me like that, Jimmy!'

'You mean you'd *marry* him, Pollyanna?'

'Oh, no! – I mean – why – er – y-yes, I suppose so,' she admitted faintly.

'Pollyanna, you wouldn't! You couldn't! Pollyanna, you – you're breaking my heart.'

Pollyanna gave a low sob. Her face was in her hands again. For a moment she sobbed on, chokingly; then, with a tragic gesture, she lifted her head and looked straight into Jimmy's anguished, reproachful eyes.

'I know it, I know it,' she chattered frenziedly. 'I'm breaking mine, too. But I'll have to do it. I'd break your heart, I'd break mine – but I'd never break his!'

Jimmy raised his head. His eyes flashed a sudden fire. His whole appearance underwent a swift and marvellous change. With a tender, triumphant cry he swept Pollyanna into his arms and held her close.

'Now I *know* you care for me!' he breathed low in her ear. 'You said it was breaking *your* heart, too. Do you think I'll give you up now to any man on earth? Ah, dear, you little understand a love like mine if you think I'd give you up now. Pollyanna, *say* you love me – say it with your own dear lips!'

For one long minute Pollyanna lay unresisting in the fiercely tender embrace that encircled her; then with a sigh that was half content, half renunciation, she began to draw herself away.

'Yes, Jimmy, I do love you.' Jimmy's arms tightened, and would have drawn her back to him; but something in the girl's face forbade. 'I love you dearly. But I couldn't ever be happy with you and feel that – Jimmy, don't you see, dear? I'll have to know – that I'm free, first.'

'Nonsense, Pollyanna! Of course you're free!' Jimmy's eyes were mutinous again.

Pollyanna shook her head.

'Not with this hanging over me, Jimmy. Don't you see? It was Mother, long ago, that broke his heart – *my mother*. And all these years he's lived a lonely, unloved life in consequence. If now he should come to me and ask me to make that up to him, I'd *have* to do it, Jimmy. I'd *have* to. I couldn't *refuse*! Don't you see?'

But Jimmy did not see; he could not see. He would not see, though Pollyanna pleaded and argued long and tearfully. But Pollyanna, too, was obdurate, though so sweetly and heartbrokenly obdurate that Jimmy, in spite of his pain and anger, felt almost like turning comforter.

'Jimmy, dear,' said Pollyanna at last, 'we'll have to wait. That's all I can say now. I hope he doesn't care; and I – I don't believe he does care. But I've got to *know*. I've got to be sure. We'll just have to wait, a little, till we find out, Jimmy – till we find out!'

And to this plan Jimmy had to submit, though it was with a most rebellious heart.

'All right, little girl, it'll have to be as you say, of course,' he despaired. 'But, surely, never before was a man kept waiting for his answer till the girl he loved, *and who loved him*, found out if the other man wanted her!'

'I know; but, you see, dear, never before had the other man *wanted* her mother,' sighed Pollyanna, her face puckered into an anxious frown.

'Very well, I'll go back to Boston, of course,' acceded Jimmy reluctantly. 'But you needn't think I've given up – because I haven't. Nor I shan't give up, just so long as I know you really care for me, my little sweet-heart,' he finished, with a look that sent her palpitatingly into retreat, just out of reach of his arms.

30

John Pendleton Turns the Key

Jimmy went back to Boston that night in a state that was a most tantalizing commingling of happiness, hoped exasperation, and rebellion. Behind him he left a girl who was in a scarcely less enviable frame of mind; for Pollyanna, tremulously happy in the wonderful thought of Jimmy's love for her, was yet so despairingly terrified at the thought of the possible love of John Pendleton, that there was not a thrill of joy that did not carry its pang of fear.

Fortunately for all concerned, however, this state of affairs was not of long duration; for, as it chanced, John Pendleton, in whose unwitting hands lay the key to the situation, in less than a week after Jimmy's hurried visit, turned that key in the lock, and opened the door of doubt.

It was late Thursday afternoon that John Pendleton called to see Pollyanna. As it happened, he, like Jimmy, saw Pollyanna in the garden and came straight towards her.

Pollyanna, looking into his face, felt a sudden sinking of the heart.

'It's come – it's come!' she shivered; and involuntarily she turned as if to flee.

'Oh, Pollyanna, wait a minute, please,' called the

man, hastening his steps. 'You're just the one I wanted to see. Come, can't we go in here?' he suggested, turning towards the summer-house. 'I want to speak to you about – something.'

'Why, y-yes, of course,' stammered Pollyanna, with forced gaiety. Pollyanna knew that she was blushing, and she particularly wished not to blush just then. It did not help matters any, either, that he should have elected to go into the summer-house for his talk. The summer-house now, to Pollyanna, was sacred to certain dear memories of Jimmy. 'And to think it should be here – *here*!' she was shuddering frantically. But aloud she said, still gaily, 'It's a lovely evening, isn't it?'

There was no answer. John Pendleton strode into the summer-house and dropped himself into a rustic chair without even waiting for Pollyanna to seat herself – a most unusual proceeding on the part of John Pendleton. Pollyanna, stealing a nervous glance at his face, found it so startlingly like the old stern, sour visage of her childhood's remembrance, that she uttered an involuntary exclamation.

Still John Pendleton paid no heed. Still moodily he sat wrapped in thought. At last, however, he lifted his head and gazed sombrely into Pollyanna's startled eyes.

'Pollyanna.'

'Yes, Mr Pendleton.'

'Do you remember the sort of man I was when you first knew me, years ago?'

'Why, y-yes, I think so.'

'Delightfully agreeable specimen of humanity, wasn't I?'

In spite of her perturbation Pollyanna smiled faintly.

'I – I liked you, sir.' Not until the words were uttered did Pollyanna realize just how they would sound. She strove then, frantically, to recall or modify them and had almost added a 'that is, I mean, I liked you then!' when she stopped just in time: certainly *that* would not have helped matters any! She listened then, fearfully, for John Pendleton's next words. They came almost at once.

'I know you did – bless your little heart! And it was that that was the saving of me. I wonder, Pollyanna, if I could ever make you realize just what your childish trust and liking did for me.'

Pollyanna stammered a confused protest; but he brushed it smilingly aside.

'Oh, yes, it was! It was you, and no one else. I wonder if you remember another thing, too,' resumed the man, after a moment's silence, during which Pollyanna looked furtively but longingly towards the door. 'I wonder if you remember my telling you once that nothing but a woman's hand and heart or a child's presence could make a home.'

Pollyanna felt the blood rush to her face.

'Y-yes, n-no – I mean, yes, I remember it,' she stuttered; 'but I – I don't think it's always so now. I mean – that is, I'm sure your home now is – is lovely just as 'tis, and –'

'But it's my home I'm talking about, child,' interrupted the man, impatiently. 'Pollyanna, you know the kind of home I once hoped to have, and how those hopes were dashed to the ground. Don't think, dear, I'm blaming your mother. I'm not. She but obeyed her heart, which was right; and she made the wiser choice, anyway, as was proved by the dreary waste

I've made of life because of that disappointment. After all, Pollyanna, isn't it strange,' added John Pendleton, his voice growing tender, 'that it should be the little hand of her own daughter that led me into the path of happiness, at last?'

Pollyanna moistened her lips convulsively.

'Oh, but, Mr Pendleton, I – I –'

Once again the man brushed aside her protests with a smiling gesture.

'Yes, it was, Pollyanna, your little hand in the long ago – you and your Glad Game.'

'Oh-h!' Pollyanna relaxed visibly in her seat. The terror in her eyes began slowly to recede.

'And so all these years I've been gradually growing into a different man, Pollyanna. But there's one thing I haven't changed in, my dear.' He paused, looked away, then turned gravely tender eyes back to her face. 'I still think it takes a woman's hand and heart or a child's presence to make a home.'

'Yes; but you've g-got the child's presence,' plunged in Pollyanna, the terror coming back to her eyes. 'There's Jimmy, you know.'

The man gave an amused laugh.

'I know; but – I don't think even you would say that Jimmy is – is exactly a *child's* presence any longer,' he remarked.

'N-no, of course not.'

'Besides – Pollyanna, I've made up my mind. I've got to have the woman's hand and heart.' His voice dropped, and trembled a little.

'Oh-h, have you?' Pollyanna's fingers met and clutched each other in a spasmodic clasp. John Pendleton, however, seemed neither to hear nor see. He had leaped to his feet, and was nervously pacing up and down the little house.

'Pollyanna,' he stopped and faced her; 'if – if you were I, and were going to ask the woman you loved to come and make your old grey pile of stone a home, how would you go to work to do it?'

Pollyanna half started from her chair. Her eyes sought the door this time openly, longingly.

'Oh, but, Mr Pendleton, I wouldn't do it at all, at all,' she stammered, a little wildly. 'I'm sure you'd be – much happier as – as you are.'

The man stared in puzzled surprise, then laughed grimly.

'Upon my word, Pollyanna, is it – quite so bad as that?' he asked.

'B-bad?' Pollyanna had the appearance of being poised for flight.

'Yes. Is that just your way of trying to soften the blow of saying that you don't think she'd have me, anyway?'

'Oh, n-no – no, indeed. She'd say yes – she'd *have* to say yes, you know,' explained Pollyanna, with terrified earnestness. 'But I've been thinking – I mean, I was thinking that if – if the girl didn't love you, you really would be happier without her; and –' At the look that came into John Pendleton's face, Pollyanna stopped short.

'I shouldn't want her, if she didn't love me, Pollyanna.'

'No, I thought not, too.' Pollyanna began to look a little less distracted.

'Besides, she doesn't happen to be a girl,' went on John Pendleton. 'She's a mature woman who, presum-

edly, would know her own mind.' The man's voice
was grave and slightly reproachful.

'Oh-h-h! Oh!' exclaimed Pollyanna, the dawning
happiness in her eyes leaping forth in a flash of ineffable joy and relief. 'Then you love somebody –' By an
almost superhuman effort Pollyanna choked off the
'else' before it left her delighted lips.

'Love somebody! Haven't I just been telling you I
did?' laughed John Pendleton, half vexedly. 'What I
want to know is – can she be made to love me? That's
where I was sort of – of counting on your help,
Pollyanna. You see, she's a dear friend of yours.'

'Is she?' gurgled Pollyanna. 'Then she'll just have to
love you. We'll make her! Maybe she does, anyway,
already. Who is she?'

There was a long pause before the answer came.

'I believe, after all, Pollyanna, I won't – yes, I will,
too. It's – can't you guess? – Mrs Carew.'

'Oh!' breathed Pollyanna, with a face of unclouded
joy. 'How perfectly lovely! I'm so glad, *glad*, GLAD!'

A long hour later Pollyanna sent Jimmy a letter. It
was confused and incoherent – a series of half-
completed, illogical, but shyly joyous sentences, out of
which Jimmy gathered much: a little from what was
written; more from what was left unwritten. After all,
did he really need more than this?

Oh, Jimmy, he doesn't love me a bit. It's some one else. I
mustn't tell you who it is – but her name isn't Pollyanna.

Jimmy had just time to catch the seven o'clock train
for Beldingsville – and he caught it.

31

After Long Years

Pollyanna was so happy that night after she had sent her letter to Jimmy that she could not quite keep it to herself. Always before going to bed she stepped into her aunt's room to see if anything were needed. To-night, after the usual questions, she had turned to put out the light when a sudden impulse sent her back to her aunt's bedside. A little breathlessly she dropped on her knees.

'Aunt Polly, I'm so happy I just had to tell some one. I *want* to tell you. May I?'

'Tell me? Tell me what, child? Of course you may tell me. You mean, it's good news – for *me*?'

'Why, yes, dear; I hope so,' blushed Pollyanna. 'I hope it will make you – *glad*, a little, for me, you know. Of course Jimmy will tell you himself all properly some day. But *I* wanted to tell you first.'

'Jimmy!' Mrs Chilton's face changed perceptibly.

'Yes, when – when he – he asks you for me,' stammered Pollyanna, with a radiant flood of colour. 'Oh, I – I'm so happy, I *had* to tell you!'

'Asks me for you! Pollyanna!' Mrs Chilton pulled herself up in bed. 'You don't mean to say there's anything *serious* between you and – Jimmy Bean.'

Pollyanna fell back in dismay.

'Why, Auntie, I thought you *liked* Jimmy!'

'So I do – in his place. But that place isn't the husband of my niece.'

'*Aunt Polly!*'

'Come, come, child, don't look so shocked. This is all sheer nonsense, and I'm glad I've been able to stop it before it's gone any farther.'

'But, Aunt Polly, it *has* gone farther,' quavered Pollyanna. 'Why, I – I already have learned to lo– c– care for him – dearly.'

'Then you'll have to unlearn it, Pollyanna, for never, never will I give my consent to your marrying Jimmy Bean.'

'But w–why, Auntie?'

'First and foremost because we know nothing about him.'

'Why, Aunt Polly, we've always known him, ever since I was a little girl!'

'Yes, and what was he? A rough little runaway urchin from an Orphans' Home! We know nothing whatever about his people, and his pedigree.'

'But I'm not marrying his p-people and his p-pedigree!'

With an impatient groan Aunt Polly fell back on her pillow.

'Pollyanna, you're making me positively ill. My heart is going like a trip-hammer. I shan't sleep a wink tonight. *Can't* you let this thing rest till morning?'

Pollyanna was on her feet instantly, her face all contrition.

'Why, yes – yes, indeed; of course, Aunt Polly! And tomorrow you'll feel different, I'm sure. I'm sure you will,' reiterated the girl, her voice quivering with hope again, as she turned to extinguish the light.

But Aunt Polly did not 'feel different' in the morning. If anything, her opposition to the marriage was even more determined. In vain Pollyanna pleaded and argued. In vain she showed how deeply her happiness was concerned. Aunt Polly was obdurate. She would have none of the idea. She sternly admonished Polly-anna as to the possible evils of heredity, and warned her of the dangers of marrying into she knew not what sort of family. She even appealed at last to her sense of duty and gratitude towards herself, and reminded Polly-anna of the long years of loving care that had been hers in the home of her aunt, and she begged her piteously not to break her heart by this marriage as had her mother years before by *her* marriage.

When Jimmy himself, radiant-faced and glowing-eyed, came at ten o'clock, he was met by a fright-ened, sob-shaken little Pollyanna that tried ineffectu-ally to hold him back with two trembling hands. With whitening cheeks, but with defiantly tender arms that held her close, he demanded an explanation.

'Pollyanna, dearest, what in the world is the meaning of this?'

'Oh, Jimmy, Jimmy, why did you come, why did you come? I was going to write and tell you straight away,' moaned Pollyanna.

'But you did write me, dear. I got it yesterday afternoon, just in time to catch my train.'

'No, no; – *again*, I mean. I didn't know then that I – I couldn't.'

'Couldn't! Pollyanna' – his eyes flamed into stern

wrath – 'you don't mean to tell me there's anybody *else's* love you think you've got to keep me waiting for?' he demanded, holding her at arm's length.

'No, no, Jimmy! Don't look at me like that. I can't bear it!'

'Then what is it? What is it you can't do?'

'I can't – marry you.'

'Pollyanna, do you love me?'

'Yes. Oh, y-yes.'

'Then you shall marry me,' triumphed Jimmy, his arms enfolding her again.

'No, no, Jimmy, you don't understand. It's – Aunt Polly,' struggled Pollyanna.

'*Aunt Polly!*'

'Yes. She – won't let me.'

'Ho!' Jimmy tossed his head with a light laugh. 'We'll fix Aunt Polly. She thinks she's going to lose you, but we'll just remind her that she is – she's going to gain a – a new nephew!' he finished in mock importance.

But Pollyanna did not smile. She turned her head hopelessly from side to side.

'No, no, Jimmy, you don't understand! She – she – oh, how can I tell you? – she objects to – to *you* – for – *me*.'

Jimmy's arms relaxed a little. His eyes sobered.

'Oh, well, I suppose I can't blame her for that. I'm no – wonder, of course,' he admitted constrainedly. 'Still' – he turned loving eyes upon her – 'I'd try to make you – happy, dear.'

'Indeed you would! I know you would,' protested Pollyanna tearfully.

'Then why not – give me a chance to try, Pollyanna,

even if she – doesn't quite approve, at first? Maybe in time, after we were married, we could win her over.'

'Oh, but I couldn't – I couldn't do that,' moaned Pollyanna, 'after what she's said. I couldn't – without her consent. You see, she's done so much for me, and she's so dependent on me. She isn't well a bit now, Jimmy. And, really, lately she's been so – so loving, and she's been trying so hard to – to play the game, you know, in spite of all her troubles. And she – she cried, Jimmy, and begged me not to break her heart as – as Mother did long ago. And – and, Jimmy, I – I just couldn't after all she's done for me.'

There was a moment's pause; then, with a vivid red mounting to her forehead, Pollyanna spoke again brokenly.

'Jimmy, if you – if you could only tell Aunt Polly something about – about your father, and your people, and –'

Jimmy's arms dropped suddenly. He stepped back a little. The colour drained from his face.

'Is – that – it?' he asked.

'Yes.' Pollyanna came nearer, and touched his arm timidly. 'Don't think – It isn't for me, Jimmy. I don't care. Besides, I *know* that your father and your people were all – all fine and noble, because *you* are so fine and noble. But she – Jimmy, don't look at me like that!'

But Jimmy, with a low moan, had turned quite away from her. A minute later, with only a few choking words, which she could not understand, he had left the house.

From the Harrington homestead Jimmy went straight

home and sought out John Pendleton. He found him in the great crimson-hung library where, some years before, Pollyanna had looked fearfully about for the 'skeleton John Pendleton's closet'.

'Uncle John, do you remember that Packet Father gave me?' demanded Jimmy.

'Why, yes. What's the matter, son?' John Pendleton had given a start of surprise at sight of Jimmy's face.

'That Packet has got to be opened, sir.'

'But – the conditions!'

'I can't help it. It's got to be. That's all. Will you do it?'

'Why, y-yes, my boy, of course, if you insist; but –' He paused helplessly.

'Uncle John, as perhaps you have guessed, I love Pollyanna. I asked her to be my wife, and she consented.' The elder man made a delighted exclamation, but the other did not pause, or change his sternly intent expression. 'She says now she can't – marry me. Mrs Chilton objects. She objects to *me*.'

'*Objects to you!*' John Pendleton's eyes flashed angrily.

'Yes. I found out why when – when Pollyanna begged if I couldn't tell her aunt something about – about my father and my people.'

'Shucks! I thought Polly Chilton had more sense – still, it's just like her after all. The Harringtons have always been inordinately proud of race and family,' snapped John Pendleton. 'Well, could you?'

'*Could I!* It was on the end of my tongue to tell Pollyanna that there couldn't have been a better father than mine was; then, suddenly, I remembered – the Packet, and what it said. And I was afraid. I didn't dare say a word till I knew what was inside that Packet. There's something Dad didn't want me to know till I was thirty years old – when I would be a man grown, and could stand anything. See? There's a secret somewhere in our lives. I've got to know that secret, and I've got to know it now.'

'But, Jimmy, lad, don't look so tragic. It may be a good secret. Perhaps it'll be something you'll *like* to know.'

'Perhaps. But if it had been, would he have been apt to keep it from me till I was thirty years old? No! Uncle John, it was something he was trying to save me from till I was old enough to stand it and not flinch. Understand, I'm not blaming Dad. Whatever it was, it was something he couldn't help, I'll warrant. But *what* it was I've got to know. Will you get it, please? It's in your safe, you know.'

John Pendleton rose at once.

'I'll get it,' he said. Three minutes later it lay in Jimmy's hand; but Jimmy held it out at once.

'I would rather you read it, sir, please. Then tell me.'

'But, Jimmy, I – very well.' With a decisive gesture John Pendleton picked up a paper-cutter, opened the envelope, and pulled out the contents. There was a package of several papers tied together, and one folded sheet alone, apparently a letter. This John Pendleton opened and read first. And as he read, Jimmy, tense and breathless, watched his face. He saw, therefore, the look of amazement, joy, and something else he could not name, that leaped into John Pendleton's countenance.

'Uncle John, what is it? What is it?' he demanded.

'Read it – for yourself,' answered the man, thrusting the letter into Jimmy's outstretched hand. And Jimmy read this:

The enclosed papers are the legal proof that my boy Jimmy is really James Kent, son of John Kent, who married Doris Wetherby, daughter of William Wetherby of Boston. There is also a letter in which I explain to my boy why I have kept him from his mother's family all these years. If this packet is opened by him at thirty years of age, he will read this letter, and I hope will forgive a father who feared to lose his boy entirely, so took this drastic course to keep him to himself. If it is opened by strangers, because of his death, I request that his mother's people in Boston be notified at once, and the enclosed package of papers be given, intact, into their hands.

John Kent

Jimmy was pale and shaken when he looked up to meet John Pendleton's eyes.

'Am I – the – lost – Jamie?' he faltered.

'That letter says you have documents there to prove it,' nodded the other.

'Mrs Carew's nephew.'

'Of course.'

'But, why – what – I can't realize it!' There was a moment's pause before into Jimmy's face flashed a new joy. 'Then, surely now I know who I am! I can tell – Mrs Chilton *something* of my people.'

'I should say you could,' retorted John Pendleton drily. 'The Boston Wetherbys can trace straight back to the Crusades and I don't know but to the year one. That ought to satisfy her. As for your father – he came of good stock, too, Mrs Carew told me, though he was rather eccentric, and not pleasing to the family, as you know, of course.'

'Yes. Poor Dad! And what a life he must have lived with me all those years – always dreading pursuit. I can understand – lots of things, now, that used to puzzle me. A woman called me Jamie, once. Jove! how angry he was! I know now why he hurried me away that night without even waiting for supper. Poor Dad! It was right after that he was taken sick. He couldn't use his hands or his feet, and very soon he couldn't talk straight. Something ailed his speech. I remember when he died he was trying to tell me something about this packet. I believe now he was telling me to open it, and go to my mother's people; but I thought then he was just telling me to keep it safe. So that's what I promised him. But it didn't comfort him any. It only seemed to worry him more. You see, I didn't understand. Poor Dad!'

'Suppose we take a look at these papers,' suggested John Pendleton. 'Besides, there's a letter from your father to you, I understand. Don't you want to read it?'

'Yes, of course. And then' – the young fellow laughed shamefacedly and glanced at the clock – 'I was wondering just how soon I could go back – to Pollyanna.'

A thoughtful frown came to John Pendleton's face. He glanced at Jimmy, hesitated, then spoke.

'I know you want to see Pollyanna, lad, and I don't blame you; but it strikes me that, under the circumstances, you should go first to – Mrs Carew, and take these.' He tapped the papers before him.

Jimmy drew his brows together and pondered.

'All right, sir, I will,' he agreed resignedly.

'And if you don't mind, I'd like to go with you,' further suggested John Pendleton, a little diffidently. 'I – I have a little matter of my own that I'd like to see – your aunt about. Suppose we go down today on the three o'clock?'

'Good! We will, sir. Gorry! And so I'm Jamie! I can't grasp it yet!' exclaimed the young man, springing to his feet, and restlessly moving about the room. 'I wonder, now,' he stopped, and coloured boyishly, 'do you think – Aunt Ruth – will mind – very much?'

John Pendleton shook his head. A hint of the old sombreness came into his eyes.

'Hardly, my boy. But – I'm thinking of myself. How about it? When you're her boy, where am I coming in?'

'You! Do you think *anything* could put you to one side?' scoffed Jimmy fervently. 'You needn't worry about that. And *she* won't mind. She has Jamie, you know, and –' He stopped short, a dawning dismay in his eyes. 'By George! Uncle John, I forgot – Jamie. This is going to be tough on – Jamie!'

'Yes, I'd thought of that. Still, he's legally adopted, isn't he?'

'Oh, yes; it isn't that. It's the fact that he isn't the real Jamie himself – and he with his two poor useless legs! Why, Uncle John, it'll just about kill him. I've heard him talk. I know. Besides, Pollyanna and Mrs Carew both have told me how he feels, how *sure* he is, and how happy he is. Great Scott! I can't take away from him this – But what *can* I do?'

'I don't know, my boy. I don't see as there's anything you can do, but what you are doing.'

There was a long silence. Jimmy had resumed his nervous pacing up and down the room. Suddenly he wheeled, his face alight.

'There *is* a way, and I'll do it. I *know* Mrs Carew will agree. *We won't tell!* We won't tell anybody but Mrs Carew herself, and – and Pollyanna and her aunt. I'll *have* to tell them,' he added defensively.

'You certainly will, my boy. As for the rest –' John Pendleton paused doubtfully.

'It's nobody's business.'

'But, remember, you are making quite a sacrifice – in several ways. I want you to weigh it well.'

'Weigh it? I have weighed it, and there's nothing in it – with Jamie on the other side of the scales, sir. I just couldn't do it. That's all.'

'I don't blame you, and I think you're right,' declared John Pendleton heartily. 'Furthermore, I believe Mrs Carew will agree with you, particularly as she'll *know* now that the real Jamie is found at last.'

'You know she's always said she'd seen me somewhere,' chuckled Jimmy. 'Now how soon does that train go? I'm ready.'

'Well, I'm not,' laughed John Pendleton. 'Luckily for me it doesn't go for some hours yet, anyhow,' he finished, as he got to his feet and left the room.

32

A New Aladdin

Whatever were John Pendleton's preparations for departure – and they were both varied and hurried – they were done in the open, with two exceptions. The exceptions were two letters, one addressed to Pollyanna, and one to Mrs Polly Chilton. These letters, together with careful and minute instructions, were given into the hands of Susan, his housekeeper, to be delivered after they should be gone. But of all this Jimmy knew nothing.

The travellers were nearing Boston when John Pendleton said to Jimmy:

'My boy, I've got one favour to ask – or rather, two. The first is that we say nothing to Mrs Carew until tomorrow afternoon; the other is that you allow me to go first and be your – er – ambassador, you yourself not appearing on the scene until perhaps, say – four o'clock. Are you willing?'

'Indeed I am,' replied Jimmy promptly; 'not only willing, but delighted. I'd been wondering how I was going to break the ice, and I'm glad to have somebody else do it.'

'Good! Then I'll try to get – *your aunt* on the telephone tomorrow morning and make my appointment.'

True to his promise, Jimmy did not appear at the Carew mansion until four o'clock the next afternoon. Even then he felt suddenly so embarrassed that he walked twice by the house before he summoned sufficient courage to go up the steps and ring the bell. Once in Mrs Carew's presence, however, he was soon his natural self, so quickly did she set him at his ease, and so tactfully did she handle the situation. To be sure, at the very first, there were a few tears, and a few incoherent exclamations. Even John Pendleton had to reach a hasty hand for his handkerchief. But before very long a semblance of normal tranquillity was restored, and only the tender glow in Mrs Carew's eyes, and the ecstatic happiness in Jimmy's and John Pendleton's, was left to mark the occasion as something out of the ordinary.

'And I think it's so fine of you – about Jamie!' exclaimed Mrs Carew after a little. 'Indeed, Jimmy – (I shall still call you Jimmy, for obvious reasons; besides, I like it better, for you) – indeed I think you're just right, if you're willing to do it. And I'm making some sacrifice myself, too,' she went on tearfully, 'for I should be so proud to introduce you to the world as my nephew.'

'And, indeed, Aunt Ruth, I –' At a half-stifled exclamation from John Pendleton, Jimmy stopped short. He saw then that Jamie and Sadie Dean stood just inside the door. Jamie's face was very white.

'*Aunt Ruth!*' he exclaimed, looking from one to the other with startled eyes. '*Aunt Ruth!* You don't mean –'

All the blood receded from Mrs Carew's face, and from Jimmy's, too. John Pendleton, however, advanced jauntily.

'Yes, Jamie; why not? I was going to tell you soon, anyway, so I'll tell you now.' (Jimmy gasped and stepped hastily forward, but John Pendleton silenced him with a look.) 'Just a little while ago Mrs Carew made me the happiest of men by saying yes to a certain question I asked. Now, as Jimmy calls me "Uncle John", why shouldn't he begin right away to call Mrs Carew "Aunt Ruth"?'

'Oh! Oh-h!' exclaimed Jamie, in plain delight, while Jimmy, under John Pendleton's steady gaze, just managed to save the situation by not blurting out *his* surprise and pleasure. Naturally, too, just then, blushing Mrs Carew became the centre of every one's interest, and the danger point was passed. Only Jimmy heard John Pendleton say low in his ear, a bit later:

'So you see, you young rascal, I'm not going to lose you, after all. We shall *both* have you now.'

Exclamations and congratulations were still at their height, when Jamie, a new light in his eyes, turned without warning to Sadie Dean.

'Sadie, I'm going to tell them now,' he declared triumphantly. Then, with the bright colour in Sadie's face telling the tender story even before Jamie's eager lips could frame the words, more congratulations and exclamations were in order, and everybody was laughing and shaking hands with everybody else.

Jimmy, however, very soon began to eye them all aggrievedly, longingly.

'This is all very well for *you*,' he complained then. 'You each have each other. But where do I come in? I can just tell you, though, that if only a certain young lady I know were here *I* should have something to tell *you*, perhaps.'

'Just a minute, Jimmy,' interposed John Pendleton. 'Let's play I was Aladdin, and let me rub the lamp. Mrs Carew, have I your permission to ring for Mary?'

'Why, y-yes, certainly,' murmured that lady, in a puzzled surprise that found its duplicate on the faces of the others.

A few moments later Mary stood in the doorway.

'Did I hear Miss Pollyanna come in a short time ago?' asked John Pendleton.

'Yes, sir. She is here.'

'Won't you ask her to come down, please?'

'Pollyanna here!' exclaimed an amazed chorus, as Mary disappeared. Jimmy turned very white, then very red.

'Yes. I sent a note to her yesterday by my housekeeper. I took the liberty of asking her down for a few days to see you, Mrs Carew. I thought the little girl needed a rest and a holiday; and my housekeeper has instructions to remain and care for Mrs Chilton. I also wrote a note to Mrs Chilton herself,' he added, turning suddenly to Jimmy, with unmistakable meaning in his eyes. 'And I thought after she read what I said that she'd let Pollyanna come. It seems she did, for – here she is.'

And there she was in the doorway, blushing, starry-eyed, yet withal just a bit shy and questioning.

'Pollyanna dearest!' It was Jimmy who sprang forward to meet her, and who, without one minute's hesitation, took her in his arms and kissed her.

'Oh, Jimmy, before all these people!' breathed Pollyanna in embarrassed protest.

'Pooh! I should have kissed you then, Pollyanna, if you'd been straight in the middle of – of Washington

Street itself,' vowed Jimmy. 'For that matter, look at – "all these people" and see for yourself if you need to worry about them.'

And Pollyanna looked; and she saw.

Over by one window, backs carefully turned, Jamie and Sadie Dean; over by another window, backs also carefully turned, Mrs Carew and John Pendleton.

Pollyanna smiled – so adorably that Jimmy kissed her again.

'Oh, Jimmy, isn't it all beautiful and wonderful?' she murmured softly. 'And Aunt Polly – she knows everything now; and it's all right. I think it would have been all right, anyway. She was beginning to feel so bad – for me. Now she's so glad. And I am, too. Why, Jimmy, I'm glad, *glad*, GLAD for – everything, now!'

Jimmy caught his breath with a joy that hurt.

'God grant, little girl, that always it may be so – with you,' he choked unsteadily, his arms holding her close.

'I'm sure it will,' sighed Pollyanna, with shining eyes of confidence.

POLLYANNA
Eleanor H. Porter

As soon as Pollyanna arrives in Beldingsville to live with her strict and dutiful maiden aunt, she begins to brighten up everybody's life. The 'glad game' she plays, of finding a silver lining in every cloud, transforms the sick, the lonely and the plain miserable – until one day something so terrible happens that even Pollyanna doesn't know how to feel glad about it.

ALICE'S ADVENTURES IN WONDERLAND
Lewis Carroll

Alice is an ordinary little girl who lives an ordinary sort of life, until the day she finds herself in the most wonderful world of mad tea parties and remarkable characters like the Mad Hatter, the Duchess, the Cheshire Cat and the Mock Turtle. As everything grows 'curiouser and curiouser', Alice is delighted to find that nothing in Wonderland is the least bit ordinary.

ANNE OF GREEN GABLES
L. M. Montgomery

Anne Shirley is skinny, red-haired, and never stops talking – and she is a girl. The Cuthberts, who had meant to adopt a boy to help on the farm, are both exasperated and entertained by her constant chatter and romantic imaginings, and don't know what to make of Anne. But they soon find it hard to remember what Green Gables was like without her.

EMILY OF NEW MOON
L. M. Montgomery

When Emily is sent to live with her horrible Aunt Elizabeth at New Moon after her father's death, she is sure she's going to hate it. But New Moon is such a beautiful place – and there are so many new things to do and people to meet that the rebellious, imaginative Emily soon finds that life is far from unbearable.

THE MAGIC WORLD
E. Nesbit

A thoughtless boy is taught a lesson by his cat; a
girl sent upstairs in disgrace is whisked to the
world of her dreams; a magic telescope brings two
boys a fortune; some very sensible princes and
princesses outwit wicked fairies and usurpers . . .
These twelve spellbinding stories open the door to
the magic world of the imagination.

SELECTED CAUTIONARY VERSES
Hilaire Belloc

The naughty children in these poems suffer
horrible fates as a result of their bad habits –
Matilda, who told such dreadful lies that nobody
believed her when the house caught fire; Jim, who
ran away from nurse and got eaten by a lion; John,
who lost a fortune by throwing stones. Here are
also some eccentric peers, and little-known 'facts'
about the llama, rhinoceros, tiger and other beasts.

BLACK BEAUTY
Anna Sewell

Black Beauty himself is handsome and sweet-
tempered but strong, spirited and with fine
instincts. His various owners make him do all
kinds of tasks, from being a carriage horse on a
country estate to a cab horse in town. Black
Beauty's tale must be one of the best-loved animal
stories ever written.

GREYFRIARS BOBBY
Eleanor Atkinson

Bobby, an active Skye terrier, adores his master
Auld Jock, and when the old man dies, Bobby
refuses to leave his grave in Greyfriars Churchyard
in Edinburgh. By day, he plays with the local
orphans and eats at a nearby tavern, but, in spite of
anything even the Lord Provost himself can do,
every night for fourteen years Bobby returns
faithfully to sleep by his master.

THE FAMILY FROM ONE END STREET
Eve Garnett

The Ruggles family, of Number 1, One End
Street, are experts at finding entertainment that
costs no money – but often leads to unexpected
adventures . . . From stout Lily Rose, whose good
deeds don't always work as she intends, to baby
William, who earns glory at the Baby Show, the
seven Ruggles children are lovable and individual –
and their adventures are endlessly enjoyable!

THE RAILWAY CHILDREN
E. Nesbit

When Father goes away unexpectedly, Roberta,
Peter, Phyllis and their mother have to leave their
happy life in London to go and live in a small
cottage in the country. The children seek solace in
the nearby railway station, and make friends with
Perks the Porter and the Station Master himself.
But the mystery remains: where is Father, and will
he ever return?

THE WIND IN THE WILLOWS
Kenneth Grahame

When Mole goes boating with the Water Rat
instead of spring-cleaning, he discovers a world he
never knew about. As well as the river and the
Wild Wood, there is Toad's craze for fast travel –
which leads him and his friends on a whirl of
trains, barges, gipsy caravans and motor cars, into
a lot of trouble, and even a battle.

THE WATER BABIES
Charles Kingsley

Tom, an ill-treated chimney-boy, jumps into a cool
stream to clean the soot off himself – and becomes
a water baby, cleaner and happier than he has ever
been, in a fairy world under river and sea. Meeting
beautiful and frightening creatures, getting into all
sorts of mishaps, and learning some lessons along
the way, Tom travels to the Other-end-of-Nowhere
on an unforgettable voyage of discovery.

PUFFIN 🐧 *CLASSICS*

THE JUNGLE BOOK
Rudyard Kipling

Here are the famous stories of how Mowgli came
to the wolf pack, learned the law of the jungle from
Baloo the bear, Bagheera the Black Panther, and
Kaa the python, and killed the evil tiger Shere
Khan. And here too are Rikki-Tikki-Tavi, the
snake-fighting mongoose, Little Toomai, who sees
the elephants' secret dance, Kotick the white seal,
and the varied characters in the horse lines of an
army camp.

JUST SO STORIES
Rudyard Kipling

From the 'satiable curiosity of the elephant's child
to the crab who played with the sea, from the
ingenious invention of the alphabet to how the
rhinoceros got his wrinkled skin, these stories of
strange happenings in the High and Far-Off Times
brim with life, humour and magic – a wonderful
collection that will hold you spellbound!

AROUND THE WORLD IN EIGHTY DAYS
Jules Verne

For a bet, Phileas Fogg sets out with his servant
Passepartout to achieve an incredible journey –
from London to Paris, Brindisi, Suez, Bombay,
Calcutta, Singapore, Hong Kong, San Francisco,
New York and back to London again, all in
just eighty days! There are many alarms and
surprises along the way – and a last-minute set-
back that makes all the difference between winning
and losing.

KING SOLOMON'S MINES
H. Rider Haggard

Three men trek to the remote African interior in
search of a lost friend – and reach, at the end of a
perilous journey, an unknown land cut off from the
world, where terrible dangers threaten anyone who
ventures near the spectacular diamond mines of
King Solomon . . .